the
Substance
of
God

a spiritual thriller

PERRY BRASS

Belhue Press

Belhue Press, First Edition
Copyright © 2004 by Perry Brass

Published in the United States of America by:
Belhue Press
2501 Palisade Avenue, Suite A1
Bronx, NY 10463
Electronic mail address: belhuepress@earthlink.net

The following is a work of fiction. All the characters, specific settings, and events in it are purely fictitious and have no relationship to actual specific personages, living or dead, or business entities except when described as part of a fictional narrative.

Cover and overall design by M. Fitzhugh
Cover photo by Jack Slomovits

ISBN: 1-892149-04-4
LIBRARY OF CONGRESS CONTROL NUMBER: 2003106047

"Stand and unfold yourself."

Hamlet, Act I, Scene I, William Shakespeare

"For in that sleep of death what dreams may come . . .
But that dread of something after death,
The undiscover'd country, from whose bourn
No traveler returns, puzzles the will,
And makes us rather bear those ills we have,
Than fly to others that we know not of?"

Hamlet, Act III, Scene I

"Hail to you, Lord of the Light, preeminent in the Great Mansion, in charge of the twilight! I have come to you spiritualized and pure. . . . may you give me my mouth with which I may speak, and may my heart guide me at its hour of destroying the night."

The Egyptian Book of the Dead, the Papyrus of Ani,
translated by Dr. Raymond Faulkner

Does genius trump reality?

For my father, Louis Brass, who taught me early on that life was an adventure;
and my mother, Helen, whose own rage has impelled me to write the truth.
And for those readers who find your own texts in your hearts,
and have found me with you, I thank you.

Other books by Perry Brass:

Sex-charge (poetry)

Mirage, a science fiction novel

Works *and Other 'Smoky George' Stories*

Circles, the sequel to *Mirage*

Out There: *Stories of Private Desires. Horror. And the Afterlife.*

Albert *or The Book of Man*, the third book in the *Mirage* series

Works *and Other 'Smoky George' Stories*, Expanded Edition

The Harvest, a "science/politico" novel

The Lover of My Soul, *A Search for Ecstasy and Wisdom*
(poetry and other collected writings)

How to Survive Your Own Gay Life, *An Adult Guide to Love, Sex,
and Relationships*

Angel Lust, *An Erotic Novel of Time Travel*

Warlock, *A Novel of Possession*

chapter one

I came back squirming, wide-awake, alone. Completely naked, all twitching muscles and shooting nerves, my eyes filled with grit. I kicked my way out of the black covering I'd been left in, as my body pulled itself up into the dark cold air from a cold metal table. Every joint in me cracked.

My stomach sucked in a shocking gasp of cold air. I sat up as straight as I could, looking at the white tag dangling from my right big toe. Pulling up my knee, I bent towards it, my fingers stiffly struggling to remove the narrow card. My toe had swollen around it, but I managed to loosen it, bringing it up to my nose. Eyes barely focusing, in the dim light I read who I was.

A half-sob rattled through my dry mouth.

Springing off the table, I hit the tile floor on the balls of my feet, reborn. Then a pain sliced through me, shooting straight up my legs to my head and I crumpled to the floor, holding on to my skull and weeping from the agony of it. Better to be dead.

The pain ebbed away, and I was just alive. Beautifully.

I got up, weightless, with that pure lovely lightness you think will happen after death. The room was dark and still with no windows. Suddenly a light so real that it flooded my eyes seemed to pour in all around me, pushing back the rush of fear I'd felt with that burst of pain.

I felt normal in the most transcendent, truthful way.

And I was, if I'd read the tag right, Leonard Jason Miller.

It was like meeting an old friend, someone you'd recognize in a crowded bar. *He's over here.* At least I was no longer alone. I now had an identity to claim for myself.

I rubbed the residue of dried grit from my eyes. How had this happened to me? How was an atheistic, Jewish scientist-cocksucker, once dead, now bouncing off a steel table in the dark? There was no time to breathe in my light. I had been marooned in death. But now I had rescued my identity myself, or that self had been saved for me. Creaky after being in one position for so long, I felt a wave of jubilant energy hit me.

I wanted to dance. Do a little turn. Experience myself unwinding from the corpse I had been, some of that tense twitching finally relaxed. With my arched feet and toes on the cold floor, I performed a few motions, a glowing white fleshy jiggle, penis flopping side to side, the love handles that stayed on me no matter what doing a little bump, grind, and shimmy. In the dark, my hands glided over smooth slabs, formica counters, an extended metal sink, cabinet drawers, then the blurred profiles of a few stiffs laid out under sheets. I wasn't even afraid; they only seemed like more furniture.

I almost broke down giggling. Even after my killing pain, I was alive—ecstatic—I was going to be Leonard Miller once more! I knew it! That was his—*my*—name! As I performed my little impromptu gestures of redemption, my elbow knocked over a small glass beaker from the edge of some counter. It crashed to the floor.

I jumped out of my skin.

Breathing through my mouth to keep from throwing up, I took slow breaths. The terrifying crash of that glass lacerated me, like a child trapped against his will, forced back into the corner of his worst punishment. I tried to hold on to myself. I had to keep from falling apart—I had to do something.

I would replace myself.

None of the corpses left out on the slabs would do. Somebody would miss them. Finally I was able to read the label "UNCLAIMED" on one of the body drawers, and pulled it out all the way.

Inside was a shrunken old man, bony and toothless. He looked like a plucked chicken on ice, with a wrinkled sagging belly attached. I was saving him from Potter's Field, I thought, popping off the tag attached to his rubbery big toe. I put my own tag on it. Then with a grunt, I hoisted him up out of his drawer onto my back. Even with my new surge of energy, it was an effort.

Breathing hard and almost falling over, I managed to haul him to the table where I'd awakened. I struggled to unzip my bag all the way, still holding on to the guy, who kept shifting about awkwardly like a big sack of beans.

Both elbows squeezing down on his cold, ribby chest, I managed to clamp him onto the table while I disengaged the metal zipper, then stuffed him back into my bag. In a flash I'd zipped it all the way back up.

I was almost out of breath. My heart was pumping furiously. Even naked I was ready to make a run for it, when I heard footsteps approaching from outside.

A flashlight beam caught me through a narrow window in the door. I scrambled from it like a startled rat. Towards the back of the room, I spotted another rolling table with a white sheet tossed over it. Grabbing the hem, I stretched it down almost to the floor and crawled under it, scrunching my stomach and hips against the cold tiles.

My head began to throb again. I lowered it. The cold tiles felt good against my cheek. My heart pounded as the door clicked open and a flashlight's beam drew a trail of rippling light over the pale front of the sheet. For a moment, all I could do was listen to the pounding inside my body, echoing in my ear against the tiles.

As the beam left the outside of the sheet, I raised the side of my head just enough to make out the click of footsteps in the front of the dark room.

"Seymour! Ain't nobody 'live in here. I don't care what you heard!"

"Yes, ma'am. But I heard somethin'. I don't know what, but I heard it."

A light switch snapped on. Extremely bright overhead lights bounced off the white tiles, the glare assaulting my eyes even through the sheet. The woman's heels moved in quickly towards me.

"Seymour! See anything special in here?" Her click-click got more impatient.

"Seymour! You take one more drink on your shift and it's gonna be all over with for you. You can switch places with some of these poor folks here. Understand?"

I watched her shoes walk away from me.

"Yes, ma'am. But I tell you, I heard somethin' funny."

"Yeah, and you been seein' pink, too." Her heels paused. "Honey, this is the kind of place where we all hear strange things. We all get rattled sometimes. But they ain't nothin' in here."

"You're right."

"I am?"

"Yes, ma'am."

Click-click-click in a circle.

"Wait a minute. Seymour?"

"Yes, ma'am?"

"Look at this mess! Did you see this? Somebody's broke a glass and they're gonna just leave it for the next shift!"

"Yes, ma'am."

"Uh-uh-uh!"

Footsteps halted; lights snapped off.

"I got a lotta paperwork to do, Seymour. Don't mention that broken glass to nobody. 'Else I gotta write it up."

The door closed. I waited in the dark under the sheet as their voices and footsteps disappeared into oblivion.

Oblivion was a destination I knew: footsteps. Voices. A hellstorm of glass . . . waiting for me in the recent past: Me, alone at night, in a small brightly lit corner of my lab. The delicate, near-perfect silence of state-of-the-art equipment, expensive gauges and pumps measuring and moving micro-quantities of materials. Hushed tick-tick of the large black clock on the wall, above orderly rows of desks and tables.

I saw myself examining a small fragment of ancient human tissue sent to me in secret by an old friend.

For weeks I had been trying to pierce its well-guarded mystery, my face glued to digital microscopes and slides; my brain already over-steeped from the volumes of files I had prepared from it. I had been dazzled by the gradual unfolding of its DNA, the seductive fan dance of its genetics, which suggested that even to the most untutored mind, this tissue might be, by any definition, as alive as I was.

The cells in it were still living, and I still had no idea how.

It hypnotized me: this bit of human flesh that had remained alive, centuries and centuries past the extermination of others. My brain took on its secrets, its ability to regenerate itself beyond any borders of time that we knew. I was intoxicated with it, gorging on my own expanding knowledge like a ravenous bee in a bed of the rarest pollen, an activity that is to scientists intellectually provocative on one hand, and shamelessly close to sexual on the other.

Very late that night, I was close to becoming unraveled myself by my own exhaustion, so I ignored a muffled stirring from beyond the door, the steady advance of a distant storm.

Footsteps. Then whispers.

I shrugged and let it go as the sound moved quickly, past the reception area and the once tomb-quiet hallway. Then the click outside the lab of the main light switch.

The big clock stopped.

I got up in the dark, by reflex palming the tissue, quickly jamming it inside the high black elastic top of my right sock. A swarm of men in dark ski masks surrounded me.

"What do you want? What d' you—!"

They grabbed me and hit me with something hard, over and over again on my neck, head, and body.

"Wha-? Wha-? Wha-?" I tried to say.

Hands choked the scream out of me.

I was flailing as they fanned out to cover the place, shattering glass, hurling logbooks, equipment, files and documents to the floor. There were four, five, maybe six of them; they took turns punching and striking me. Obviously they had known when I'd be alone, when the tissue I carefully guarded would be out.

Someone with I.D. must have let them in, past the guard twelve flights down, who was contracted from the outside and basically unreliable. He would not be doing another round for at least an hour, unless they had cornered him and tied him up. Under one of those masks was a Trojan horse in my own lab, who was evidently prepared to kill me.

Playing dead, I hit the floor, squeezing my eyes shut. As racks of test tubes and glass petri dishes crashed down on me, their cultures exposed like oysters pried from their shells, the thugs grabbed my head, banging it again against the floor until I passed out. Somehow I came to again, rolling on to my stomach. Blood from inside me surged up into my throat.

The beating stopped. Still I couldn't open my eyes, like they'd been nailed shut. The darkness was like a wintry polar midnight, squeezed dry of all light. Next, a kind of pale hazy glow dropped towards me and I felt a comforting silence blanket me, as off in the distance I heard the chaos of destruction continue. Through the haze, figures appeared: Mom and Dad, dead, their index fingers on their lips, as if they were warning me to stay quiet at a movie.

Don't get up, Lenny. We'll take you out ourselves. We have all sorts of things for you at home. Your little black-and-white TV set. Your favorite macaroni-and-cheese dinner from the box, with the toasted crumbs on top. That new Schwinn bike with the white fringe on the handlebars that you always wanted. We got it for you. Come on, it's going to be yours.

They both took me by the hand, leading me towards home and my new bike, until an iron rod cracked the back of my skull like an eggshell, and my life stopped.

I saw Jesus.

He seemed endless, like the sky, and shirtless. I drifted right up to his face, to his lips. He was smiling at me, his skin all beams of white light waving towards me. He told me something without words, but I was right there, floating towards him as if gravity itself were pulling me to him and the message was streaming directly from his lovely head and into mine.

This will be easy. Easier than we had thought.

Or was that me at twenty with long hair when I thought I knew everything? He was so beautiful. Never had I seen anyone so beautiful. (Could this be me? I was enchanting . . .)

Don't worry. You've been lucky.

I contracted. Became small, heavy, no longer floating. Sinking down towards the bottom, suddenly I couldn't reach up to him, but sank into a bog of blood. *Lucky?* I'd been murdered and was sinking through the catacombs of my own death, lined with tormenting fear, hard, real, tightening. The lights, those little glowing flickers at the far physical edges of me where Mom and Dad had offered their hands, went out. I stopped sinking.

The fear stopped, replaced by something else.

Gratitude for the end.

It was over.

I crawled out from under the sheet. The people who had killed me would do it again. There was no telling where they came from and how many they were. I would be followed. This was no intuition: I knew it. My own self was speaking to me: I couldn't just come back to life—*presto!* Somewhere out there were my murderers, and they wouldn't let their work go undone. Once you've been killed as violently as I had been, you can never really escape.

I'd been given a reprieve, but there was no way of telling how long it would last, or what I was now.

How alive was I? Was I really Leonard Miller? Or had that tiny bit of tissue created something else entirely?

My head began to hurt again. Funny idea: Me, my own clone! I chuckled. If fate's distant bell were calling me forth from death, there was no telling how much time I had in front of me, before the same bell rang again.

I did not want to hear it.

Suddenly I smiled in the dark morgue. Being Dr. Leonard Miller might be an iffy proposition, but I realized I'd returned as the same horny goat I'd been before. Despite the pain in my head, I was starting to get hard after raising my genitals from the cold floor. Maybe it was all the same urge: the urge towards life, towards sex, even towards God or everything that we want to call *God*. I was experiencing all these urges together and could not separate a single one of them.

Not that I have anything to report about God personally. All that happened in my Afterlife was that the lights went out. It was over.

Then point-blank, I was alive again. Legs, toes, and shoulders all worked. My pulse felt like a detonation, its throb emanating from my heart as all my systems started back again. It was as if the Titanic had suddenly pieced itself back together and resumed its way to New York.

I farted—can you believe that? That was the first thing that shocked me out of the bag, out of my void. I squirmed and managed to kick off the bag, which hadn't been zipped up all the way. Thankfully, I hadn't been autopsied or embalmed, so maybe my vision of Jesus was right: I *was* lucky.

Could it be I hadn't died at all? Perhaps on some last, cellular level, I had remained alive even after my brain, kidneys, liver, and heart had stopped.

No, that miraculously-preserved tissue inside my sock had done it. Without even touching it, I was convinced it was now grafted to me.

It itched—even tickled. I bent my knees slightly, leaned over, turned, and traced the veins going up my right leg. The back of my lower calf felt warmer than the rest of me. It *must* be grafted to me. I half-expected it to glow, like something out of a "B" horror movie.

I *was* glowing—with being alive! I stood up, gently squeezing the head of my cock, feeling it warm, expanding between my fingers. I felt like some vast city seen from a jet at twilight, as its pulsing lights came on. In this moment I was all of God's magnificence, holding this energy before me and offering it again to me, Lenny Miller. I leaned against the wall by the rolling table and held my awakening sexual parts in both hands.

I was prepared to leave now.

I needed something to wear. In a janitor's closet by the door, I found a T-shirt, some loose pants, and sneakers. Maybe Seymour's. I felt bad for the guy—not only had I almost cost him his job, but I was swiping his clothes, too.

Everything was a little too big, but better that than too small. I found the stairs, and in a minute I was out. Free. The city morgue was in the basement in the old part of Bellevue, on First Avenue near Twenty-Sixth Street. A sleepy-looking guard holding a paper coffee cup at the front door even did a brief "good-bye" wave, like he knew me.

But then, I was alive. So why not?

Dawn had not broken and the streets were empty, the lights on only for me. It must have rained while I was dead, because the pavement was wet. The sounds of my too-big sneakers smacking and slopping on the sidewalk enchanted me. I was suddenly in love. If it were possible to fall in love with your own self as you would with another person, I did that— and also with the world.

I wanted to dance. Happiness spilled out all over me, now that I had enough strength really to experience it. I started to run. I was breathing, my lungs taking in air like a blacksmith's bellows, in big, big gulps! I was skipping, turning, jumping like a clown in the big shoes.

There was a subway station on Lexington Avenue, and I hurried down into it. The token booth clerk was half-asleep, balding, and about a hundred years old. I jumped the turnstile, then ran down to the end of the platform and found a recess in the wall to hide in. I gazed up and down at the empty platform and the tracks. A man in an off-white raincoat stood waiting twenty feet from me, his face buried in the *Times*, his back to me.

A fat little rat came running out of the wall from the far side of my end of the platform, hurrying directly in front of me. Then it sped along the platform's edge, directly in front of the man with the *Times*. The man kept turning the pages of his paper, as the rat, who seemed more alive than either of us, jumped into the tracks and disappeared.

chapter two

*T*here was my apartment near Columbia, but I had no keys to get in. And there was my lab: I wanted to go back, but people with access to it had killed me. One of them might still be there. I didn't know who he was. Or, actually, who was I?

"I'm still here!" the old showgirl in *Follies* proclaimed.

Was I incarnated from myself, or just on loan from that place that no one really comes back from?

The train roared into the station. The man with the *Times* and I got in. The train was empty, except for a few exhausted night-riders and homeless people. One of latter sat across from me, fidgeting, our eyes just eluding each other like submarines warily crossing under ice. He was tall, rail-thin, young, late twenties, early thirties perhaps, with a tangled mop of dull dirty-black hair on his head, hollow cheeks, and a narrow, Goth-white, bird-skull of a face that made his lips look crimson by comparison. He looked like a scarecrow doll in rags, but buzzing with his own quirky energy so that his whole body jumped with every jolt of electricity that moved the train.

I tried to look away from him. Still, he was so alive, fanning an intense curiosity in me; I almost moved towards him. I, who'd been cold-dead such a short time ago! Our eyes met and he grinned a smile like a wolf puppy, with dark gaps between his broken teeth.

Besides his rags, he wore dainty, black, flat-soled shoes, like the kind sold in Chinatown or dancers wore, on his long narrow feet. No doubt next, he would pop up and do an elegant little dance from *The Nutcracker*; or was I just half-drunk on my re-born self, thinking that the whole world was there to entertain me?

He noticed my gaze. Both feet left the floor, and he began tapping them together, keeping time within himself. I smiled. He had been a dancer once, I decided, long-limbed and beautiful, until drugs or the hardships of life had got to him. Ah, the dance . . . I could feel it again pulling me into something, in my first hours of awakening.

His feet stopped fanning the air. Losing interest, he turned from me and went back to that place that was obviously not *The Nutcracker*. The hammering pain returned to my head and I placed my hands on it and tried to make it go away. I didn't want to acknowledge its existence. It reminded me too much of the blow that had split my own fragile skull.

His hands fished into one of the bloated plastic shopping bags piled next to him. There were bags inside bags, some of the handles reinforced with wads of tape and cord. Pulling an old brown paper sack out of the bag, he stuck his fingers into it. The sunken beads of his eyes focused on the sack, then swept suspiciously towards me.

I turned my head away, ashamed of my interest in him. I was laughing inside at him. What kind of person would—

He lunged towards me.

My body jumped. I tried to grip the seat as a thin scared shriek broke out of me. Twitching, he towered above me, skeletal, reeking of garbage odors and street fumes. Silvery crystals of dried-up urine caked his pants. I felt trapped. Why couldn't he scram! Get back to that closet full of smashed-up doll heads that the homeless live in, exactly where my own head had been placed; but I'd escaped.

He pressed in closer to me, his sharp shin bones into my knees.

"I know you, Mister! You can't fool me!"

He—*what*?

I stopped breathing. He *knew* me? I was sure that every eye in the car was riveted on me, that everybody knew my secret. That I was dead.

I gripped my head, the pain splitting my skull as he aimed dirty clenched hands at me. With each thunderous jerk of the train, more and more glass shattered, the car filling with broken test tubes and smashed equipment. The lights went out. Darkness spilled out all over me like a flood of black blood. Then I heard a high-pitched sound like birds screeching:

"Cheeeeeeeeese!"

Tears filled my eyes, but I forced them open. He uncurled filthy palms to show me broken chunks of Ritz crackers.

"Come on, eat some cheese. Eat it! Come on, I'll share wit' you."

Pushing the crackers towards me, he dropped drifts of crumbs into the air. Like a kind of blessing, some hit my head lightly. The pounding pain stopped, and I managed to get my breath back. Did he really recognize me? I wanted to take his hand and eat the crackers directly from it. I would have; I was that unhinged and just grateful to be alive with him.

"No thanks," I mumbled. "Kind of you, but no."

"Sure, man? They're on me. They're free!"

"I'm sure."

I looked down embarrassed at his Chinese shoes. He bent over me, his pee-stained crotch almost pressing into my face. I shrank back from him, going into that stone-faced act all New Yorkers know, and he danced away, returning to his shopping bags. He didn't look at me again.

The passengers at the other end of the car ignored us as I watched him munching crackers, licking his fingers, and scratching himself. His dark eyes looked sunken into his white face beneath his mop of hair. I could still smell him. His odor lingered even more strongly on me than the morgue's did; I felt suffocated.

I got up. The wind blew through me as I walked to another car and found a seat all by myself. Exhaling slowly, I tried to calm myself.

Tears streamed out of me. Was I mourning that part of me that had died and I could never bring back: the part that believed knowing was everything, and at some point I could know it all? The Ritz cracker man in the other car, with his Chinese ballet shoes, did he know this?

That I was dead, and hungry? Hungry for life. Hungry for anything that let me know I was here.

People want to believe there's some climactic moment, like a big-bang last orgasm, when you "pass over." They want to believe it's that pronounced, that "cool." But that's not what you feel when you pass at all.

What you feel is relief that this helpless drift towards the unknown, with only glimmers of recognition along the way, has stopped.

The fear and drifting is over, and you're grateful because there's no fear now: for that alone you're grateful.

Then, even being grateful stops.

Oh, for the comfort of my own stupidity, when I thought I knew just about everything, and not knowing only excited me. I needed to stop crying. I was embarrassing myself, something I didn't think I could do after waking as I did, with a fart no less. At the next stop more people rushed in, each one a little detail: New York. I was back into it. I needed a plan.

I *had* been stupid. I'd made the genuinely stupid mistake of breaking up with Josh Moreland, my lover, six months before. We'd been together for six years, until I'd had my premature "Seven Year Itch." I started feeling there were things I was supposed to have—things that Josh, good as he was, was never going to give me.

It started out as curiosity. I was turning forty-five and had recently discovered the kinky Personals ads in the backs of glossy New York bar magazines with names like *Me, Too* and *Homofide*. The ads were basically about men who offered to do *anything* for you if you didn't ask any questions beyond how long, how big, and sometimes, as in money, how much? It was about nitty-gritty sexual connections, without any emotional component, with guys who at twenty-two knew more about sex than I would have known at a hundred-and-twenty-two.

They were born hot.

These ads were in the same magazines you could get for free on certain corners. They proved that a lot of the young men that I used to see on the streets and pant after were available by touch-tone phone. Although many of the ads turned out to be "dry holes," most of these dudes had a simple, off-hand, supple style and a concentration of brain matter that, no matter what, seemed to be centered solely on their dicks. Who could resist? I'd spent so much of my life in near monastic cerebral pursuits, that now I wanted to be drenched in sex.

Luscious, brainless sex! What better prescription after squeezing my middle-aged brain through the lab's daily meat grinder, then scurrying around to impress the nitwit money men whose approval I needed to continue my work?

Soon I was addicted to the ads, as well as any unexpected friendly glances from good-looking men on the street. They came just when I felt sure that my days of getting those looks, which once flowed aplenty, were about to stop on a dime.

Queers, I had told myself, have the life span of those ragged mutts you find at the pound: at a certain point, it's over. *Finito.* They aren't taken out to be re-groomed like nice straight dogs with a pedigree. Instead, when the time's up, they take you to a grubby room down the hall, flick the "Disposal" switch and quickly burn what's left. You're over; invisible.

I was middle-aged and teetering on the edge of that growing invisibility, my image no longer reflected in the gay world's clear blue pool of young Speedo-clad beauties. Not that aging heteros are that much more visible in America's "reality show" Winner-Take-All culture.

I wanted a reprieve from banishment from that tribe of hot young men, some appreciation, some delicious bit of kindness for being me, Dr. Leonard Miller. I was still rather good looking in a lively, Eastern-European-Jewish way, smart after all; five-foot-ten and a couple of tenths left over, thinning a bit on top, graying, of course, getting that wayward little paunch and those love handles that would not submit to discipline. Cock, as demonstrated, still working, but the legs—one could not make the legs appear twenty years younger anymore. Maybe some could fool their legs, but not I.

I was still in love with Joshua.

A high tide of gorgeous, romantic love broke over me. Lovely Josh. I remembered how cute he was when I first saw him; that small, impossibly tense, clever mouth waiting for me to kiss him, like I did that first time. He'd been a little shy, and I thought I was going to cream all over myself. There was a light now on his adorable face; I could reach for it.

The train ground to a station stop, with Josh's light still on.

But was I really feeling love for Josh Moreland? Or was it for myself, going through these huge mood swings after death, for finding myself so happy to be alive?

But why ask? Why could I never stop asking?

I hadn't expected any of this, but you don't really expect anything when you're dead. All you expect is—I decided to go to his place and ring his bell. I got out at the stop near Bloomingdale's, and walked over in the early-morning shine of the still-dark city, past uniformed doormen in great buildings, who sometimes nodded to me; the street sweepers; some men quietly going through garbage cans; and a couple of big truck drivers who looked like mastiffs. Josh lived on the outskirts of what used to be called Hell's Kitchen, on Fifty-Seventh Street, in a new doorman building. The building was characterless, towering, and reminded me of a college dormitory. We had never lived together; sometimes we traveled together, but that was all.

I told the doorman, who, luckily, had never seen me, that I was Eric, a mutual friend. I was too embarrassed to say who I really was. Afterall, I'd been dead. Dawn was now coming up: the first dawn after my reprieve from death.

The first dawn of this life, whose ever it was.

After some talk over the house phone, the doorman, an older man with a resigned Irish face, shrugged and announced, "Your friend told me, 'This had better be good.' Go on up."

There was a woman in the elevator with a small pooch, part Pekinese and maybe part-chimpanzee, that looked like her. The two had similar stringy brown hair and squashed, wrinkled little faces except that hers had traces of pink lipstick on it. She pretended not to look at me, but I could feel her staring at me even harder than the man on the subway had. True, it was way too early for normal people to be up, and I was wearing clothes that did not fit. With a sneer on both their faces, she and her dog got off on the eighth floor.

Josh was on the tenth, down a long, too-bright hallway with sentries of black doors, some bedecked with the gleaming silvery mezuzahs favored by religious Jews. Josh was blandly sweet, white bread material from the Midwest, but he'd been in New York for so long that some of the color of the city had bled off onto him.

Eyes still so deep in sleep that I could not see them, he opened the door part-way in his burgundy bathrobe, ready to release a well-deserved *kvetch*.

I got closer. He opened his sky-blue eyes a fraction more, his lean face etched with dime-sharp dimples blanching, as his nostrils flared. They did that when he was shocked; he was trying to breathe.

"You're . . . ?"

I nodded and walked in. Taking his hand, I closed the door. I touched his face, the slim sculpted nose, the cheeks that felt soft even when he needed a shave, the chin that turned up slightly with its little cleft. I was overpowered by him, as this infinity of love engorged me.

"I'm dreaming, right? I'm in bed and I'm dreaming, Len?"

"You're not dreaming. Please don't be scared, Josh. Just—" I wanted to say *hug me, hold me*. My legs shook.

He started crying. "It is you, right?"

Now he did hug me. I'd wanted it so much I started crying again myself.

"I almost didn't want to answer the bell," he cleared his throat sniffling. "I thought what kind of nut would get me up now? *Eric*? You're right. Maybe Eric would. He's so crazy! He'd be out slutting someplace, then try to wake me up with the details. Jesus-God, Len? Tell me, how—?"

I sat down for a second on the couch, then realized I had to pee. It had been so long I was afraid I was going to pee on his pretty couch. It was soft and deep brown, like bitter-sweet chocolate; comfortably made for napping. I had admired it new. Excusing myself, I went into his bathroom.

After I peed, I grabbed his toothbrush and some toothpaste and took a few swipes at my teeth to clean my breath. I felt pretty grotty. I could still smell the sharp whiff of a chemical disinfectant the morgue had used on me, even over Josh's "ever-fresh floral" room deodorizer. The shower tempted me, but first I had to explain myself to him.

Josh had a cup of coffee waiting for me on an end table by the couch, where he was sitting. I wasn't sure how he had got the coffee. Maybe he'd microwaved it, perhaps to occupy himself while waiting for me. He looked shaken; his eyes searched me.

"Does anybody else know you're alive?"

I shook my head. "I'm not even sure I believe it. I should be dead. I *was* dead. They did this thing to my head, it was cracked open. I've got bruises all over, and something on my leg. I want you to look at it."

"Okay" He blinked twice. "You're here. Am I hallucinating this? I can't believe I'm not."

"You're not hallucinating. Believe me."

I pulled the T-shirt off and he got up. Using the wall mirror in his living room with sufficient light from a marble table lamp, both of us looked steadily at me. Although somewhat near-sighted, I could function without glasses. Miraculously, most of the ugly discolorations on my body had already begun to heal.

There were still faint blue outlines of broken veins, but the progress was impressive. Another victory for the amazing substance. My face was even more improved. My left cheekbone was still splotched with an indigo stain, and I had a two-inch scar on my right temple, but it looked like it could have happened a year ago.

I asked Josh to look at the top of my head. I bent towards him, and he felt my skull with his hands. He was quiet.

"What's there?" I asked.

"A crack. Just a thin one, but I can feel it under your hair."

"That's all?"

"Yes, and something else. Dried blood, I guess. But not a lot."

I raised my head, exhaling. Good, the outside was healing—but what about the inside? Storms of raw feelings were still rumbling through it. But at least my skull had come back together. I could almost pass as a "regular person," about as much as I ever could.

I pulled down the baggy pants, so we could look at the back of my right lower calf and the rest of me. My thighs had not done as well as my ribs and chest; they were still splotched with black-and-blue marks.

I made Josh run his hand over the place where the tissue was grafted, to feel the nubby bump on my skin. The color was an unnatural, dull grayish shade, but firm, with the thick, rubbery texture of orange peel.

Thanks to this grafting, I was alive. But it looked repulsive.

I felt funny standing there with my privates hanging out in front of Joshua. Maybe even *more* so in front of Joshua, who definitely wasn't a trick. I pulled the pants back up, but hated the morgue smell, especially in Joshua's always tasteful apartment. I let them drop once more, no longer concerned with my modesty.

Looking back into the mirror, I rubbed my face just to convince myself that I was alive. Didn't Hamlet ask the possibility of dreams after death: "To sleep, perchance to dream?" One of those lashing storms bounced through my head hard. I hated the dead man I was, grotesquely come to life here in Josh's apartment, of all places. Why was I making him go through this with me? What was I—

"Shit! I should be dead!" I screamed.

"Len!"

I stopped. I looked at his face. The concern on it shamed me. "Sorry."

"Why?"

"I'm not sure this is my real self. I don't know what I'm putting you through. Please forgive me."

"For what? Being a miracle?"

He smiled at me, putting his hand on my bare shoulder and stroking my neck softly.

"What's not real?" he asked. "You look good to me, Dr. Len. All of you. I'm happy to see you, no matter how."

"I guess you can say I look rested."

"You do. You used to work like a machine. Keyed up, exhausted, flying off the handle, making up excuses."

"I was a dumb shit, wasn't I? A perfect screw-up, a—"

"You were never dumb. You were so smart it awed me. You could talk about anything, and you always knew what you wanted. It's just that there wasn't much room for me in it."

"I feel terrible. I want to make up for everything. I want to—"

"You do?" He hugged me close against his bathrobe, kissing my cheeks lightly and then my mouth. "I feel like I'm kissing a miracle. But what are you, if you're not yourself?"

I tried to put it into words that Josh, a corporate law librarian who had majored in English, could understand. Nothing too theoretical, no pages of biochemical formulae that even I had to stretch my wits to follow. He'd never really understood my work. Some of it, like experiments I did with animals, repulsed him. We'd had that strange attraction of the arts, him, to the sciences, me. Or was it vice versa? Maybe he had a soul, whatever that meant, that I didn't. He had a genuine purity, while I was all appetites, urges, and an intellect whose relentless curiosity drove me crazy.

Drawing slightly away, I told him about placing the specimen in my sock, just before the thugs had got to me. Josh stopped hugging me.

"The tissue I'd been studying regenerates itself, as well as other cells it becomes attached to. It must have taken over inside me, replicating enough to bring me back. It must have started with my blood, then gone on into my organs, even my brain. What's incredible is that this 'substance,' this advancing colony of cells, actually *understood* the moment of my death and was able to process what had to be done at that moment. How long it's going to last, I don't know. I was dead, I think. But how can you know you're dead when you're dead?"

"Doesn't that depend on how you feel?" Josh asked. "Some people believe that the dead know they're dead. And that someone is waiting for them. They believe in a consciousness after life."

"Not me. I never believed in the Afterlife, the eternal soul, anything like that. I believed in science. I always believed that this was *it*."

"So what do you think now, Doctor?"

"I don't know."

"You don't sound as certain as you used to be."

"I'm not. Maybe it depends on your definition of death. At this point

I don't know what that is. Maybe we're just a part of a vast pattern of elements that replicates itself over and over, over eons of time. And life and death only represent a series of complicated variations in the pattern, like the buildings in a town."

"What do buildings have to do with it?"

"Buildings are basically brick, mortar, pipes, tiles—stuff like that. They may look different, but they're all built of the same basic materials. So they get built, torn down, rebuilt. No matter how you work it, you use the original elements over and over again, and just put them into new forms. The bricks over time get reduced to clay again and get refired, the—"

"Wait. How did that save you?"

I put my hands on my head. "Biologically speaking, this substance recognizes all of this and knows how and when to speed up the life process. It also knows when to hold itself back in a stable formation, so that it can support life again at the necessary time. In other words, it knows when to retract, as well as when to proceed."

"Wow!" His head jumped.

It did seem amazing, but it had happened so why deny it? The whole idea of cloning itself seemed pure Buck Rogers a few decades ago, but then so had cell phones.

"Josh, the substance *knew* I was dead and what it would have to do to bring me back. Doesn't that put it in your 'God' realm?"

"I don't know," he said. "I feel like I'm lost suddenly."

"Imagine how *I* feel."

He looked at me. His eyes were puzzled, and slightly scared, as if the ground was starting to shift too quickly under him.

"But death is still *real*, isn't it?" he asked. "I mean . . . everything disappears?"

"Maybe. Or maybe it just goes someplace else we can't see."

"Len, I can see and feel you."

I smiled. He pulled me to him, hugging me again as if to make sure I was solid, really there. Now I felt funny about Seymour's big sneakers and the pants down around my ankles.

"At least you can for now," I said. "Thanks to God, or whatever brought me back."

Josh let go of me. "I told you, you should have been Episcopalian, Len.

It's much easier than being Jewish. Plus you get all that nice scotch, high teas, plum cakes, good things like that."

"All right. I'm convinced. I thank the Episcopalian God."

"He's called Jesus. Thank Him and his Father." He looked lost in thought. Suddenly his small lips pursed. "Remember, we spoke on the phone a couple of weeks ago? I called you. I thought we could go to the opera. You talked about this stuff and told me not mention it to anyone— that it was constantly cloning itself."

"Sure, I was just starting with it. What opera did you see? I couldn't go, could I?"

"*Don Giovanni*."

"Right, the one I could never make through the last act." I laughed, then said, "Yeah, I guess I did use the word 'cloning' with you. I wouldn't have with most people. Using it sets off all sorts of alarms, but that's how this substance from Turkey has been preserved for two thousand years. It was a small piece of a foot. You'd expect to dig something like that out of an ice cap, not perfectly preserved in a warm dry climate."

He shivered. "You're giving me the willies!"

"Wait. Doesn't my being here do that to you?"

He shook his head. "I know you. I can accept you, Len—not some foot from two thousand years ago. Now I remember: you wouldn't tell me on the phone how you got it, or who sent it to you."

"Alvin Jurrist, an old friend of mine, an archeologist. We met in San Francisco at a conference on working with ancient tissues. At the time I thought he was kind of weird, like a character out of one of those old 'Ah, Dr. Miller! Now we meet the Mummy' movies. So, of course I was drawn to him. He never expected to find anything human this old in a distinctly-living state. He knew that I was doing genetic research involving regeneration, so he sent the specimen to my lab about a month ago.

"Naturally, since we were afraid the government and the media would go crazy, we had to keep Jurrist's discovery a secret. First, it could have contained viral material, maybe plague or some other ancient disease.

"And second—it was possible the tissue would let us reproduce life from its own period, the time of the Bible. I could see those headlines in the supermarket tabloids."

"You're right. That would have turned your lab into a circus."

I nodded. "Unfortunately, some of the business suits at my company were eager to do that. There's nothing cheap about running a research operation, so BioStart wanted to let the word out as fast as it could. They'd already started working on the spin for it. The right wingers scared me. They're against cloning completely. They don't mind destroying thousands of species, whole eco-systems. But cloning, Sir, that *be* against God."

He sat down and looked at me. His gaze made me draw the floppy pants back up.

"My immediate staff at BioStart was with me. They wanted to keep the lid on it. The suits were itchy to release it, but we held back. Anyway, the more I worked with it, the more miraculous it became. People are happy to get a bit of hair from a few hundred years back. But this tissue was still alive, still active on a cellular level. At the very least, it would give us a true biological picture of the characteristics of humans, their immunities, *everything*, in the age of the Caesars.

"I wanted to publish my results scientifically in journals, but the popular media would have exploded, either villifying me, or distorting what was going on so that all sorts of crazies would have come banging on my door. 'Can you bring back Uncle Solly and my dog Pishkie? I have a piece of toenail and some whiskers!' I could hear that starting. I was already notorious enough among the straight scientists who thought I was a queer kook. For years the academics who handed out the big grants and prizes looked down their noses at me. That's why I got into private industry.

"Two weeks ago the lab started to run seriously out of cash. We were borrowing on top of borrowing. Then our financial partners walked in and demanded to know when were we going to bring in the real 'gusher' on their investment. Something to make Viagra look like dog vomit. They talked in 'linear and non-linear strategic planning.' 'Non-sharable percentages of future market shares,' blowing their cigar smoke right up my nose and threatening to shut down my lab. I didn't have a Christopher Reeve to do a quick photo op with—him in his wheel chair, me holding his hand. But I was sitting on this pot of gold. The question was, when would I release it? And of course, what kind of curse came with it?"

Josh took my hand; I was more upset that I'd expected to be.

"It's okay," he said, softly. "I'm sorry."

"I was . . ." I couldn't hold back the tears. I'd been alone in my lab, where I had spent so much of my life, and I'd been murdered violently. I'd died by myself, after more panic than I ever knew existed.

After an agonizing minute, I pulled myself together. "I *had* to show them what it was, Josh. Give them the full show with most of my staff around. I tried to beg for time. A week later, give or take a day—they killed me."

Josh softly stroked my head.

"I can't imagine it. I feel so bad for you."

"It was like drowning, sinking to the bottom of this lake, except that the lake was my own carnage. You're looking up from that bottom and you see someone familiar. He's you. But you're helpless. You can't even say good-bye to him."

"I wish I could have done something." Josh was crying. He gave me a handkerchief from his robe pocket. I used it on my eyes, and handed it back to him and he blew his nose with it.

"What could you have done?" I asked. "All I want is for you to be here now for me."

"Good, I am," he whispered. "It made the front page of the *Daily News*, Len. They called it a suspected drug robbery. 'Frankenstein of Cloning Murdered in Drug Heist.'"

"They called me *Frankenstein*? Everybody's got to be a 'Doctor Something' nowadays. I guess it's better than 'Dr. Death.'"

"Do you want some more coffee? Do you want to eat something? You must be hungry."

I did not want to tell him about the scene on the subway. Maybe I just looked transparently hungry.

I smiled at Josh. "That's what I love about you, Josh. You're more of a Jewish mother than the one I had. Mine couldn't cook, thought 'bake' was spelled 'Sarah Lee,' and her worst four-letter word was—"

"Yes, I know, 'iron.' You told me that years ago. Her other one was 'dust,' as in she never did it. How about some eggs? The last thing you have to worry about is your cholesterol."

I sat down at a table in his small kitchen as he scrambled several eggs for us. We held hands while we ate. His hand was so clean and warm and I kept kissing it, loving the touch of his fingers and knuckles on my lips. I'd never tasted anything as wonderful as those eggs. Just being with him again gave me an erection.

By the time I had finished my eggs, I was all over him, too.

I pulled my tongue out of his mouth.

"I can't help it," I said, out of breath. "All I can think about is you right now."

"It's okay, Len. Maybe I can't help it, too."

We dropped our clothes in the kitchen and raced into his bed. His bedroom was meticulous; the bed looked unslept in, like he remade it habitually every ten minutes.

He stroked the thick dark hair on my pale legs.

"I love the hair on your legs, the way it curls up in scallops when it's wet."

His skin was smooth, really nicely tanned. He had been away in Florida—I had known that, okay, before . . . my murder. He'd just come back. I sank into him. His soft, slightly raised nipples. His smooth stomach, groin, and silky, lovely cock. Bodies were made for this, that moment when nothing happens in your brain except the physical thing. I was so happy for it; my whole insides were grinning.

We showered afterwards. I had Josh's semen with his lovely, slightly salty, almost buttery taste in my stomach; better even than the scrambled eggs. At first the water spray hurt my chest. Josh turned it down, gently lathering me up with a soft acrylic sponge filled with a lemony liquid shower soap. I felt so tired I could barely hold myself up, even with his help.

"Let me get you washed off."

He turned me around under the light spray, then knelt to help me wash the soapy foam off my legs. I closed my eyes to the pulse of the water and his tender hands on me. When I opened them, he was turning off the water. I went blank.

I fell to the hard floor of the tub.

"Oh, God, Len!"

I couldn't move. He threw several thick towels over me, patting me until I was dry.

"Can you get up? Let me help you."

I was too exhausted to answer. With his help, I managed to pull myself up over the tub, then I sank to my knees and threw up breakfast on the white tile floor. My head pounded. The spattered tiles tilted up and spun around me. When they finally quit spinning, I could see the panic on Josh's face.

He ran out. I heard some clatter in the kitchen, then he returned with a clean plastic bag, a fresh dish sponge, paper towels, and a bottle of pine-oil disinfectant. Still naked, on his hands and knees, he scrubbed away every trace of the vomit except for the slight lingering odor. I sat inside the tub, my hands and chin locked around my knees. I would have felt embarrassed schmutzing up his bathroom, if I weren't so empty inside, so removed from myself. Everything that resembled the old in-control Dr. Leonard Miller had disappeared and gone some other place, perhaps back to the morgue.

I heard Josh toss the sponge and soaked paper towels into his kitchen garbage can. Then he returned with a stack of blankets and arranged them around me to warm me, though I was burning up with fever.

Taking his cordless phone into the bathroom, Josh called his office to announce he was sick and not coming in.

"Thanks," he said into the phone. "I must have what's going around. I'll take care of myself." He hung up.

Still naked, he knelt down next to me. For a moment, I was afraid he'd catch something, maybe what I had.

But *what* did I have? I was too weak to get those words out, but that question and the fear behind it raced through me, the way that fever boils your brain into a delirium.

Or does your brain merely slow down, so that all the fears you normally attempt to hide overwhelm it?

chapter three

I woke up in Josh's bed with him sitting next to me, fully clothed. He wore attractive silk bow ties at work and nice shirts. He had on one of those shirts, of elegant fine white cotton with thin shiny blue stripes in it. I touched the shirt, and pulled him to me, kissing him softly on the cheek.

"My mouth tastes terrible!" I managed to spit out the words.

"In case you missed it, Len, you threw up. I got your face as clean as I could with a wash cloth, before I got you into bed."

I pulled myself up a little. My head still hurt but not so much. I no longer had that running-on-empty feeling that had hit me in the bath.

"My body must have started rejecting the work of the new cells in that substance," I said, theorizing that it must have gone as far as it could with them, then started fighting them. I lifted my hands, palms up. "Life and death are in a funny balance. Once it surrenders, the body doesn't snap back to life so fast, even if on some level it really wants to. There must be a force in us towards death, just as there is a force towards life."

Josh stared at me. I don't think he actually understood what I was saying. There was only this complete simplicity and love in his eyes.

"It does," I explained, "fight to stay alive, the body does. But it's still hard to overcome death. A point of stasis—inertia—happens, and the question is, which force will overcome it? Aspects of you, like your sperm for instance, remain alive for a considerable time after you've been proclaimed dead. But they're cells that don't need the kidneys, liver, and other systems to function. That's why 'clinical death' is a strange term. I always asked, 'Whose clinic are we talking about?' Maybe the one where Pluto is the chief physician. He's the god of the dead, you know."

Josh smiled. "That I know."

"Good. His clinic, you know, usually got the final say. But nowadays there are other questions."

He nodded. "I get what you mean, Doctor."

The fever had passed as quickly as it had come. I threw off the sheet and blanket and raised my leg to examine the tissue again. Twisting about to study it, I wondered how it had grafted itself so fast to the skin cells on my calf. Grabbing the skin, I pressed it towards me.

The universe has consciousness: I was aware of that. *It*, the orchestrated cells in the substance, knew exactly what was called for. All of those little soldiers must have jumped to my rescue, but first they had to disguise themselves as a part of me, an innocent welt on a hard-to-see part of my flesh. That's why there had been no questions raised in the Office of the Medical Examiner, a.k.a., the morgue. I had not been turned over and closely examined yet.

I'd always believed there was intelligence in the universe; that the grafting had started at the moment of my death, only underscored that feeling. Usually this natural intelligence works very slowly: evolution is proof of that. But something had happened here to kickstart the process. Could it have been my own reaching out towards something, that consciousness embodied in that figure of light who resembled me at a younger age, which triggered the onset of regeneration within the cells?

Nature is always reaching towards a desired direction. Physicists call this "handedness," meaning that everything moves either towards the right or the left. Most of the cosmos works in a balance between clock-wise and counter-clockwise. But does human consciousness have a "handedness" of its own? A direction, say, clock-wise towards life, or counter-clockwise towards death? Perhaps in a part of my own "handed" consciousness, I had set the "hand" of this thing to start at my own biological midnight: that precise "tick" of my own death.

The welt had swollen, going from its former dull gray to a slightly more pinkish color. It was sweating and generating heat; I could feel it.

"That looks pretty gross," Josh said.

I started laughing, I couldn't help it. "You think *this* is gross? You should have—" I wanted to say he should have been beaten to death, then come back to life in a morgue. "I was always just a bit too human for you, wasn't I, Josh?"

"Jesus, Len! You'd fight with me after death, wouldn't you? You've got to admit, it does look kind of—"

"Gross? Sure." I shut up. I felt awful. Why was I lashing out at Josh, of all people?

"I wish I weren't such a defensive asshole," I apologized to him. "I love you. I want to be a different person now."

He got up and shrugged. "Maybe you are. Are you sure you're really Leonard Miller?"

"I'm sure not Leonard Bernstein."

He smiled. It was our first joke. When we'd met at a pick-up joint in the Village, he had asked me my name. I told him, then added, "Like Leonard Bernstein."

"You're *not* Leonard Bernstein," he said.

Actually, Josh had met Bernstein once, years before, and had flirted with the Maestro, who turned out not to be interested. But I was interested in Josh, extremely so. He was a true gentleman with real sweetness; maybe he'd been *too* good for me. He just didn't have that mustang wildness I pursued in my fantasies, the ones where bound and gagged, I "forced" myself to do everything and everything was done to me.

I looked around the room. There were still several framed pictures of me in it.

At times I hated my fury towards life, my own raging appetites. Was I angry because, like a lot of queers, I never thought I'd been a real boy, or a real man—only a pretender at both? Looking at Josh's pictures of me, I didn't see a pretender. I had been real. Unfortunately, it had taken my dying to figure that out.

I flashed onto myself as a kid: smart, alienated; then as a young man: wandering, lost. I started crying again, really blubbering. Josh brought me a handful of Kleenex tissues.

"I'm sorry." I took one, brought it to my eyes, then blew my nose loudly. "I must be in grief for me, too."

He sat down again on the bed, taking my hand.

"Can you remember anything else about what happened?"

"I was working late at night, the way I often did, alone. My assistants had gone. I didn't hear anyone get in. Then I heard really loud—'Where is it? WHERE IS IT!!!' I froze, just stopped breathing. It felt like the earth had opened up and all I wanted to do was to shrink and become invisible. They were going to kill me! I could feel it coming, like a bomb had exploded in my face. They were going to rip me to shreds."

I tried to get my breath back, shaking as if I were back there again.

"They were wrecking things, scattering everything, my files, all those documents and lines of cell tissues we've been working on for years. I kept hearing glass crashing, and they were jumping on me over and over again. I pretended to be dead—"

"It sounds to me like they wanted to take that substance you were working on, and make sure that no one knew for a while what had been taken."

My head felt like it was being cut by a saw. I kept hearing glass shattering and their voices approach . . . this infernal buzz that got louder. I felt nauseated again.

Josh squeezed my hand and I looked into his clear blue eyes. The darkness and hell of the lab slowly disappeared. I tried to relax.

"Did you recognize any of them?"

"No. They wore ski masks."

"Did you know that the cops spoke to me?"

I tried to smile. "*Know*? Josh, I was *dead*, wasn't I?"

I was a scientist, I was supposed to know what death was—or was it possible that by pretending to be dead, I had kept myself from going into shock, which made their "murder" of me easier to revive? Though if I weren't dead, they didn't—God!—Or *Whatever!*—What an idiot I was! Could I never stop questioning anything? You'd think I'd not look this one gift horse in the mouth. Accept it, believe in it.

I should have simply dropped all my scientific defenses and believed in this miracle that had brought me back.

But I couldn't.

The pain was back, from concentrating, thinking, analyzing. No wonder I got involved with weird scenes and way-out degrees of kink. Bondage like medieval tortures. Flogging—I had tried that, but decided it hurt too much. Clothes pins, crocodile clamps, equipment you'd use on horses, heavy domination, piss. Anything to halt for a moment that surtax on my brain of excessive intelligence that kept me from simply being a part of the Universe. I put my palms on my face, softly rubbing my head.

"They spoke to you?"

Josh nodded. "They got my name from your receptionist. Remember, he used to call me and give me excuses why you had to break dates? 'Dr. Miller can't make the opera this evening.' 'Dr. Miller is going to be late.'

The police wanted to know if I knew about any of your enemies. Hell, I hardly knew about your friends."

I laughed big.

"What d'you want to know? 'Sex pig looking for fat dick in my pussy-hole.' I always thought that was a fun one. Though, 'Latin dwarf ISO white guy with horse dong, must be straight-acting.' He spelled it 'S-T-R' then the numeral '8.' Know what I mean?"

I removed one hand from my head and did a figure "8" in the air. I'd got into sex ads initially because I liked the verbal quality of them: gay lit in its most elemental form. Magical incantations. Uncensored wishes. Like the little rhymes children pass down from generation to generation to skip rope with. (I could hear queer playground chants like: "Ring around the ROSEY / I need a hot HOLE-sy / I'm a hunky DADDY / who'll FUCK you in the BUTT!")

Aside from that bit of anthropology, they were also fun.

"So I told them I didn't know any of your friends. At least not any who weren't friends of both of us. Did you have any?"

"Only playmates," I answered. "You know, like kids have?"

"Sure." He looked wisely at me, reminding me that in the long run he was smarter than I was.

"Got any aspirin? I've got a killer headache. Nothing like having your head split open to produce one."

Josh went into his bathroom, bringing back two Extra-Strength Tylenol and a small paper cup of water. I swallowed them with the water.

"I couldn't seem to keep friends," I admitted.

He ran his fingers through my hair. I took his hand, kissing the palm. I felt that moment between us so intensely that it could not have been the old, easily jaded Dr. Leonard Miller feeling it. Whatever I was now was just floating there, trying to grab onto something as good and lovely as Josh.

Josh said, "What will we do about—"

"What?"

"Eventually, they're going to figure out you're not dead. At least not like you were."

I stopped floating. Thank God, or *It*, for Tylenol. Extra Strength. "Will you claim my body?"

"What?"

"I can't suddenly be alive now. Look, there's an old guy there with my name tag on his big toe: I put it there. They would have just thrown him into Potter's Field. I know I'm asking you to do something impossible, Josh, but please, will you?"

"Are you afraid they'll try to kill you again?"

"Sure, of course I'm afraid of that, horribly afraid. But I have another fear, and it's really hard for me to get a grip on that one, too. The truth is, I don't really know now who or what I am exactly. Or how much time I've got to figure it all out. See, I think this is just a reprieve. It's what I asked for. What I reached for, and got. You see, I don't think *I* have really been revived."

"You mean I shouldn't get too used to having you around?"

I nodded.

He looked at me, his face just barely holding its composure.

"Okay, Len. What do I need to do?"

"You're being very brave." He only looked at me, waiting. "We need to arrange a cremation. I'll call Watkins on West Fourteenth Street. They're like a gay funeral home. I went to a funeral there once for one of my—"

"Playmates?"

I nodded again. "He was murdered, too. Like me. It was awful. A nice Hispanic kid, about thirty. They had an open coffin, but you could tell he'd been really cut up. That's why we need the cremation fast, in case they're holding me to do an autopsy. Morgues get crazy, though. There're all sorts of slip-ups. Sometimes you can get away with things, if you claim to be the next-of-kin."

"I'll do it," Josh said. "I've just got to look at him and say he's you. That's all, right?"

I smiled. For the first time, I began to relax. I could even joke about this.

"Sure, Josh. Just call it, 'Papa's got a brand new bag!'"

After looking up the numbers, I arranged for my cremation with a woman at Watkins, then Josh spoke to a clerk at the Medical Examiner's Office. He told her he was my cousin and he'd come by, claim the body, and sign any papers necessary. She gave him no problems.

I was now up and walking about, dressed in some of Josh's freshly dry-cleaned and fashionable clothes. Even his shoes fit me—the joy of having a boyfriend your own size!

"We'd better do this fast," I told him. "I'll take a cab over to Bellevue with you, but I won't go in. It'd be my luck that someone hanging around there saw me in that other condition."

"You mean, like dead?"

I nodded to him.

chapter four

$\mathcal{I}$ held Josh's hand in the back seat of the cab. His hand was cold and damp. About a block or so below the Bellevue complex, we stopped in front of a Greek coffee shop with a large plate-glass window on the east side of First Avenue. It looked fairly inviting. Josh paid for the cab, and without my asking, handed me a twenty dollar bill.

"You might need this," he whispered.

We got out and I hugged him on the sidewalk. "Do you know what you need to do?"

He nodded, swallowing hard. "Uh huh. But I've never done anything like this."

"Sure, it would scare the crap out of me, Josh, and I'm used to stuff like this. But it's one thing to do this in a lab setting, I mean work with dead things, and another to do it when it means something to you. You're being wonderful; I mean that."

He lowered his head and walked off. I went into the coffee shop, and sat down at a table with a window view. I ordered some coffee and a piece of warm apple pie with lots of whipped cream. I had not had whipped cream in a year. Like Josh remembered, I'd been watching my cholesterol.

We used to joke about that when we went out, because I liked eating cum. I know that being a sperm *maven* sounds funny, but it's an almost perfect food with an amazing range of tastes: buttery, salty, lemony, sharply tangy, acidic, even sugary, depending on diet, and a man's age. Younger men have higher concentrations of zinc, copper, and other trace elements, which leave a bitter taste, while older men seem to have better-tasting cum. Some men get off on that, though—that wild, zincy taste of young guys with the toned skin and muscles that go with it.

Despite big AIDS warnings about oral sex, I'd always found the odds of getting the virus orally to be minimal. At least my odds were. I sipped the coffee, luxuriating in the deep, aromatic warmth of it. Then the waitress brought the pie and I thought I was going to cry.

Simply from tasting it. I am a big man for the senses: I really love all of them, especially in those brief moments when the senses totally take over. I stuck two fingers into a thick, airy cloud of whipped cream and carefully licked them. People were grabbing a peek at me and I winked at them. I've always enjoyed the voyeuristic pleasure of catching people off guard, of interacting with the city's strangers and even laughing at its insanity. What I was doing was insane enough: waiting for my own body to be identified and then picked up.

I ate the pie slowly, and afterwards felt all right; certainly nothing like how I'd felt earlier after the eggs. A man came in selling the *New York Post* and I bought a copy from him. I liked all the dirty gossip and tabloid headlines in it. I turned to "Page Six," and then spotted an item. "No Killer Yet for Doc Frankenstein."

They were talking about me.

I'd taken one of Josh's ballpoint pens with me and I circled the piece, which was written by a reporter I didn't know. With publicity now such a part of research, I had got to know a lot of journalists, but usually these were science journalists, not tabloid ghouls trying to tweak the morbid fascination circling around a high-profile death.

They say dead men tell no tales, but often what is left of us is a real account of ourselves, more truthful than what we told while we were alive. I remembered in school working for a lab that did pathology work. Coroners from all over the area would send us tissues, revealing all sorts of secrets: a sober judge drank like a fish; a straight-laced, moralizing minister had contracted gonorrhea ten years earlier.

Yes, organic evidence does remain in our blood and tissues. No one can fool us, the scientists, the pathology queens, for very long. Deeply hidden mysteries unfold right in front of us. Now there was the unfolding mystery of the substance Alvin Jurrist had sent me from Turkey, from an area so ancient that the layered soil had become a veritable encyclopedia of history. Dig straight down several feet and your shovel starts to clang against the iron work of the Crusades; several feet more, Roman bronze; still further, crumbling clay idols from the time of Abraham.

Alvin had dated his discovery close to the time of Christ. Archeology, he explained to me, was much like detective work: mostly it was constant boring surveillance. You take measurements, make working drawings and photos of a site; you dig some, look some, then dig some more. If what comes out shows promise, you'll hire more people to dig and hope that they don't screw up the evidence, or rip you off every chance they get. You could be in a squad car sloshing bad coffee, and waiting for the action to start.

Then suddenly, blood racing, you've found it. I tried to envision it fully, my mind recalling the words he had used, to see the place, the excitement of the find, and the fear.

"*Ne? Ne? Ne demek?*" the diggers screamed—*What does it mean? What? What?*—as Alvin, already out of breath, came running towards them. A chief digger was bent over, whisking dust with a soft badger-hair brush from a small globular specimen, still on the ground. An eerie, golden glow popped up towards him and the digger's eyes bulged in his head. It was a distinct piece of human flesh, from the heel and part of the sole. It was ghoulishly fresh, and looked as if it had been severed only yesterday.

The diggers looked at each other, then up into the clear blue sky.

"*Ne demek?*" they demanded to know over and over. What *does* it mean? Was this cruel, isolated thing evidence of a murder, perhaps a fragment from a young woman, or a child?

Alvin couldn't answer them. The site had been left untouched for millennia. The geological stratum around it—dirt, sand, clay, ground rock, minute bits of material from the period—showed no change in texture, a sure sign that someone had recently tampered with the area, perhaps hiding the specimen there.

He felt certain of only one thing: this specimen wasn't new.

And also, it resembled nothing he had ever seen before. Taking out a clean handkerchief, he carefully picked up the piece and put it into a large, air-tight plastic container. Then, without looking back at his diggers, he brought it to his tent.

It was noon, near the sparkling Aegean coast, in early fall under the low trees of a running brook whose fresh-water source, from springs in the nearby hills, flowed clear even through the summer. In the shade, his men broke for lunch. Normally they would have fished or horsed around as they sipped sweetened mint tea, sharing the local dark wine from wineskins. They would have munched on salty white cheese and green olives, played dominos, clapped hands, and sung out loud to each other.

At the opening to his tent, Alvin looked back out towards them, hearing only the brook and the hiss of the wind in the bent little trees. The men stared silently back at him, then they turned away and began to speak softly among themselves.

Deep within his tent, Alvin nervously opened the plastic. A neutral smell came up. There was no indication of corruption on the tissue, no evidence of maggots, stains from minerals, or worms. Putting on rubber gloves, he picked the specimen up, washed it with bottled water, and felt the engaging, rounded plumpness of it. It had retained much of a normal flesh color, mirroring the dark, sun-tinted bronze of the men outside. But its surface was glazed with a slight golden blush that had produced that initial glow the men had seen, and that had frightened them.

Fearless now, Alvin touched it to his bare cheek.

It felt warm. He kept it there, pressing it with his fingers, close to crying.

He could imagine the uproar from the University of Chicago's justly famous archeology department, which had sponsored his dig. They would say he was crazy, that something like this thing couldn't possibly happen, that this was in the domain of bad pop movies. He removed it from his cheek and stared at it.

He transferred it into another, cleaner plastic container, then took it into his nearby field hut, which contained a narrow wooden table supporting a portable microscope. He squeezed his eye into the eyepiece and gave the surface of it a look. His head felt dazed. There they were in front of him: these were living human cells from two thousand years ago, when the Romans were *the* superpower and soon rumors would spread about a young teacher named Jesus. In this azure-skied part of Turkey, by some accident that might *not* have been an accident, his men had dug up a small but still living piece of that tumultuous era.

Alvin kept the specimen near him for two days, hating to part with it. He waved off the repeated questions and hostile faces of his diggers, appealing to their fierce pride, telling them that real men were not bothered by gossip and superstitions. Late at night in his closed tent and in his field hut, he did all the tests he could on both it and the stratum around it. Working alone, he became certain that, indeed, this human substance was as old as he had believed it was.

Next, the question was what to do with it? How to bring it to the world, without bringing suspicion and ridicule to himself? He thought about me. This was no longer in the dusty realm of archeology, but from my part of science. Packing the specimen in surgical cotton soaked with a mild, sterile, saline solution to keep the living tissue fresh, he put it in a small glass lab dish with a gas-permeable seal on it, so that it could still have oxygen.

Later he called me in the early evening, from a small village several miles up the coast from his dig. It was still morning in New York and I had just arrived at my lab. From the way his sentences gushed and stumbled, I could tell he'd already had several drinks. Maybe he needed them to deal with the stress from his discovery. He was bursting with excitement, but still we refrained from saying anything too confidential over the phone. After he had hung up, he sent it on to me by an express courier who made a special stop at the village.

Before opening the package, I made sure everyone was out of my lab. As evening approached, I studied it in increasing wonder for an hour in the dark, with only the light from my microscope. How had something like this remained in the earth and survived? And how could a piece of human flesh regenerate itself over and over, ignoring the normal obliteration of time?

Mummified humans had been found almost intact in the glaciers of the Alps or the Andes, but that was simply due to freezing. This was not frozen, and no one had touched it with the preservatives the Egyptians used. Sharing the secret only with my chief lab assistant, Tom Zhang, we examined the tissue more closely, extracting one-cell-thin sections from it, then poring over the slides. I wanted to keep as much of it whole as I could, and I made sure the specimen was kept cool, protected, and under constant lock and key.

I only brought it out when I was alone, or with a few trusted colleagues.

But with so much of my time devoured by it, word began to leak out. Jasper Englestein, the lab's bookkeeper, approached me one afternoon. A tall guy in his mid-thirties who looked like a telephone pole with a little potbelly jutting out of its middle, Jasper resembled a slightly-born-too-late suburban hippy, wearing ill-fitting, cheap suits that were always bunched-up and wrinkled. He had coarse, unruly, dirty-blond hair that stuck out in long corkscrew curls, and big blue eyes that opened into a "Like wowie, Man!" flash when he got excited.

"Len! We can name our ticket!"

Jasper's eyes were doing cartwheels, while he pitched that we should stage a media conference—

"As soon as possible! You got any idea what we got here? This is living proof that human cloning is not only possible, it's one-hundred-percent completely natural! We knew Mother Nature had been cloning herself forever—but not *human* nature. This is so cool, man, this is—"

I wanted to stick my fist into Jasper's mouth to silence him, but somehow Englestein was related to someone with money and influence, so he carried this whiff of fear around him as the bumbling, good-natured, poor-relation, house busybody. Even his being there stood as a witness that in my field of bio-research, where science closely followed the trail of politics, money had started to get tight.

Perhaps you might remember the old Sputnik hysteria in the fifties: because the Russians were beating the pants off us in space, America put everything at the disposal of scientists to get ourselves up there. Science education zoomed; labs popped up like toadstools after a spring shower. The toad, actually, is a good analogy, because they're amazingly self-regenerative. An organism that starts out as an amphibian tadpole can replace a dismembered foot. American labs had to do that: make up for lost time.

After Kennedy put us into space, big business decided that we weren't going to make a lot of money up there and the Space Program started to suffocate. During the Reagan years, only research attached to defense was funded, so you needed a defense contract to survive. Labs became attached to universities, with their nearby business schools; or spun themselves off as research and development departments of big drug companies. Dollars were expected to pop out of every microscope and when the dollars did not pop fast enough, the microscopes were quickly turned off.

Under Bill Clinton, private labs like my own were funded by roving venture capitalists, following the greed incentive that one of us might stumble upon the successor to Prozac or Viagra. Since that kind of Holy Grail is not easily sightable, scientists were forced to apply to the government for additional help. Now with the re-surfacing of other Republican toads in the White House, money for non-defense research was again tumbling out of the picture.

"This could fund you for years, Len!" Jasper announced.

"Or kill us."

"*Kill*? Wow, Man! That's a bummer."

What did his parents wean him on, the Beatles' *Sergeant Pepper* album? "I think so," I said.

"You mean, like some fundamentalists may actually come after us?"

"Not us, Jasper. *Me*, big boy. Whenever you dig into human cloning, they get pissed off. Especially when it's a queer man doing the digging."

He shook his head. "So you think they'd really come after you?"

I looked into his spacious blue eyes, which should have been connected to his blond head with antennae, and rubbed my hands to make the point.

"They might, if we go public about this too soon. That's why I want to wait on this, then get a few other high-profile, science talking heads to back me up on it. If not, I'll go from being seen as a TV sideshow, to the lavender Devil himself."

Since I'd been doing research on cell regeneration and cloning for close to ten years, our "Let's-Make-It-Simple" media had decided that my real goal was to clone gay men, so we could start reproducing "parthenogenetically." Meaning: *alone*, like the "virgin" goddess Athena, who'd been produced from Zeus's naked brain waves. For gays, the idea of being able to reproduce "conceptually"—that is, through the brain alone—was exciting. It harkened back to the "gay" idea of Platonic existence, an existence based on mental and physical perfection.

But I was never exactly behind that, either.

Human cloning was exciting to me, but as a "gay"-specific idea it was a dud. I wasn't even sure if I had any "gay"-specific ideas, or did I? In short: I didn't think that cell regeneration, leading to the *repro* of humans, should be limited to gay men and lesbians; nor did I feel we should be barred from it, either.

However Jasper got his way. The business side couldn't hold out any longer, and we were scheduled to have the big media conference *exactly* the day after my murder.

Wowie!

Finishing my pie and the *Post*, I paid the bill and went out for some air. I'd walked to one end of the block and back again, ready to return to the coffee shop, when Josh showed up.

He looked upset. The color had bleached out of his smooth face. At first, he couldn't speak, then he said mumbling:

"We're too late, Len . . ."

I took his hand. It felt even icier than it had in the cab.

"It's been done, honey," he blurted out. "Somebody else claimed the body!"

chapter five

I couldn't believe my ears. "What?"

"This nice African-American lady told me somebody else had come in to claim it. She told me she thought they'd better wait for an autopsy. But somehow they had got somebody to sign what looked like a release from the D.A.'s office to take it."

"Did you tell them you were my next-of-kin?"

He nodded.

"Who took it?"

"I asked that myself. I said I wanted to read the release papers and she brought them to me. It was your brother—Robert Miller."

My head started to tighten with pain.

"Josh, I don't *have* a brother named Robert. My brother's name is Stephen, and he wouldn't claim my body. Believe me, he would feed it to the turtles before he'd claim it."

Josh's face flooded with anxiety. The noise of rush hour overtook us, as a stampede of people and honking cars hit the avenue.

"Let's get out of here." I grabbed his arm and pulled him to the street, then put out my hand to hail a cab.

Taxis whizzed by us, a blur of yellow, all filled with passengers. Suddenly that nauseated feeling came back to me, and I wished that man on the train with the Ritz crackers were there—anything to divert me at the moment. I didn't feel like I was going to throw up again, but I was having a hard time holding myself together.

Josh looked at me. Much of the normal color had returned to his face. He seemed more concerned about me than anything else.

"You don't look right," he said. "We've got to do something."

All I could do was nod.

I wanted to go back into the coffee shop, but I was afraid I'd collapse on the sidewalk. I felt embarrassed to be sick in New York, losing that control you need to survive there on the streets, sure that people hurrying by were staring at me. A few of them did. What could they be thinking? Had they seen my picture in the papers also, or was I just frightening myself? I needed to get off the street fast.

A big black luxury car-service sedan, windows heavily smoked, drove up slowly beside us, coming to a stop. The front passenger-side window rolled down and the driver, a handsome Mediterranean-looking young man with a black mustache, smiled.

"Would you like to come in, sir?"

Without speaking, I opened the back passenger side door for Josh, then I got in after him.

Inside, it was dark; soft, easy-listening music played on the radio. As I settled in, I noticed a man in a sharply-pressed business suit sitting on Josh's left. I couldn't really see his face. Another passenger, I decided, as I closed my eyes and exhaled slowly, hoping the pain in my head would go away.

"Everyone comfy?" the driver asked. "Where can I drop you gentlemen off?"

Josh gave him his address on West Fifty-Seventh Street and we headed uptown. My headache began to ebb. I opened my eyes, put my head back, and quickly squeezed Josh's hand. He squeezed mine back. From the backseat, I could see little through the side windows, just through the windshield, but I allowed myself a moment to relax, knowing that we were going to be all right.

The businessman flicked on a reading lamp and snapped open the *Wall Street Journal*. Everything seemed normal in a distant, slightly threatening New York way. I hoped Josh had enough money on him for the fare. We hadn't even asked the cost of it—usually you negotiated that first with private cars or you'd really be taken for a ride.

The driver, in the rear-view mirror, smiled at us.

"Everything all right, gentlemen? More air conditioning back there? How's the music? Does it bother you?"

Josh mumbled that it was all okay.

I rolled my window down a bit to look out. Traffic had become snarled on the avenue. The driver took an exit to F.D.R. Drive, along the East River, weaving in and out of lanes quickly, as if he were in a real hurry to take us someplace. We passed the U.N., then Sutton Place and the exit closest to

Fifty-Seventh Street. The businessman put down his paper, and I realized we were heading towards the Fifty-Ninth Street Bridge into Queens.

With his reading lamp still on, I could see that this other passenger had a short, neatly trimmed, reddish, cinnamon-shaded beard with dashes of silver in it, dark brows and eyelashes, a thin, neatly shaped nose, and a pair of prim, tightly held lips. Except for the dry lips, he might have been some banker who easily traded his three-piece pin-stripes for complete leather drag on weekends. He glanced over at us, smiling briefly as if he were beginning a stale joke, then snapped off the light.

"So? How are you gentlemen this evening?" he asked.

Neither of us answered.

From the corner of my left eye, I saw him looking straight ahead. His fingers tapped his bearded chin, then he said casually, "I thought you might like to come home with me for a while."

I shook my head in disbelief. "What?"

"I said I thought you'd like to come home with *me* for a while. Didn't you hear that? You know, relax? Put your feet up?"

"No!" I turned to him in the dark. "We're getting out of here!"

I tried to open the locked door of the moving car.

"Don't even try," the man said softly. "We're both armed."

It was not nearly so dark that I couldn't see the service revolver he showed us in a shoulder holster inside his jacket.

"I don't think we're going to need this. Right, Dr. Miller?"

I couldn't answer him. I didn't even nod.

"Jesus Christ!" Josh screamed. "What are you, Arab crazies? I swear—I want you to know this, I've never done anything against you people. I want you to know—"

"Please, Dr. Miller. Would you calm your friend down? And tell him *never* to swear and use the Lord's name in vain in my presence? We're Christian businessmen, not Moslems. We respect the sons of Mohammed very much—they're zealous people—but we are not Moslems."

I took Josh's hand, squeezing it gently; Josh started crying. "He's scared," I said. "This has been a lot of stress on him."

"I can understand. You've been hard to deal with, Dr. Miller. You know that?"

"Sure, I know. Just tell me who you are, and what you want from me."

"Where to, Mr. Nathan? Your office or your house?"

"I'm going to take them to the house, Tonio."

Tonio—the driver—started along a wide avenue, then turned onto an expressway. After almost a lifetime in New York, I knew the direction we were heading, towards Belle Harbor and the Rockaways, the beach parts of Queens. A good place, if you needed one, to get rid of bodies.

"Mr. Nathan," I said calmly, "You don't need to hurt Josh. I mean that. If you need to hurt me, okay. But why hurt him, too?"

"We'll treat your friend with the utmost respect, Dr. Miller. I gather he's a professional, too, like you are. He must have a sense of ethics. That's what we look for in anyone."

By now my eyes had become adjusted to the dark. I struggled not to be afraid. Fear, I was coming to learn, was an automatic reflex, like anger, and I needed to learn how to control that reflex. What use was fear to me, if this "second lease" on my life were going to last only a short time? I couldn't be afraid for my life, since I wasn't even sure I had one. But obviously Josh was terrified. All I could do was grip his hand, squeezing it softly.

"He's extremely ethical," I said.

"Good. I'm a businessman, Dr. Miller, but one who works in the ways of the Lord. Have you any idea how many Christian businessmen there are in America, or the world?"

"No."

"We're like a big, powerful family. We're *the* family that runs the country. And we're everywhere, like you gays. So you never know when you're going to run into one of us. Our life's mission is to do God's work in a zealous way. Science has no mission, and I know you homos don't. You'd sell your own mothers for a—"

"What's this about, Mr. Nathan? Just tell me what you want and why you have to involve Josh in it."

He edged forward in his seat and turned to me, so that I could see more of his face. The tip of his tongue moistened his dry lips.

"Okay, cards on the table, Dr. Miller, time to fess up. You've been involved with a substance that comes from God. We know it dates back to the time of Jesus and we know it's holy. No man should have the right to degrade it as you have."

"So that's why you tried to kill me?"

"We did not *try*, Dr. Miller. My men *killed* you, plain and simple. They made sure you were dead. You did some kind of trick with that substance and now you're back. We need that substance from God Almighty Himself, and we're going to get it."

"I don't have it," I said.

"Lying contravenes the Ten Commandments, Dr. Miller."

"So does murder."

"For those who trespass Levitical law, the price is death."

"Which Levitical law? You mean like not mixing milk and meat?"

"You know which one. The one about man lying with—"

"You're the one lying, Mr. Nathan. When I think about the lies people like you have told about people like us, when I think about—"

"Stop!" Josh cried out. "Who cares what Leviticus says? *Leviticus*? You're going to kill me because of Leviticus? This is crazy!"

"Son," said Nathan, as if addressing an unruly child, "I can see you're upset. Highly strung, artistic men like you become upset easily. But don't blaspheme the Bible. We won't hurt you, I promise. Like I said, I'm a businessman. In business, rule number one is, 'Don't involve people who don't need to be involved.'"

I smiled. "I thought rule number one was, 'Make all the money you can.' And it's also rule number two *and* rule number three."

"Maybe in your business, Dr. Miller. But not in mine."

Josh dropped his face into his hands, sobbing openly. I placed my hand on his head, and kissed him softly on his ear.

"I wish you guys wouldn't do that. It repulses me."

I stared over at Mr. Nathan. "Sure. You don't mind killing people, but this repulses you. Didn't Jesus kiss his disciples?"

"Not like you do, Dr. Miller. We won't allow you to play God, or play with His handiwork. As a professional scientist, you probably feel you have no boundaries. But that sort of arrogance doesn't sit well with us."

We were skirting the various terminals of J.F.K. Airport. I could see police cars all around us, but I wasn't sure if any of them would do me any good. I clutched Josh's hand.

"If I was so against God, who detests me, how come God allowed me to live? Can you tell me that?"

"God did not 'allow' you anything, Doctor. It was trickery. The Devil has tricks, too. We see them everyday."

Flashing police lights shone through Nathan's window.

"Tonio, slow down! We have to be careful here. The cops in New York have a lot of holiness in them, but they still work for a godless government that won't even let kids pray in the schools."

"Yes, sir," Tonio said and we slowed down.

Josh looked up at me.

"Sorry, Lenny, I couldn't help it. I freaked out." He turned to Nathan. "So what sort of business are you in, sir?"

"More like 'businesses,' friend. Like I said, we're all over the place. We import running shoes and other types of casual clothing, and export food and other essentials. I'm also seriously involved with health care. The poor of the world need that, you know."

I continued to stare coldly at Nathan, hardly believing the man could use a term like "health care" like that, with his veneer of compassion, and then have me killed so brutally.

He smiled to himself, bringing his fingers together as if in prayer.

"That's how I make a *living*, gentlemen. But Christ is my real living. I live for Him. For a while, in my youth, I could have been like you. Someone only out for his own gratification. Sex, drugs, those kind of temptations. My family, I confess, was not the best Christian family. There was waywardness in it. But I found the Lord, or He found me. In this modern world where everything is without meaning or a compass, God has told me how I need to live and where I need to go."

Joshua nodded emphatically at his words, but I could detect a sharp edge of tension rising in him, something he normally concealed under his stylish facade.

"Okay, I understand, Mr. Nathan." He swallowed. "Let me tell you this, I'm no druggy. Most of my life, I've thought about other people. I'm a librarian. Books, learning, the truth—that's not drugs." Josh paused, then snapped at him, "I'd like to tell you where to go. You know that? I mean it. I could—"

The genial, smiling mask dropped instantly from Nathan's face. He yanked the pistol from his shoulder holster, striking Josh's nose violently with its butt. Josh flinched and struggled to catch his breath, as blood trickled down his face.

Nathan replaced the pistol casually in his holster, and the tight, smiling mask returned. He grabbed a wad of tissue from a box near his reading lamp and helpfully offered it to Josh, who pushed some of the tissue up into his left nostril, holding his head back until the bleeding stopped. Then Josh stared ahead, his expression glazed and hurt.

I placed my hand on his icy fingers. I wanted to warm him, to do anything I could. I hated myself for putting him through this, but I hated Nathan even more.

"That wasn't necessary," I said, when I was finally able to speak.

"Dr. Miller, let me and the Lord decide that. The Lord has spoken many times through me."

"Sure," I said. "And I bet He loves your method of getting people to listen."

Nathan turned his face from me. I watched his profile in shadow. A revolving blue light from the top of a speeding emergency vehicle pierced my darkened window, rolled across Josh's crushed features, and landed on him. A loud, repeated siren blast exploded in from outside, then vanished. I could see bitter rage smouldering on Nathan's face. We rode on in silence for several miles. I held Josh's cold hand, vowing to myself that I'd do anything I could for him, and keep fear as far away from me as possible, no matter what.

Really, how could I be afraid now? All I could do was hate a man like Nathan. That hatred, with Nathan's prim face behind it, suddenly gave me a strength I didn't have before. I wanted so much to give that strength to Josh, just peel it off me and hand it to him.

Outside, the landscape changed from high rises to houses. We were on an attractive residential street with sloping lawns, shrubs, and big dark shade trees along clean sidewalks. Tonio stopped the car. He got out and opened the back passenger side door for me. Then Mr. Nathan, pistol in hand, nudged Josh out.

On the sidewalk, Josh looked at me. I smiled, nodding calmly. I wanted so much for him to know that I wasn't afraid, and wanted to convince myself as well. Tonio got back in his car and drove off.

It was a clear night; the air had a bracing tang of salt in it. I'd always liked this part of New York. I remembered it from when I was in my twenties and used to explore every area of the city that I could. People forget that New York has beaches as well as concrete canyons and crowded sidewalks. Despite a gun steadfastly pointed at us, I took Josh's hand as Nathan motioned for us to walk up to his house.

chapter six

The house, a fairly spacious, two-story, family residence, was no mansion. Many showy places graced Belle Harbor, but this wasn't one of them. Mostly, it showed its age as we marched down into a living room stuffed with sagging plaid furniture sunk into a brackish expanse of dirty pink wall-to-wall shag carpeting. Grainy, 1950s rice-paper plastic ceiling fixtures only accentuated the deep cracks and chipping paint in the lime-green walls.

I felt like I'd been dropped into some improvised rented college pad, the kind with the drugs stashed inside the stereo and the grown-ups a hundred miles away; not in the home of morally-upright people. There were, though, enough bad pictures of Jesus to start a museum of truly bad pictures of Jesus. They all made him look like the touch-football coach at "St. Swigham's," one of those fabled New England boys' schools where the jock-ish, fair-haired instructors slept tightly locked each night in their own private closets.

That Jesus C. might have been a short, excitable, swarthy-skinned Jewish guy with a big nose, acid stomach, and skin problems had never occurred to the faithful here.

I'd only had a moment to check things out, when three drab-looking men and one Hispanic-looking woman in the mid-stages of pregnancy appeared from another part of the house. I stared at them, while Josh sat down, his eyes turned away.

The pain in my head had stopped and, frankly, just being there was starting to feel strangely comical. Maybe I was only becoming accustomed to the insanity of my situation.

One of the men, in an ugly gray suit and a tie that looked ripped from the plaid upholstery, approached me, slowly shaking his head.

"So, if it isn't Dr. Miller!" he spat out at me. "It looks like you can't die, you Jew-queer!

In the dull yellowish light, I put him back into a white lab coat. He was Oren Tillman who had worked with me for two months as a "tech," or low-level lab assistant, mostly cleaning equipment and checking gauges. I had hired him myself. He'd had a good resumé, but a jumpy temper that sometimes popped right off its leash.

Usually he brought his anger quickly under control, apologizing afterwards. I'd never thought much about him, since I was too busy working. But I remembered how two days before my last night at the lab, he had exploded at me.

We'd had an argument about cloning itself. He revealed a vehemence against it in any form that I hadn't expected. If cloning did occur in Nature, he informed me, it should stay there. "Who are we to intervene with this?"

If he thought this, what was he doing in my lab? He'd been a good worker, a bit testy, okay, but I'd had no forewarning about his feelings. The next day, prior to my last night on earth, he had quieted down considerably, even treating me extra-pleasantly as he went scurrying about his business.

I hated the way he grinned at me now, as if he had taken the mask off me, instead of the other way around.

"I don't know how you did your trick, Doc—got the other corpse into the bag. You're certainly clever. God doesn't like clever people. The Devil does, but not our Lord."

"I never knew you were on such close terms with the Devil, Oren."

"I should be, after working with you!"

He turned to Nathan, who looked impeccable next to him.

"I thought we'd killed him, Henry. I thought we'd killed this monster. The homos, the abortionists, it was my job to infiltrate them. But I had to pray hard every night to keep their filth away from my mind."

"Did it work?" I asked calmly. "I mean, it's never easy to pray hard. I can barely pray soft."

"Shut up!" Tillman spat at me.

I wiped his saliva quickly off my face. "Hey, I thought they did that to Christ!"

"I told you to shut up, you Jew-bastard!"

"Oren!" Henry Nathan said, "Anger is not the way of the Lord. And I was born a Jew, but I declared myself for Jesus, so let's not denigrate the Children of Israel. Consuela, can you bring us something for these men to eat? Can we offer you anything, gentlemen? It's going to be a long night, and we will not harm you if you behave. Please take our word for it."

Josh looked at them. There was still a trace of blood under his nose. "What *are* you going to do, Mr. Nathan? I mean, what do you want from us?"

"We want what Dr. Miller has, that substance that regenerates itself. We put Oren into his laboratory to spy for the Lord and he told us about it. Spying is an honorable vocation when you it do for the sake of God. Tell me, Dr. Miller, have you ever noticed how many homosexuals become spies, all of those English gay-types? Ever noticed that, Dr. Miller?"

"Pretending to be what you're not is a lifetime avocation with us. People like you, *Henry*, have made it part of the territory."

Nathan's eyes dropped to the shag carpet, but he did not lose his temper this time. The woman came in with a bowl of fruit, an unopened box of Sarah Lee cheese danishes, and several glasses of fruit drink on a tray. The men took the fruit drinks, so I figured they were not trying to poison us. I took a glass and drank it down, but Josh wouldn't take anything.

"Sure you won't have anything to drink?" Nathan asked.

Joshua stood up. "Maybe just some water. What I'd like to do is use the bathroom."

Nathan agreed. He handcuffed Josh's hands in front of him. One of the other two men, who was slope-stomached, balding, and in his mid-thirties, was directed to go with him. This strange-looking geek had his pants hitched up about three inches below his armpits, and a premature-ly-wrinkled, bird-beaked face attached to a skinny, macaroni-pale neck.

"Don't try anything funny," Nathan warned as they walked out.

Josh glanced back at him. "Like what?"

"He means, don't offer this gorgeous hunk of man-stud here a blow job for your freedom," I said, chuckling. "I have a feeling these boys don't get much of anything."

"That's real funny," Tillman said. Then he socked me in the jaw, and I knew instantly he'd been the first one to attack me after the lights went out. It was the feel of his fist; I couldn't forget it. I wanted to kill him so much, it was painful. I buckled to the floor, so he could see how much he had hurt me, pretending to be even more hurt than I was, just as I'd pretended to be dead then. Not that his blow hadn't hurt, but at a certain point you get used to physical pain. Perhaps I was at that point.

"Oren, you need to control that temper," Nathan warned. "The Lord does not care for intemperate men."

"He's not partial to people who screw around with His work, either," Tillman replied.

I eased myself up from the floor, then found a chair. Consuela offered me a danish. "Gracias," I said. She smiled at me.

"My wife appreciates your efforts," Mr. Nathan said. "It seems you can be a well-bred person when you need to be, Dr. Miller."

I thanked him for the compliment, then Josh came back from the bathroom. I asked if I could have a turn. I was handcuffed and the bird-looking wonk, who walked like an ostrich and was named Tommy Lee, paraded down the hall with me. He flicked on the light in a small john, then closed the door behind us.

I smiled broadly at him.

"What's so funny?" he asked.

He had a peculiar voice. I imagined it coming out of a hillbilly goldfish, since it was high, sounding like it had nervous little bubbles popping out of it.

"Oh, just that I noticed they always seem to send you with us to the john, Tommy. You think there's a reason for that?"

"Dunno, sir. I'm from West Virginia, a bitty place near Wheeling. My main thing is to serve the Lord and make sure they stop killin' the little babies, and do good stuff like that."

I looked around. It was a regular-looking bathroom; it could have been anyone's. I went over to the medicine cabinet, opening it with both handcuffed hands.

"Think they got any aspirin here, Tommy? Your friend Oren did not do a nice thing to my head. Ever get a headache?"

"Sure. I get 'em. Who don't? Lemme look."

He went over to the cabinet and started rummaging through it. Aspirin, tooth paste, a small can of Right Guard spray deodorant, bobby pins, Peptol Bismol, nothing that could be considered revealing. He handed me two aspirin tablets and a paper cup from a bathroom dispenser.

Unable to fill the cup with my cuffed hands, I asked Tommy to do that, then swallowed the aspirin and took the cup from his hand. I moved in close enough to him to smell his stale breath. He edged away.

"Thanks for the water, Tommy."

"Was nothing."

I unzipped my pants and took my penis out, even though I was not close to the toilet. "Mind if I pee in the sink, Tommy?"

"*Whaa*? Tha's not a nice thing t'do, Doc."

"I won't miss, if you don't mind. I got one of those dicks that can't aim right. Ever see a peter like that?"

I waved it at him, and I could see him turn beet red in front of me.

"I hate cleaning up bathrooms, so I always piss at home in my sink."

He looked at me in stark horror.

"Y'do?"

I nodded.

"Well, remind me never to drink outta yer sink!"

"Sure, Tommy. I'll be happy to remind you of that."

I held my cock over the sink, then ran the cold water. He turned his head away from me.

"Some people have a funny thing about bathroom sinks," I said grinning. "You know that old saying, 'Everything but the bathroom sink'? I guess they think it's sacred or something."

He remained turned from me. "T'tell you the truth, sir," he confessed, "I don't like no-how to mix th' sacred in with th' bathroom. Know what I mean?"

"I know exactly what you mean, Tommy. Never mix, never worry."

I watched the shiny back of his head, as I availed myself a bit more at the mirrored medicine cabinet.

"Finished, sir," I announced after I had put myself safely away. "Would you mind if I combed my hair a bit?"

"Doc, come on. We gotta get back."

"All is vanity, vanity, vanity!" I finished zipping my pants up.

We were back in the living room again. Josh had finished a glass of water. He smiled at me.

"They want to know if I'm your boyfriend."

"I never deserved someone like you." I pressed my handcuffed hands to his neck and kissed him. I could see the faces all the men made. Only Consuela did not mind. She smiled at us.

"I'm glad you gentlemen are becoming comfortable," Mr. Nathan said. "A van is going to pick us up very early tomorrow morning. You'll be blindfolded. We're taking you to a safe house, where you'll tell us everything about this substance you've been working with."

"He's got to have the stuff on him," Tillman said. "It's either on him or in him. I know that for sure. What I wouldn't do to take a knife and cut this queer-ass bastard apart!"

Nathan shook his head sadly.

"Oren, would you watch your language? My wife may not speak a lot of English, but she knows I do not tolerate words like that. Dr. Miller, how does cutting you apart sound to you? I mean, in the name of science?"

"Better than in the name of God. God's name seems to cause more problems. Right, sir?"

Tillman raised his fist again, but Nathan stopped him.

"He may have a point, Oren. Sometimes, Dr. Miller, I do believe that you take God seriously."

Henry Nathan was right. After my "awakening," I did take that vast mysterious entity called "God" seriously, even more seriously than I had ever suspected I would.

The men led us, still handcuffed, down into an unfinished concrete basement, where the intense white glare coming from rows of naked ceiling light bulbs almost blinded us, like walking into the sun after being in the dark. Nathan, Tillman, and the other man, who was also Hispanic, went back up the stairs. They left Tommy with us. Boxes were piled shoulder high around us, and in the middle stood an old filthy, chintz-print sofa, Delft-blue and white, with handfuls of cotton stuffing popping out of it. I figured they used this for their guest room.

We sank onto the sofa, with the blazing ceiling lights drilling down on us. I kept clenching my eyes to relieve the strain on them and the pain in my head, made worse by the glare. I kissed Josh several times on the mouth. Every time I did it, Tommy Lee turned away.

"They're going to kill us," Josh whispered. "Aren't they?"

He looked wasted. His hands were trembling. There were big perspiration stains on his nice shirt. I had never seen Joshua sweat, ever. He always seemed so calm next to my craziness. I hated the handcuffs. I wanted to put my arms around him, just to calm him and keep the awful lights out.

"Why don't you try get some rest." I motioned for him to lie down.

"I'm too scared, Len."

I kissed him softly again. "I wish I could do something so you wouldn't be. I won't let them hurt you. I'll do anything, Josh. They can kill me again. They can crack my head open one more time, but I won't let them hurt you."

He nodded. More blood came from his nose and he wiped it on his sleeve. I slid across the couch to the end, and he stretched out, putting his head on my lap. I stroked his face with my chained hands. Tommy was getting more embarrassed, I could tell. Placing my hand over Josh's eyes, I bent over and kissed his face, while Tommy Lee moved further away from us. Finally there was a moat of lacerating light between us, a glare that literally dissolved him from us.

"Try to get some rest," I whispered, lifting Josh's head so that I could get up. He shifted his body, facing the back of the sofa to shield his eyes.

I got up and started looking around. Some of the boxes were marked DANGEROUS CONTENTS. I knew that they contained explosive chemicals. Beside them were stacked boxes of ammunition. The place was a bunker and we were captives in it.

I ran my hands across the boxes, smelling the unmistakable odor of sulfur, gun powder, and metal blasting caps. The smell brought me back to when I was a small kid on Long Island. My father occasionally went shooting in New Jersey with business acquaintances. He was never crazy about it, but it was one of those things a "real man" at the time could hardly get out of. He'd bring back a freshly killed wild turkey or pheasant and my mother would bring it over to a neighborhood butcher shop to be dressed.

My brother went out with him a few times on those hunting trips, but I never did. Still there were certain distinct smells of guns and hunting that my father would return with, and they were down in that basement. I went back to the sofa. Josh had managed to fall asleep.

The geek emerged from the moat of light.

"Is your friend okay?" he asked, stooping his shoulders.

"He's sleeping."

"He seems like a nice kinda guy."

"You mean for a homo?"

"I didn't say that."

"He is nice, and I am, too." I took my cock out of my pants, and started fiddling with it.

"What are you doing!" he screamed.

"I thought you might like to see what I do. You know, queers? You never can tell what we're going to do next."

He started shaking.

"You'd like to suck this, wouldn't you?" I asked.

"Stop!!! You revolt me!"

"So why're you here, Tommy? Why don't you just get out of here?"

"I should kill you!"

"You don't have the balls," I said, then aimed some spit into my hand.

"STOP THAT!" he screamed.

Josh woke up. "What's going on?"

"Your friend's a pervert," Tommy Lee informed him.

Josh looked over at me and smiled. He shrugged, like what else was new?

"I should kill ya. I should kill both o' ya!"

"You won't," I insisted. "Because you need me alive."

"I don't need you for nothin'. I came out of Anti-Abortion, Pro-Life. They pushed me into this mess. I hate it! Lord Jesus, why've You made me consort with these perverts in Yer most holy Name?"

I put my dick away, then stood up. "I could sure use a drink of water."

"I bet you could! Ever'body in Hell wants that!"

Josh looked at me. "I guess we're close, aren't we, Lenny? To Hell, I mean."

"If you don't get me a drink, Tommy Lee, I'm gonna start jerking off again. You have a choice. What's it going to be?"

He turned around and hurried back up the stairs. The door slammed. We were alone. My head again felt like it was going to split open. The strain on my eyes after being dead was torture. I decided then that no matter what, everything was going to change. It was definitely not going to be good; and I was no longer going to be nice.

I told Josh that.

"What are you going to do?" he asked.

"Try anything to get you out of here alive."

"All right," he said. He started crying again, which didn't help his bleeding nose. I used my sleeve on his face, then immediately smiled. I would get him out, no matter what—I'd made up my mind.

A few seconds later, Oren Tillman came back down by himself. He was holding a revolver and no water.

"What are you trying to do, Dr. Miller? Some kind of queer sex act in front of Tommy Lee? He's just a country boy, what do you think you're doing?"

I starting laughing. I couldn't help it.

"Yep, a sex act. I can do a strip, too. Want to see, Oren? Anybody ever tell you you have a name like a cookie?

"You're one funny faggot. Shut up!"

"Maybe you want to see my dick, too! Did Tommy Lee tell you how nice it looks? Want to taste it? All of you guys are secret homos—I know it!"

"I should shoot you right here, you Jew-faggot!"

"Wait a second, Oren," I said, shaking my head. "You need me alive. Remember, you guys want to cut me apart while I'm still alive, 'in the name of science'? Right, Oren—or is it Oral? Are you oral, Oren? Do you like to suck dick? Is that your thing, you just can't do it for the Lord?"

He raised his pistol, aiming it at me. He couldn't shoot me; they needed me alive, if only to know where the substance was. They had no idea how easy it would be to spot. Then he aimed it at Josh, now standing up but leaning with one leg against the sofa.

"Suppose I shoot your boyfriend here? How's that?"

Josh's face turned to Tillman; he was speechless.

"Beats suckin' dick for a living!" I said, smiling brightly, briefly meeting Josh's tired eyes. Then after clearing my throat and lowering my voice close to a whisper, I asked, just between the two of us, "Oren? Mind if I smoke?"

He lowered his weapon. A furtive, psychotic smile came out of hiding.

"Doc? Don't tell me *you* got cigarettes!"

"How could *I* have cigarettes? But I remembered that you smoked, Oren. You used t' grab a smoke in the lab john, then open the window to let the smoke out."

"You knew that, Doc?"

"Come on, we all knew. God, I'd sure love a cigarette now! I'd die for one. I'd crawl for one. I'm a secret smoker myself."

"Really?"

I nodded my head. "Like I've never wanted anything in my life. Oren, if you gave me a cigarette now, you could shoot me right afterwards.

Firing squad style. You know, like the French do?"

"Shit. Really, Doc?"

I nodded again, smiling at him, eye to eye.

"Henry Nathan won't allow me to smoke. No smoking. No drinking. Jesus, these people! I mean, the damn Arabs smoke. They don't drink, but they sure do smoke. As much as I love Jesus, you have no idea, Doc, how much it sucks working for Christians. I'd kill for a cig now, too. You really want one?"

I told him I did. Passing the revolver from his right hand to his left, he scrounged in his jacket pockets for a secret pack of smokes. Finding the pack, he flicked out one cigarette for me. I took it. He lit it for me, then lit one for himself.

Gray smoke started swirling around us through the intense glare. I took several drags, blowing a fat puff right at him, then brought out the little aerosol can of Right Guard I'd found in the john. I aimed a full blast of it into his eyes.

He screamed, "JESUS CHRIST!"

I jumped at him, grabbing for the revolver. Blinded, Tillman turned and pulled the trigger, firing directly at Josh. Josh must have got very close—I couldn't hear the gun go off. He jumped towards Tillman, coming between us. I saw only Josh's back, with the light exploding like a halo through the gray smoke around him. I grabbed him to push him to safety. He was soaking-wet from sweat, and slipped away from me, blood oozing onto my hands. Then he fell straight down to the concrete.

Tillman's eyes blinked. I lunged at him, grabbing his left wrist with both hands, kicking him as hard as I could in his shins and groin, squeezing him, until he dropped the gun. I scooped it up, shooting him in his face.

They both looked up at me from the floor, with Tillman's eyes wide open, frozen in surprise next to the gore of the bullet hole. I bent over Josh. He was dead; I'd known it even when I'd tried to grab him. There'd been nothing left alive to grab, just the blood on my hands. I closed Josh's eyes. He'd tried to help. I felt blank inside, though my legs were shaking all over, but had to take a few more seconds to kiss him. I'd never kissed those sweet small adorable lips enough, and now there was no more time.

I wanted to scream, but I got up, unafraid.

I was breathing so hard that I wasn't aware that I was breathing.

They'd be down in a second. What was keeping Nathan and the others? Every muscle in me twitched to blow the place up. I grabbed Josh's wallet and keys from his pants, then went through Tillman's pockets. He had keys on him. I grabbed them, too.

Tommy Lee opened the door at the top of the stairs and shouted, "The van's here!"

I shot him. He fell down the stairs dead.

Nathan would be out with the van. For a second, I felt bad about the woman. Using Tillman's plastic cigarette lighter, I lit the sofa. The cotton chintz burned fast and I threw the lighter on it. I ran up the stairs. The front door was open. I had the pistol in my hands, and I wanted to find Nathan and the other man. I'd never been so angry in my life.

I ran out to the street. The other Hispanic man saw me with the gun and ran back into the house. I jumped into the van. A young light-skinned black man, maybe twenty-two, was at the wheel. He didn't seem to be too disturbed by my gun and chained hands.

"Where's Mr. Nathan?" I demanded.

"I think back in the house with his wife, Sir."

"Drive! NOW!"

He looked at me. I put the gun right on him.

"Whoa, Mister! Whoever you are, the Lord does not want you to kill me. Let me tell you that, Sir."

He started the van.

As we began to move, the house blew up.

chapter seven

*T*he entire house exploded with a big BANG. I thought my spine was going to snap. The boy almost jumped through the roof, letting go of the steering wheel so that we swerved off the road. With my chained hands, I reached over to steady him, but he leaned forward and grabbed the wheel again.

Pain, like an atomic elbow jab, hit me in the stomach, as my head stopped hurting completely. My back was up against the wall and I wasn't sure where my front was, but that after-Bang silence, like the air had been sucked out of the world, lingered in my ears. I was only afraid that my young driver had been so rattled that he was going to get us killed.

He wasn't. His eyes stayed glued to the road.

In fact, he looked calm. Suddenly rapturously so; even close to happy.

Balls of powdery stuff, like make-believe snow, were falling out of the air. I smelled scorched paper, vaporized paint, melted plastic, charred wood, and that unmistakable odor on the wind of burned human flesh. As a scientist, I'd recognized it, but I'll never forget the way it smelled that night, with the two of us speeding in the van.

But I was alive. Life was washing over me like an intoxicating wave of oxygen, and every breath I took made me feel more expansive than I'd been only a few minutes before captive in that basement. Even without Josh, I felt truly grateful to be alive. All I wanted was for the explosion to block out that awful last image of his face on the floor: just obliterate it.

Whatever part of its regenerating cycle that substance was in, it was pushing two hundred percent now. My energy, stoked by anger, felt unstoppable. A bunch of nuts were doing their damnedest to extinguish Lenny Miller, but a totally new, spit-in-the-eye survival part of me was grabbing the world by its balls!

I'd never felt like this before. Who the hell was I?

Who-ever I was, we were bouncing down this road gutted with

fucked-up New York City potholes, as if everything were now back to normal. The young man slowed the van down, and I turned to concentrate on him: He was ... no doubt about it, really nice-looking. Bright, intelligent face. Sensuous lips. And a very appealing, narrow-bridged nose with an elegant bit of chiseling on both sides before the nostrils flared.

He turned to me and I caught a glimpse of his sparkling, light-colored eyes. I started swimming in that sparkle; it danced alone in the dark without a lot of light around him. He kept glancing over at me while I pointed the gun at him.

"Sir? You okay now?"

I nodded, grinning generously at him.

"Sir, can you tell me where you want to go?"

I shook my head slowly. "Where were *you* going to go?"

"I'd been hired to take you into Pennsylvania first of all. You'd be moved after that."

Hired? Excellent sign. "Does that mean you're not really one of them?"

"No, sir. I'm a devout, believing Christian, sir. I just don't get as bent out of shape over it as some of 'em do. I got a cousin who was supposed to be doing this, and he couldn't. So I was doing it for him."

"And the van. Is the van theirs?"

"No, sir. It's rented. Less traceable that way. Why'd you ask?"

Suddenly I had a plan. "We're going back into Manhattan. Let's take the slow way, through Howard Beach. You know that area?"

"I am familiar with it, sir. They love black people in Howard Beach, it's just that they've got a problem showing it. A problem that goes back a long way."

"Do you go back a long way, too?"

"Huh?"

"I mean, like those friends of yours who wanted to murder me. What do you think about that?"

"Sir, the truth is they're not my friends. I was s'posed to pick up a vile, evil, homosexual-abortionist-murderer and his accomplice and take them over to Pennsylvania. Like I said, they hired me. My church is involved with a lot of Christian things—that's about right for a church, right?—so they hired me to drive two dudes to Pennsylvania. I'm against abortion, but I don't think that all abortion-favoring people are murderers."

"So you can think for yourself?"

"Sure," he answered. Suddenly, he broke into a private, very interior smile. I hadn't seen such a sweet unguarded smile in a long time. "You like rap music?"

"Not at all."

"Good, neither do I. Every black dude—every dumb nigger—is supposed to dig rap music. But the truth is I don't."

"Who says you're a . . . dumb, uh—?"

"Nigger?" He shrugged. "It's just a word to push your buttons, sir. That's all it is. Another pigeon-hole to get stuck in, like you're 'sposed to like being a 'niggah.' Know what I mean?"

"I'm afraid I don't."

"I guess you wouldn't. Tell me, sir. What are you thinking?"

I looked at him. I felt blank. What could I say?

"I'm not sure at this moment," I answered. "But whatever it is, I don't believe you're a dumb anything. No matter how cool it sounds, you're not a—"

"Nigger?" He grinned broadly, with his eyes back on the road.

"No! I mean it. Believe me, you're *not* a nig—" I drew my breath in, then focusing on the word, I released it—"ger!"

Immediately I knew I *was* a nigger, too: handcuffed, a fugitive; I expected dogs to start chasing after me. I had to change the subject.

"What's your name?" I asked.

He smirked, his bright eyes dancing back and forth between me and the road.

"Benjamin. But my friends call me Benjy."

"That's nice. Benjy what?"

"Benjy Rosenbaum, sir."

"You're kidding?"

"Nope. Not kidding one bit."

I beamed. "That's more Jewish than me—I'm Lenny Miller. Dr. Leonard Miller, the vile whatever. Hey, you do look Jewish, Benjy—I have to tell you that—in the best way. You're handsome. You look like a prince, really. Right out of the Bible."

The smirk dropped from his face and he tensed up. I'd embarrassed him.

"We'd been Jews someplace," he said, about a minute later, relaxing.

"Jews were all over Africa—mostly Ethiopian. They came from the Queen of Sheba, that's what my great aunt, Esther Varshti, told me. She was Esther Varshti Rosenbaum. My theory is that a family of Jews once owned us. That's how the Jewish blood got in there. Anyway, there's no way of telling, is there?"

He paused for a second, then added, "All the same, I prefer Benjamin Rosenbaum to Rufus Johnson or Raheed Mohammed, those stock colored names. Jews aren't such bad dudes, you know, as long as they don't get too screwed up with Israel. That's their Achilles' heel. Know what that means?"

I shook my head, not because I didn't know what an Achilles' heel was, but because I was having such a hard time trying to figure out what was going on.

"It means a sensitive, vulnerable spot, sir. We all got 'em, right?"

I nodded my head, looking at him. "Would you mind if I asked you something, Benjy?"

"No, sir. Please ask."

"You're like a real person. I mean bright. Intelligent. How did you get into this story?"

He smiled. "I've been going to Brooklyn College and studying theology. The truth is I just needed the money."

We were now driving through Queens, which always looked like Los Angeles in the dark, row after row of identical streets and houses.

"Suppose I paid you, Benjy? You won't have to drive me all the way to Pennsylvania. Is that okay?"

"You're not an abortionist, right?"

I told him I wasn't and asked him to stop. He did, and I put down the pistol long enough to get out Tillman's keys and use one on the handcuffs. It felt good to have my hands free again. I put the pistol inside the belt of my pants, and shoved my shirt over it.

Benjamin lit a cigarette, then offered me one, bringing me back to that moment when Tillman had killed Josh. I shook my head slowly, refusing it, trying hard not to feel so horrible for Josh Moreland. The worst thing was that I'd have to use a lot of what that sweet man had on him, his keys, his wallet, just to stay alive.

I put my feet up on the dashboard of the van and pretended that everything was like a movie on a big screen: Technicolor, big stereo Surround-a-

Sound. It was all happening in front of me, not *to* me. Before I'd come back from the dead and all of this had happened, that was how I'd fallen into the strange byways of kinky sex—all those guys with their desires to be firmly dominated, or tickled out of their wits. I fondly remembered one adorable thirty-something cutie whose specialty was that, being tickled until he came.

I'd externalized it all: it was all one big movie, and hardly any of it ever got inside me, except for that blessed release from my daily battle with self-censorship. No tests, review boards, and censorship on those wild, aboriginal shores of sex, amongst the native "abos" of Brooklyn, the Bronx, Queens, and some of the bordering regions of New Jersey. Just a pure acceptance of me, and the physical moment. I looked over at him. "Tell me, Benjamin. Do you like getting your dick sucked?"

"Sir?"

"You know, your dick sucked? How about your ass eaten? Would you like that?"

"Sir, I thought I told you, I'm a Christian. Would you eat Jesus's ass?"

"Sure, if he let me."

His brow furrowed, as if he were really thinking about it. "Jesus"—he hesitated, then said—"probably would, wouldn't he? I mean, *if* you really wanted it, he'd do that. He wasn't judgmental. That's what I love about him. He loves me, I know it, even though I'm just a pretty ordinary black, part-Jewish kid at heart."

"You're not ordinary."

"Thank you, sir."

"But so what if you are? I was just a white Jewish nerd. Smart, probably too smart. It used to cut me off from a lot of what I wanted."

"Like getting your dick sucked?"

"Exactly. You guessed it."

"Yes, sir, I understand what you mean. Intelligence can stand in the way of many elemental things, like faith for instance. Sometimes you can be just too smart for faith."

We approached a quiet street, a sleeping village of small dark houses. With so few lights outside interfering, I could really observe his face. He was smiling, deep in thought.

His right hand was between us. I took it. He let me, without flinching. I felt thrilled. His hand was thick and work-toughened, not soft like Josh's.

"It was just meant to be a conversation starter, Benjy. I mean, here we are on the road. A house just blew up. My friend got blown to pieces. I'm torn up inside. I don't know what's next. It's like a war's happening, know what I mean?"

A shiver charged through me. In the after-shock of the explosion, I wasn't sure suddenly if I was going to start sobbing or get a hard-on. Maybe both. I wasn't used to giving vent like this. I only knew I was so utterly grateful for this kid—with whom I didn't have to be afraid. It was like he'd been dropped on me from *It*. Okay, call it Heaven; I felt so open towards him.

He glanced over to me and nodded, a genuine brightness in his eyes. I wanted to jump into that radiance, like an inviting pool of water in the dark.

I squeezed his hand, searching for something to say. "We could be in a tank together, Benjy. Locked in. The world exploding around us. Just the two of us."

"We could, sir."

"Isn't that when guys really start to think about getting their dicks sucked?"

"They do." He squinted at the road.

"Sure, Benjy, it's—'Let's pull it out and do it, because in another second it may be all over with. BANG!' Ever feel like that?"

He hesitated. "No, sir. I'm afraid not."

That image of me jumping into the moonlit water, with him, of course, evaporated. My voice fell: "Not?"

"Yes, sir. Not."

I released his hand, swallowing the little lump that came into my throat. Any stiffness in my pants fell too.

"I guess being dead is … different to you, Benjy." He nodded. "It's the Christian thing, right?"

He didn't answer me.

"Can you tell me what that's all about? Really, I want to know."

We were now cruising through Howard Beach, close to the salt inlets of Jamaica Bay. It looked as shut up as a ghost town. A couple of big dogs in very run-down front yards started barking. A few porch lights went on and clicked off. Benjy kept his shoulders locked in tension, his eyes straight on the road ahead of us.

When we got back on to an expressway, I rolled down my window.

The night air greeted me with a milky mist, as some first light started to come up around us.

"So, sir? You still want to know about the Christian thing?" Benjy glanced at me. Our eyes stayed together for a second or two. In this early light, his looked greenish, a dark, mesmerizing jade green.

I held my breath, nodding for him to go on.

"Sir, the truth is, I'm in love with God. That's why I feel like even in a tank, it's not all going to be over with for me."

"I see." I ran my tongue over my top lip. "But isn't that kind of 'queer'? I mean, isn't God, you know, our Father? Like a man?"

"Come on, it's *not* like you date Him! It's that your heart is now His. It belongs to Him. That gives you a big heart, too. Because He has such a big heart."

He lit another cigarette.

We went over a bridge that looked like something left over from the fourteenth century. In the dim morning, New York looked decrepit. I was genuinely touched by him.

"That's really beautiful, Benjy. I like the simplicity of it. Everything's so complicated now."

"Yeah, you can say that. Men and women, you can't tell 'em apart. They're starting to clone humans. It's scary. That's why I need Jesus so much. I need Him inside me."

I was touched by his openness. Not a single one of the men I'd met was ever that open with me. Not even Josh.

I took his hand again briefly, then released it.

"I hope you get Him inside you," I said.

We went back across a bridge into Manhattan; I knew I'd have to make a decision about my new friend. I told him Josh's address on Fifty-Seventh Street and he reached it. Taking out Josh's wallet, I found eighty dollars in it and handed it to him.

"I need to make more money than that, sir. They promised me two days' work."

"That's just for tonight. It's yours; you're free, Benjy. I'm not going to ask anything else from you. You can take the money and drive on. Or, if you need to, spend the night here. I don't know where you live, I don't—"

He looked directly, very seriously at me.

"Sir, that is kind. I thank you for your offer. But I must ask you this. You won't try anything funny with me, will you? You will, sir, respect my honor as a real gentleman would respect a devout, practicing Christian?"

I lifted my right two first fingers up to heaven. "Scout's honor."

"That's all I need to know, Sir."

We drove into a garage next to Josh's building. An automatic dispenser spit out a ticket. Carrying Josh's keys and ID, I felt like a vulture picking over his bones. When we walked into his building, a new doorman asked me where I was going. I told him I would be staying at Joshua Moreland's and I had his keys.

"He's on vacation," I explained.

"He is? I thought Mr. Moreland just got back."

"He came into some money. So he's enjoying it. This is my friend Benjamin. He's a divinity student."

The doorman, who was dark-skinned and sounded West Indian, smiled at Benjy who smiled back at him sweetly with those green-lit eyes. Then the doorman nodded at me.

"This is a nice building," Benjamin said, as we got to the elevator. "I wouldn't mind living in a place like this."

On Josh's floor, the hallway was suddenly so bright and stark that it reminded me of being in the morgue again. I unlocked Josh's door and flicked on a wall switch.

Someone had been in the apartment. I could tell they'd rifled through things. Not badly, nothing all over the place, but they'd been there. Perhaps some new boyfriend of Josh's had his keys. Or, had another pack of zealous Christian businessmen already made the connection between the late Dr. Miller and Joshua Moreland?

I went into the kitchen and opened the refrigerator. There was beer in it and I offered Benjamin one. He told me he did not drink, but: "If you're having one, sir—"

He took one anyway.

We both had a beer, then I found some cheddar cheese, bread, and lettuce to make sandwiches with. I was not sure if Benjy was the cheese-sandwich type, but I was not capable at the moment of foraging any further. We ate them on a table in a part of the living room where Josh entertained. The table expanded with two leaves and Josh could sit six people comfortably around it if he wanted to. I remembered him doing that once. It had been a nice evening, and for a second I was shot into that memory.

Benjy ate without looking at me, drinking the beer as if he did it all the time. I offered him another beer; when I came back with it, he was staring at me with his mouth slightly open, like he had never seen anything like me before. In the room's low lighting, I could see his reflection in the wall mirror, the soft light dancing in his greenish eyes. He looked happy, relaxed. Maybe he'd found his own instance of Jesus there; something, I could understand, we all looked for.

A lot of people were starting breakfast or still sleeping, and we were having dinner. I had no set sleep patterns anymore. We finished the sandwiches and the second beers, along with some ruffled potato chips from a bag. I didn't feel tired, just tense and dirty. I wanted to take a shower. I turned to Benjamin. "You want a shower?"

"That would be cool."

"Okay." I pointed him to the bathroom. There were fresh towels in a linen closet next to it. Josh's towels were big, thick, and fluffy, in pastel colors like aqua and fuchsia. Mine were thin, grayed, stiff, and redolent of wet feet and mildew. I kept house like a pig and changed them about once a month. Scientists aren't good at housekeeping.

In the dim light on the way to the bath, Benjy started dropping his clothes in front of me. He had a nice body, somewhat stocky but young and trim, light-café-au-lait-colored, with strong thighs and an amazingly-eatable outie belly button on a slightly rounded stomach. There was a dense field of short, black, curly hair on his muscular upper chest. He took everything off, his eyes glittering.

"You want to shower, too, sir?"

"I can after you."

He blinked, then said, "Why 'after'?"

I didn't blink.

"Okay," I said.

Taking off all my clothes, I felt suddenly more self-conscious than he did. I'm not sure why; he was the religious one. Without turning on the light in the bath, we got into the tub in near darkness. I adjusted the water to warm, then turned the shower on.

He was all over me. Like I had turned on a switch and there he was: a

72

young animal out of the cage he'd been trapped in. Hugging my chest, he took my cock in his hand and I held his, which was circumcised, boyish, and got hard instantly. He had this warm natural quality that some men, especially young ones, revealed, once you got all their clothes off. It was like their real selves, no longer hidable, were waiting for an invitation to emerge. We washed one another with Josh's liquid shower soap—all that fine-scented lather, bubbles, and foam, mixing with steam and our own heat.

Who could restrain the natural desire the suck his delightful young cock? I couldn't—he moaned as I got on my knees, worshipping this naked faun and his delightful throbbing organ.

I was all pale, middle-aged, white, like some Jewish Icelandic beast, with my own wet black body hairs wriggling and splitting into swirls in the warm spray next to him. His dark fingers guided my face as I worked on his equipment.

If you can call this wonderful play "work." Absolutely, I'd been waiting for this: a shower in the dark. For real life and the night to begin, no matter what time it was. I sucked his cock as if it were a conduit to all of Creation, which is what it was. And what was I? Only the Great Cocksucker, sucking in all of life, pulling it towards me.

I released his dick, and started eating him all over hungrily: his firm chest, his Coca-Cola-colored pointy nipples; belly; chewy outie navel; muscular young ass. Even his fingers and feet. He started laughing, giggling. So did I. Then he got quiet suddenly and knealed, and took me in his mouth—long, deep, intensely hungry, too. So hungry that both of us lost where this would lead. I came in his mouth.

He looked shocked. He swallowed. How did all this happen?

Poor sweet Josh dead! A house blows up! Me in Josh's meticulous apartment—and now this beautiful, supposedly-straight, devout young man sucks me off? My only explanation: maybe Benjy also grasped I was a miracle, and just wanted to be a part of it. Further theories: who can say, precisely, how we punch the erotic buttons of others? I went for him again.

His sperm tasted very nice: zincy, fairly citric, with a bit of cilantro and a touch of chlorine thrown in. It took him about forty seconds to climax. For a shy, religious kid, he was white hot.

"I bet you think I do this all the time," he said as I toweled him off. "Christians, you know, aren't supposed to do such things."

"How do you know Christ didn't? I'm sure nobody never talked about it, but if He were so big and cool, maybe He left nothing out."

He looked at me seriously. "Perhaps."

I liked that idea, I mean sucking dick as a ritual. Who would not really, except of course Henry Nathan and his ilk? In India, I'd heard, ritual fellatio was practiced by Brahmans to keep them strong, thus divorcing it from desire. Youths were taken by older, married religious men, then paid for each "load," like delivery boys. Since only the slightest affection was implied by it, it was kept safe from homosexual "unspeakableness." I brushed my teeth with Josh's brush and offered it to him. At first he declined, probably being taught so by his mother, then accepted it.

We walked into Josh's bedroom.

"What's going to happen now?" he asked.

I told him I didn't know. But I could see the crystal-pleated hems of the rosy-fingered Dawn coming up from Josh's bedroom window, that faced East. I suggested we sleep.

We got into bed, and I did fall asleep for a while, holding him. Then I was awake.

Too much had happened for me to sleep, and I needed something to chase that image of Josh on the concrete floor out of my brain. It kept popping up inconveniently. It was lodged in my brain, and that had always been a problem with me: turning the neurons off.

When I was younger, I used to be delighted by the fact that my brain stayed up at night, entertaining me. At school in Boston—I had gone to Harvard for a while—I used to stay up at night and watch physics formulae perform intricate dances in my head. Symbols and numbers became so real to me that they took on metaphorical characteristics. Starting out neutral or chummy, they might warily split apart, only to return for opportunities to get together, like cruising men out for the night.

"P" might pursue "X" to the Third Power, squeezing "Q," a pushy interloper, out of the way. "PX" (to the Third) remained a romantic item, until "X," arrogant with the volatility of the combination, started to believe he didn't need "P" anymore. He had too much going on on his own, at which point—

The physical world I decided then was the most amazing. I gave up on poetry. Nothing from Shakespeare or T.S. Eliot would ever come up to the purity of the measurements for the expansion of a gas, or the pull of a planet. Newton and Einstein became gods to me. How they'd been able to do what they did, using only their raw brains without computers, floored me. There had to be some place where they'd gone, some door I couldn't push open.

I wanted to open it. I believed I could. But it scared me horribly.

What if that place past that door had no bottom, and you fell all the way down into the madness of your own imagination? Could I—would I?—be ready for that, surfing through the outer reaches of my own intelligence, my imagination released from that fortress of everyday minutiae we call "reality"?

As complex formulae and theories physicalized in my head, their structures became actual bodies with weight, dimension, color, what scientists call "character." Unlike a lot of my friends, I'd never done drugs. These moments on their own were too far out, simply as they were. Though tiring, they were also incredibly seductive, like practicing a thousand years of Zen in one weekend. Later, when I began to "discover" my "gayness," which seemed like a bubble exploding into a thousand tiny droplets of various queer sexualities, drugs began to have some appeal; if only for the sorely-needed reprieve they offered to my brain.

I liked poppers. And also hallucinogens, in small amounts.

The wild, fantasy sex I explored—as in young, silken-butted New Jersey Latino boys who were testing the waters ("Javier seeks fun pal for friendship") for a good blowjob; or who, after some nocturnal soul-searching, wanted to be tied up and fucked by a dominant white Daddy—was a reprieve as well. What it was not was the polite world of the good little gay boys, like Joshua Moreland, although I loved him really, as much as I could.

I was not the first person, believe me, to find myself too smart for my own good. Einstein's personal life, with a broken marriage and several broken kids, one committing suicide, was hell. Da Vinci, the last man to know everything, was overwhelmed by waves of depression, which left him shy and insecure. I understood that fear of your own feelings, which is, I guess, why I got into "hard" science, rather than hairdressing, interior decorating, embalming old ladies, or the other gay art forms.

If science can be a lusher form of poetry than even poetry, scientists are, for the most part, not poets. Even at their most eccentric, they can be conventional, like the "creationist" scientists, devout Christians, trying diligently to prove that eons of evolution did not create the platypus; God did it in a foolish hiccup.

There were things, though, I couldn't prove scientifically or completely understand about myself. They were hard to explain, even to try to communicate, for someone like I, rational, disciplined, driven. I would experience distinct moments, "states," when I'd find myself falling into an immobilizing trance. The boundaries of all my rationalism ended, as everything around me—that constant, whirling machinery of daily enterprise with me clinging to it—would stop, totally, and everything would become . . . the only term for it was . . . *God*.

God was everything: the total pattern of existence, the movement that dictates its own movement, the full *It* and continuous *Now*. And I, the first time the "state" happened, was simply a part of it, within everything that *was* the Great Being.

That first time, I spent about two minutes in it and was left frazzled. My brain stopped all the working and identifying that a brain normally does, and it, too, became another part of this pattern of being, of *all* Being. You might think that would be restful, finally stopping the brain; that it would be pleasant.

It wasn't. It was horrifying.

Because the brain could now be itself—just another organ—and in doing so, it actually "looked" at itself, which is no small feat for any brain to do. The brain, normally, cannot look at itself while being the brain: that is its limitation. But in this "state," *it*, the brain, on its own, could.

I experienced my brain as its own drug, a collection of chemistries, a physical thing and invention happening all at once, intoxicated with itself. It was my brain, but separate from me. And it was exercising, by itself, all of its own eccentric powers, properties, and splendor.

I panicked. I had to cease this.

This was scary beyond any idea I had of scary. Initially, it seemed to come out of nowhere, perhaps from overwork, my need to escape, or even an unconscious desire to die. But it made a powerful "mind-expanding" drug like LSD look like Excedrin, as I was pitched into anxiety, experiencing that the brain could work on its own, while I was "out there," part of the vast moving pattern we describe inadequately in basic terms of Time,

Space, or Consciousness.

I became one with the vast Cosmos, and the inner structure of molecules; with my own becoming, and my own undoing.

It was too frightening to do this alone.

I needed something else with me. So I had to cobble together some kind of instinct that could pull itself into a religious presence, without any reliance on faith, dogma, or belief. The Universe, I decided, as personified in "God," was passive: merely a vast, recognizable pattern, and I could merge with this by accepting my own passive place in it. As I became used to it, the "state" became more extended. It left me me feeling both "out of it" and "into It"—the great *It*, God, at the same time.

Once, I survived almost a whole day in it, without going totally nuts. I accepted the divinity of a subway clerk, a fat cop, two delivery boys on the street, and a good-looking, mustached lawyer I saw on Madison Avenue leaving Brooks Brothers. I became invisible to myself, as I passed plate glass windows with no reflection and saw distinct auras of light flashing before me like the eruptions of gas on the sun. Was it possible that I was seeing human energy, the life energy, physicalized? For someone who had rejected religion, spotting an aura-nimbus was, well, nuts! I mean, I could accept the "state" as part of my own strange make-up, but *auras* . . . they were genuinely frightening.

It left me vulnerable. When I walked into a street sign and almost knocked myself out, I became afraid that people would think I was drunk, or an addict. I had to force myself to stop doing it, to keep the "state" from happening, except in the most protected way.

I started going on retreats, checking into a motel in the Catskills where I could safely lower my emotional defenses and, at the same time, slow the conscious machinery of my brain. I felt the way an actor feels seduced by a role he plays: at the beginning, bigger, special, very privileged; then manipulated, small. Lewis Carroll walking into Wonderland had nothing over me. But once started, stopping it wasn't easy.

There was that fear that I might not come out of it, and end up psychotic, "bumping" over and over again into my "real" self trapped in the "state."

My pursuit of sex, between these "states," helped me re-integrate myself again, bringing me back to my own human cravings. American culture wants to see God as a reaction against sex, or animal desire; but the animal, the basic and low, were all aspects of the great Being, the *It*. Sometimes I felt myself going all the way back, like the springy double helix of DNA, boring itself through time, to meet myself in that original single cell from which we all sprang. It was then that I became aware that life does not stop: only changes. After all, God "knows," and in the knowing became Itself. So why would this "knowing" stop with death?

God was in man and woman. *God* was in that single cell that, out of frustration, or ambition, or sheer meanness divided itself and became two. God was in me and in my shit, sperm, and blood. But was *I* God?

Yes, but only in those moments when I left all of my defenses and accepted me as *It*. Once I'd been tied up by this man who shaved my balls, then put alcohol on them so that they burned slightly. He blindfolded me and whipped me in the most teasing, skillful way, then fed me his dick. I started moaning from pure pleasure. When he pulled out, I begged him to do it again. He beat me harder, and rubbed his cock over my face, putting tiny electrodes on my nipples and balls, then scraping, licking, and tickling the soles of my feet until I peed on myself.

I became Atman and Brahma, the universal breath that belongs to God. I became the thing that the Egyptians called the *first* light, that glimpse of dawn that distills Creation.

I went inside myself, walking towards the extinction of death; yet it was pleasant, a curative part of the brain taking me there, unlike the stark terror of my own real death, when the men broke into my lab.

Lying beside Benjy, I thought about when the final blow came to my head. On retrospect, it felt—almost pleasant. Like a relief: a calming spring flowing to announce that God *Itself*, the whole magnificent pattern of the Universe had come. I saw *It* then as that white light surrounding my younger self, who had come to speak and assure me: *This will be easy. Easier than we had thought.*

It had come to deliver me. But to where?

I got up.

Going for a drink of water into the kitchen, I opened the fridge and took out some bottled water. The kitchen was dark, except for the refrigerator light. Leaning over and drinking there, I felt like a robber. I had taken Josh's life from him, just as much as that creep Oren Tillman had. Josh had been kind, a good man, while I was all rapturous energy; and raptor, too. I shouldn't have been allowed to live; Joshua should have. And yet, if it hadn't been for my own "raptor" self, could I have come back as I did, killed Tillman, and blown the house up?

Perhaps, I was alive for some reason.

I went into the bathroom to a pee, shuting the door and turning on the light. In the bright, theatrical glare surrounding Josh's mirror, I looked like hell. I was still alive, and kicking—but getting kicked a lot, too.

Benjy came in, half-asleep, scratching his chest. "Gotta pee."

I nodded. "It's okay."

I liked the way we looked in the mirror, with Benjy reminding me of pictures of Vishnu—the Indian version of a young, darkly beautiful Apollo—as the goatherd. The village girls are all crazy about him, and want to blow on his flute. Benjy went to the bowl and peed. A little dingle of yellow—just a drop of urine—stayed on the tip of his cock.

I bent down and licked it. He laughed.

"You're some wild dude! Lord Jesus, I'm going to go straight to Hell with you!"

"I hope it's worth the trip," I said.

We slept till almost eleven. Then I got up, put on some underwear, and made coffee. Josh had the *Times* delivered; it was outside the door. I scooped it up and went back to his table to read.

Benjy had the TV on to Channel One, for news of New York. The first story reported an explosion in Belle Harbor "at the home of a retired manufacturer, named Stewart Cooper, now residing in Mexico. Mr. Cooper has been contacted, but he was unavailable for comment." Authorities were withholding the names of the fatalities until family members were informed, one newscaster explained, but neighbors had reported strange people coming into and out of the house for the last several weeks. "The police are now sifting through the wreckage for clues, to see if this explosion had any ties to terrorists working in the United States."

I offered Benjy some coffee, and found some bagels and cream cheese in the fridge. I felt very comfortable, hardly worried at all. What was there to be worried about, after the night I'd had? Benjy chewed on a toasted bage, leafing through the *Times.*

"Your funeral's today."

"Excuse me?"

"It says here"—he was at the back page of the National section, for the obits—"'A funeral service for Dr. Leonard Miller, slain researcher in biotechnology, will be held today at Grimaldi's Funeral Chapel on First Avenue at Twenty-Sixth Street at 1 p.m.'"

"God!" I swore. "I'm going to miss my own fucking funeral!"

"I didn't know you were dead."

"Officially, I am, Benjy. I mean, some very misguided people—"

"Not Christians, I hope."

"Whatever, even Christians can do bad things, right?"

He didn't answer.

"Anyway, they killed someone else instead of me, and now they're going to bury the wrong body. I wonder who grabbed that body to bury it? If I could find that out, it might solve some of the mysteries I've been living with."

"I guess you don't want to go to the cops with this?"

I looked down at the table, then up at him.

"Let he who is without sin go to the cops, young man."

He nodded. "That's cool. So you want to do your own funeral? We can jump into some clothes and go."

My brow knitted and I stroked my cheeks. There was no telling how long I'd be alive, but the very minimum I could do for those nice folks who'd killed me was attend my own funeral. Afterall, what idiot would miss that, if he had the chance not to? I'd never considered myself much of a dresser and I hadn't shaved. Sure, I looked a sight right out of Halloween, but anyone would recognize me. I got up and went into Joshua's bedroom. He had a whole drawer full of second-hand crazy clothes and cheap make-up that he liked to keep around for parties. His "drag," he called it.

I did a quick rummage through it, then I went back into the bathroom, did a glance at the mirror, took a quick shower, and began seriously to shave.

*young usher in a black double-breasted suit and skinny polyester tie nodded to us just inside the door to the chapel where my funeral was being held. He had a long, brooding, five o' clock-shadowed, "Don't-chu-fuck-wit'-me" face, like a hunky Long Island pizza boy reluctantly dressed up for a prom.

With a gloved hand, I tilted up a pair of dark glasses, and being very careful of my wig, used a lace hanky to daube my eyes.

"I'm Leonard's aunt, Flo Rosen," I announced in my most authentically matronly voice. "How *awh* you? Such a nice boy! Bright! *Smawt*! The first to go to college in his family—and become a doctor, yet. It made us so proud! Not that Lenny was a *real* doctor, but so what? We loved him anyway!"

After escorting us half-way down the aisle, the usher pointed to two empty seats in the middle of the well-attended chapel. Suddenly, in the full crescendo of a wave of whispers that followed us, I felt kind of glammy, like Joan Collins breathlessly waiting for a bank of flashbulbs to go off at the Oscars.

Benjy grabbed my arm. "Girrrl!" he warned in a low voice, "Calm down. Easy on that Auntie Flo act, or you'll blow your cool."

I looked at him and smiled demurely. In Joshua's fashionable, navy-blue suit that was only slightly too large for him, Benjy looked dashing, while I looked schleppy as usual in a high-necked mauve Rayon frock I'd found, something you'd expect a tall shapeless woman, one who wasn't let out on her own very often, to wear. Luckily, Benjamin had watched his older sister put on make-up. Otherwise, without his help, Josh's drag drawer finds—the slightly peachy, opaque-as-paint liquid foundation, the ebony mascara, and the fire-engine red lipstick—would have made me look like Dame Edna's double, after ten days in a psycho ward.

I took regal, measured, Grace Kelly steps in my stacked heels. As I sank into a chair and barely managed not to upend myself, I felt an immediate new respect for drag queens. I did a gaze-around the large crowd.

There were people I knew from the lab, many in tears; some vague acquaintances who had probably come out of curiosity; and then, sitting up front near the closed casket, several mourners I wouldn't have known from Adam.

Or Eve, for that matter.

Among them, a woman in her mid-forties kept staring back, like she expected someone important—me, for instance?—to walk through the door any moment. Pale-skinned and tastefully groomed, she was attractively dressed in a petite burgundy suit that was flared in the right places to show off her figure. Her eyes bored down on me. I turned away, sure she was still watching me, but turned my attention to other things.

Several of my . . . okay, "co-celebrants" from my old *rites d' skin* filled the seats. Some kept their heads down, trying discreetly to hide in the back, but two of them strolled up front, wearing fitted black leather, Euro-chic motorcycle jackets and dark ties. Ah, those boys! Alex Steuben, a red-headed chef, and Chico Rodriguez, his Cuban lawyer boyfriend, both great frisky playmates, hot as hell. "Two Non-Stop Tops Seek Bottom Looking for Heaven."

I guess I fit that bill.

"If they could see me now, that old gang of mine!" I wanted to get these shoes off as quickly as possible.

A very somber-looking minister in a three-piece, gray, man-of-God suit, his pinched "American Gothic" face culminating in a stiffly lacquered, tar-black-dyed comb-over, stepped forward to begin my eulogy.

"Friends." He cleared his throat, Adam's apple bobbing. "We're gathered here on this day to mourn a remarkable life."

I would have preferred that the young "Guido"-pizza-hunk usher had done this, preferably in a very skimpy, white, guinea-"T" tank-top, flashing some cute pink nipple every now and then. But, being dead, I was in no position to make that decision.

"Dr. Leonard Miller was a man dedicated to his profession, the study of biology. We are sure he was a good man, although his ethics might have disappointed some people, who felt that he did not have the right to play God. Now, only God Himself can judge him, or judge the events that took him away from us so early."

I started to squirm. *Ethics*? Who was *he* to talk about *my* ethics?

Was this drip with the coal-dyed pate going to knock me, when I couldn't defend myself? Where were the *ethics* of being murdered? If it hadn't been for my ethics, I'd be lying in that coffin.

"There have been many stories about Dr. Miller—that he was an atheist who worked with abortionists—"

"He was *not*," I whispered to Benjy.

"—that he thought only of himself—"

"He *did* not!"

"Pipe down," Benjy whispered. "You're gonna blow it, man."

"—that he believed he was another Dr. Frankenstein, trying to re-create life in his lab. That he was arrogant, that he was—"

"He was NOT!"

Every head turned to me. Putting both gloved hands over my face, I lowered my head and murmured apologies.

"Excuse me." I waved a sweat-soaked gloved hand out in front of me. "My nephew was none of those awful things."

"Dear lady, I was going to finish by saying that although Dr. Miller might have been misunderstood, he bore the bearings of a gentleman. Someone our Christian nation could be proud of."

I'd heard enough. I jumped to my feet.

"He was NOT a Christian! And I want to see who's in that damn box!"

"Ma'am, please. This is no occasion for profanity, and this is not an open-casket service. Those features were not provided by the family. Now, if your state of mind is too upset, I'm afraid we'll have to ask you to leave if you interrupt us once more. We know you're grief-stricken, Ma'am, but here at Grimaldi Brothers, decorum must be preserved."

The petite woman at the front who'd been playing eye-tango with me, got up.

"Dear, let me help you! She's Len's aunt. I know her."

Hurrying over, she pulled me up towards her with an iron grip like a stevedore's. With Benjamin in tow, she hauled me up the aisle and out of the closed chapel.

"Aunt Flo!" she said in the dimly-lit, small lobby. "It's been so long. You must remember me. I'm Gretchen, Len's sister!"

Whaaa? I'd never seen her in my life. "Of course, dear, I remember you."

"It's been ages, I know. But my husband and I followed Len's work always. Close friends of ours told us all about what he was working on. You know, that substance that would change everything we thought about life—and God? Know what I'm talking about?"

Suddenly my mouth clamped shut. All I could get out was, "Uh-uh."

Her voice switched to ice cold. "People will do anything for such a discovery, Aunt Flo . . . there are no limits. Get what I mean?"

Two razor-scalped brick shithouses in suits, who looked like bouncers at a Hell's Angels dance, started staring at us. I swiveled away from them. Something about them did not seem kosher at a nice Jewish guy's funeral.

Even Benjy saw this. "Ma'am. I'm going to take Aunt Flo home. She's a little under the—"

"Absolutely not," Gretchen protested. "You're both to be our guests at the reception afterwards. My husband and I went to great lengths—"

I looked down at the floor. *Husband?* "Your husband?"

"Yes, a prominent businessman. Maybe you heard Len speak of him, a Mr. Nathan?"

"Uh? I thought Mr. Nathan had another wife?"

"I bet you did, Aunt Flo," she growled. "He only said he was married to Consuela to get her over here from Honduras. She was carrying child, you know. But now that poor girl's no longer with us. Now—"

She grabbed my arm, her nails clawing through my puffy Rayon sleeve. The two brick shit houses appeared right behind her.

"Gretchen?" I asked. "Aren't you missing the rest of the service for your dear brother Lenny?"

"Don't worry, Aunt Flo. They'll bury him without me. They were just going to stick him in Potter's Field anyway."

My heart started to pound. Wasn't Nathan dead? And who was this gorgon? Whatever she was, obviously she and her people knew what they were looking for. And I had it on me—worse, in me! And this time they'd kill me for good, and amputate my leg to get to it.

"He's right. I'm not feeling up to this!" I screeched, looking towards Benjy.

"Aunt Flo, there you go again with your worrying!" Gretchen declared. "Me, my husband, and the Lord are going to make you feel a lot better fast!"

"Think so?"

Before she could answer me, I jerked her claws off me, pushing her away from me as hard as I could. Either she had to let go of me, or we'd both end up on the floor. She fell into the hefty chest of one of the Hell's Angel acolytes behind her, who lurched forward. Placing both his hands under her bust, he nudged the diminutive Mrs. Nathan upright like a bowling pin.

I gripped Benjy's arm and rushed us towards the door. A close group of people exiting another service milled around in front of it, including a grieving widow and her boy-toy-pretty. bar-mitzvah-aged son in what looked like the kiddy-sized version of a $4,000, dark blue serge Italian suit. His spiked, freshly-combed, strawberry-blond locks were glistening from styling gel and his tender face glowed with a gooey, right-out-the-jar, Madison-Avenue-skin-salon freshness.

"It's all over with, Joey," she cried, her pink nails finding a few stray hairs on his head. "It's just the two of us now, Sweetheart."

He ducked away from her.

"Ma, I never liked him. Of all your husbands—"

"Joey!"

"He was mean to me!"

"*Mean*? He gave you everything, Joey. Your own floor in the apartment, a driver—"

"Big deal," the kid pouted. "When they cremate him, I wanna keep some in my room. Can I?"

"Joey!" she cried, then shrugged. "Well, why not?"

"'Scuse me, young man," I said.

"Ma, is that a man or a woman?"

I elbowed him and whispered, "Out of my way, Joey, or you'll find out."

We were at the door. The two guys rushed us, one snatching the wig right off my head.

"It's a man!" Joey screamed.

I pivoted, shoving the boy directly into the first of the two goons; then wigless, hauled Benjy with me out onto the sidewalk, just as Gretchen, followed by her muscular pals, reappeared.

She was waiting, furious, next to the same big black car that had kidnapped me to Belle Harbor. The front and rear passenger-side doors were thrown open, ready for us. Inside, I spotted two faces. There was Tonio, again at the wheel.

And, directly behind him, eyes drilling through me, sat a very alive Mr. Nathan.

How in hell had he lived through that explosion? Poor pregnant Consuela, dead! Poor Josh, dead! Poor me—I tore open my purse, pulling Tillman's pistol from it, and pointed it straight at Gretchen.

"I'm going to murder your wife, you bastard!" I screamed.

She reached to the sky. "Lord, I pray! If I must die, let it be as Your servant!"

Every sweaty finger on me itched to squeeze that trigger.

"Cut the crap, you hussy!"

Her eyes bulged at me. "What did you say, YOU PERVERT?"

Nathan's head popped out towards us.

"Gretchen, please," he called softly. "What's going on? I thought we'd just—"

"HUSSY? HUSSY? I've never been so—!"

Before I could duck, she cocked her fist back and delivered a haymaker into my left cheekbone. Everything around me started spinning. Stars flashed. I could barely stand in Josh's stacked heels. What a punch this broad had!

Grabbing Benjy, I tried to get my breath back as the two goons gathered in closer. Benjy tried to steady me.

In the midst of the blinking stars in my head, I saw Gretchen grinning triumphantly at Nathan and then at me. She was convinced completely that I was as good as in the car. And as good as dead: twice.

Nathan slipped out from the passenger-side rear door, grabbing Benjy's arm. Benjy tried to jerk away from him, but the two bald goons stopped him.

I got my breath back. The blinking stars in my head faded just enough. Still, all I could see was that smile glued tight on Gretchen's face, like a missionary converting a topless dancer.

My itchy fingers quickly won.

I shot her in the stomach.

chapter nine

*G*retchen screamed, "Lord! Lord! Receive Your Servant Now!"
Tonio leaped out of the driver's seat, then jumped back in again.
Grabbing his bleeding wife, Nathan pulled her into the backseat, just as a
near-riot of confused mourners stormed out of Grimaldi Brothers' Funeral
Home, some following my very plain "Funerals-R-Us" wooden box with
that other unfortunate's corpse inside it.

Cops suddenly appeared. Gretchen's two vulture-headed body-
snatchers raced from them, and in the middle of all this, Benjy and I dashed
around the corner into a multiplex movie theater about a block away.

The box office was inside, the lobby empty, and no one questioned my
strange get-up while Benjy paid to get us in.

We dashed into the men's room where Benjy and I got into a spacious
stall reserved for gentlemen in wheel chairs. He grinned at me as I eased
up the dress, then helped me unhook a bra I'd carefully packed with
Kleenex. After pulling out the T-shirt I'd hidden inside the elastic waist to
my pantyhose, I rolled down a pair of chinos I'd worn over the black
stockings.

With the help of some premoistened towelettes, we got all of Josh's
foundation and party make-up off me. I took a pair of rubber flip-flops out
of my purse and felt fairly presentable again.

We sat down in the theater in the middle of a loud action movie, close
to a flock of about thirty hyperactive kids in Catholic school uniforms. On
the screen, Arnold Schwarzenegger was pretending to be an actor, but
who cared?

"Want some popcorn?" Benjy asked.

"I'm about broke," I whispered.

He took my hand shyly in the dark. "That's all right. You're really a
nice guy. I've been wanting to tell you that, Len."

"Thanks."

"Eef you geev me any prahblems, it's all over mit," Der Arnold threatened on the screen.

"There's something else I've got to tell you," he said, trying to keep his voice low and still be heard.

"What's that?" I whispered.

"I love you."

"What?" I turned to him.

The light from the screen lit up his green eyes and danced across his face, making him really look like an Eastern god, so exotic, so alluring, I had to catch my breath.

"It's true, I mean it," he said. "I just realized it. When that lady socked you, all I could feel was hurt inside. I was so scared something was going to happen to you, I would have gotten right into that car with you. I was so—"

Two Hispanic girls with braided hair and little butterfly barrettes were sitting in front of us. One looked back and asked, "Would you two dudes please be quiet back there?"

I turned to Benjy, and kissed him very softly.

"I'll get some popcorn," he whispered, and got up.

I told him I'd go with him. He peeled off the jacket of Josh's suit and handed it to me. We walked out the movie theater and I took hold of his hand. People stared at us; even in New York people only pretend not to be interested. Benjy hailed a cab and it took us back to Josh's apartment.

Someone was following us, I felt sure of it. It was a feeling I'd never be able to shake. I also felt totally nuts, but at least I didn't feel alone.

"What do you want to do?" I asked, when we were by ourselves in the elevator.

"Do you like to get fucked?" he asked. "I'd really like to do that."

I nodded. "Okay."

There's something about having a younger man, even as beautiful as he can be, screwing you that opens you up to all sorts of . . . wondrous possibilities. First, there's the voluptuous release from all the boundaries of set rules and "normalcy" in it. My legs over his shoulders. Him cautiously inside me; me stroking his chest. Then him, arching down to kiss me. And soon he gets a little bolder and starts to move some; then there's that feeling of me letting go even a bit more, but holding onto him at the same time and still having him right up there, with his lips, arms, and hands all over you. It's like being given all the candy in the world—just because you've been such a sweet ol' boy and have let Junior have what he wants.

In my life, I've learned to fuck from about thirty-two different angles, either in the "active" or "passive" positions—though there's nothing "passive" about a man getting fucked who really likes it and becomes a full partner in it. Or particularly "active" about a young man like Benjy doing it. Since screwing is so natural to them, they don't have to exert a lot of energy in the act, once they get rid of any taboos about not doing it.

First I went down on Benjy, then put a rubber over his cock after he got hard. Standard white latex, the rubber glowed like a night light against his dark skin. Josh had a lot of lube in the house, and we were on his bed in the darkness, with just the lights of the city coming in through his bedroom window when he entered me.

He let out a great sigh. "Wow. This is nice."

I nodded.

"Sure I'm not hurting you?"

"I'm sure," I answered.

"I don't want to do anything rough."

"Maybe I do."

"Yeah?"

"Yeah."

I lifted myself up, until I was almost riding his shoulders. He pushed his dick further up me. As I lowered myself down, it felt as if we had just met there, at that point where all of those tingly nerve endings inside me met the sheathed head of his cock.

Benjy was doing this very well, as if he knew, instinctively, what it was all about.

I'd done enough screwing to know that you can relax into it and let it happen: just let yourself become a part of the whole flow of energy between two men as it circulates through them. I let go of Benjy and we lay for a while, with him doing this neat, soft, rhythmic hump inside me that became mesmerizing. Bad as they are, I wished I'd had some excellent poppers.

I remembered, for a moment, the Golden Age of poppers, all of those delightful "amyl" concoctions. Back in the late seventies, several of my chemist friends made batches of it in their bathtubs. The formula was simple but volatile: a couple of wrong moves and you could have a window-shattering explosion.

I was exploding myself, countless little synaptic responses were firing off in me. Where was I? Oh, yes: most Western men, in our modern, germ-hysterical, toilet-phobic culture, have no idea how pleasurable anal sex can be. So many nerves terminate in there that just sticking a little finger up his butt, and doing a little wiggle with it, can drive a man *meshuga*. We have this thing (Benjy was really getting into it now, long and lovely) about the fact that poop comes out your rear end that revolts a lot of people. Nevertheless, shit is basic. It returns us to the animal, fleshy aspect of human beings. So this man-man connection takes place at the central point of a universal, intimate, and intrinsically healthy activity.

In rural India and parts of Southeast Asia, men crap together, squatting and gossiping on the roadsides. They will talk frankly about their "movements"—how it comes out and what form it takes; constipation and what to do for it; and the firm, healthy fitness of their butts—in a way that's hard to imagine American men doing with other men (or women, for that matter).

Four thousand years ago, the Egyptians were using a sheep's bladder with a silver tube attached for enema douching, to keep that area clear and ready for penetration. I'm sure no one "tut-tutted" about it in the shadows of the Pyramids, where Thoth, the ibis-headed god of magic, was also the protector of the anus. Still, it's hard for us to believe that something that has one purpose can be used for another, as if your mouth should be used only for eating and talking, but not for kissing, licking, and sucking.

While Benjy was going at it, I began to wonder: if I had been "cloned" from myself—*alone*—perhaps there were others who'd experienced the same thing.

Therefore, I might go all the way back in time. But to what? We started out as single-celled creatures that divided at their own rate. These merged to become larger organisms, until their cells became too complicated to replicate through division. Sex had to have been started by some very ambitious, aggressive cells that began dividing too fast for their own good. What these cells needed was to *create* a more complicated, even potentially risky situation in which to fulfill their more complicated roles. They needed a challenge; they needed a quest.

But for what? Mates?

Okay. But then, what was my quest? Was it to find others like me—possessed with my own drive, simple curiosity, and strange, complicating queerness? If the very first uni-celled creatures on dividing resulted in perfect replications—"clones"—of themselves, were these "clones" composed of the very primal, original substance of God *Itself*?

If this were true, then *God* would at some point flow through all of us; and we could go back to *It* . . . if we just knew how.

Did Moses know? Jesus? Walt Whitman?

Perhaps *It* talked to them, in a language so simple that only they could hear it.

I was ready to "shoot" (a great term: kids use it, and so do porno stars). Suddenly, I wanted Benjy to take me, eat my cum, my own explosive seminal trail back to the original substance. It was still hard to believe this had happened to me, a close-to-atheist Jewish cocksucker. I hadn't even thought deeply enough about these questions to be a *bona fide* atheist. But here I was, reborn, of God's own substance: *It*. Wow . . . double wow.

I felt ridiculously inadequate, though my "brilliance" had been recognized: Columbia, Harvard, more Columbia. Gay Mensa. But, *if* I should now be part of this . . . very thing of God, shouldn't this have happened to someone more religiously inclined?

The question itself only made me feel stupider, as the answer consistently eluded me. No matter how I approached it, I wasn't getting any closer to it; but now Benjy, after climaxing inside the rubber, was kissing me.

"I guess you'd like me to suck you now?" he said.

"Naw," I answered, always trying to be a mensch. "You've done enough."

The truth was, I was floating far too up there in the celestial brainsphere for a mere blow job to work. I wanted blast-off cosmic sex. I got up, cleaned myself off in the bathroom, and then opened Josh's fridge. A little brown bottle labeled "Pig Sweat" was on the door.

I went back into the bedroom. Benjy had got rid of the rubber. His cock was lying like some dark-fleshed, napping lotus bloom amidst the damp curls of his crotch.

"Ever do these?" I asked.

"What?"

"I guess you haven't."

I unscrewed the cap and gave him a short whiff. "Lord God!" he cried, his cock awakening instantly, stiff-in-a-jiff. I took a deep snort, then began sucking him and jerking off. He came in my mouth, just as I did in my hand. My brain went blank, that post-climax, *petite mort* quick abandonment of the scene.

Where were my ambitious little sex cells now, the ones primed for a full-bent dive into the deep-wet pussy sea? Were they angling somewhere out there, through my own history?

For a second, I thought I was returning to one of those frightening "states" from my past. But no: I was elsewhere this time. Instantaneously inside Leonardo's quattrocento studio-*cum*-bedchamber. Together in one brain, we were drawing this beautiful dark barechested youth in tight white hose, his almost bursting codpiece barely fastened by elegant loops of bright silk ribbon, its contents aching to be released. Now, making oral love to the boy, we were, da Vinci and I, acting as one brain, tongue, penis, body; but my presence, too, was singularly there.

Pray how, you ask?

Only too simple: I'd gone to him; and Leonardo, as I went back, had embraced me as something new, exciting in the ink-charged passages of his brilliant mind.

How shy this genius must have been—and sad—writing all of his thoughts backwards, hoping that only God would read them. Uncommonly, famously attractive as a youth, he'd been a snappy dresser, adept at the flute, the lute, the arts of anatomical, architectural, and mechanical drawing, as well as that of fleshly *embouchment* (okay, cocksucking). I felt his Italian tongue sensitively licking the dark Jewish stubble at my throat; I had come directly out of his psychic balls to claim my place as his peer and lover, despite a paltry separation enforced by the illusions of time.

(Ahhh, those pushy, thrill-seeking neurons, enriched by the blood of orgasm!)

Couplings of this nature are unimaginable to heteros: what do straight men really have in common, other than screwing women and competing with each other on the same march towards the repro-goal, where only *one* blessed fucker will get in? In contrast, the hidden queer population brought itself into being by a continuing, pervasive awareness of itself, despite the darkness of ignorance all around us. This is our own true "coming out" into light, which we repeat generation after generation, sometimes only in our most private embrace.

We do incorporate what came before us: sometimes up the ass or down our throats.

"I'm getting hungry," Benjy said to me, shattering the post-coital trance I was in. "Let's go out."

We did a quick shower together. As Benjy got dressed, I realized that Josh's death would get out at any moment, and I'd have all sorts of strange questions to answer. I could barely answer them to Benjamin who, certainly, would begin asking them soon enough.

I needed to get into my apartment. I had paid the rent through the month, and there was my deposit. The lab, I was sure, would take care of things later, arrange some place for my "effects" to be stored. I had too many records from work there, too many things to incriminate people. Joshua had a set of my keys that I'd given to him, and luckily not asked for back after we'd split up. While Benjy finished primping over his hair, I went through the living room, still jaybird naked, trying to remember where the keys were and find them without my glasses.

He came in, holding out my keys. "Is this what you want?"

I nodded. "Where were they?"

"In the bedroom, on his bureau, next to your picture. Didn't you know? I guess that was his shrine to you. Poor guy."

"A good lesson. Those who dump the gods end up clueless, and keyless!"

Benjy smiled, smacking me on my rump. Seeing him dressed again, I realized I had no idea who he really was. As I did with some of my sex-ad connections, I could let my imagination off its leash, turning him into some hot piece of forbidden scenario/mythology for which my scientific mind starved. The green-eyed god I'd seen at the movies? Or some gorgeously dark, fellow galley slave, chained next to me, on our forced voyage back from . . . what else, I wondered, had to be clean in Josh's closet?

His closet was so neat and orderly that it made me miss my own messiness, where I could put my hands on everything. Here, the choices! All sealed in see-through-plastic dry cleaning bags. I hated to schmutz up one of his imported, professionally-cleaned shirts just to go back uptown. But I did, ripping one out of its bag. It needed cufflinks, but I just rolled the sleeves up and found a pair of close-to-virgin, spanking white underwear and some pleated navy blue pants.

Once I had dressed, Benjy smiled at me. "Papi, you are something!"

"Thanks," I said. "You probably say that to all the older men in your life."

"It's part of being a Christian gentleman."

"Must be the good part. Speaking of Christian gentlemen, did you ever see that man in the car before, the one who tried to grab you?"

"Nope. Can't I say I did. I didn't like him very much. He sure didn't act like a Christian to me."

"If you never saw him before, who hired you to drive the van to Pennsylvania?"

"Nobody really. I mean, my cousin Anthony was supposed to do it. Anthony Johnson."

"The one from the *goyishe* side of your family?"

"*Goyishe*? You mean, as in not Jewish?

"You got it."

"He's not Jewish, but he praises the Lord all he can. Anthony got into crack a couple of years ago, but Jesus got him out of it, and he's belonged to the Lord ever since. Some funny-sounding guy named Tillman contacted him and offered him the job."

"Ah, the good Mr. Tillman. Oren. He—" I had to speak carefully. "He tried to murder me. Mr. Tillman is not the best example of Christianity either, I think."

"I'm disappointed, Len. When men who say they're following Jesus do such things, it sorely hurts my heart."

"Didn't do much for my head, either." I placed his fingers on the break in my skull. He stroked it softly. I loved the way his hand felt. There was a knock at the door. I thought my heart would stop.

Benjy looked at me. A key turned, and a very well-dressed African-American man walked in. Two other men came in behind him.

"Excuse us, sir," the black man said. "We thought the apartment would be empty. I'm Johnny Williams, the building's manager. Are you a friend of Mr. Moreland's?"

"Joshua? Yes. I'm his—"

"Cousin!" Benjy broke in, smiling directly at Mr. Williams, who was very distinguished-looking, with a little gray mustache. Benjy turned to me. "Milton, you told me your cousin was out of town."

"He is," I said, nodding. "Josh is away. Benjamin and I've been visiting from Boston."

"That's strange," Williams said. "Mr. Moreland didn't tell us anything about this."

"He told us it was just for the weekend," I explained, even though I was hardly sure what day of the week it was. "The Hamptons. He's in the Hamptons, or someplace like that."

"Yes," Mr. Williams said, nodding, "Mr. Moreland does have friends in all kinds of interesting places. Nice gentleman, he—"

"You got any I.D.?" asked one of the men, who looked like a police detective.

"I've got some," Benjy offered. "Milton, I told you not to leave yours in the car."

I pretended to hit my head.

"I'm Professor Rosen," I said. "Harvard. Benjamin and I came down for a conference. Josh is a cousin on my mother's side. What's this all about? Is he in trouble?"

"He's dead, Professor. He got blown up in a house in Queens. We were able to trace him through a laundry mark on his shirt. I'm Detective Roberts. The whole thing's been odd. Mr. Moreland was a friend of Dr. Leonard Miller, who was killed a few days ago. Both of them died violently. No connection to the deaths that we can see, but it's still odd."

"Joshua . . . dead! What's this world coming to?" I dropped to the brown couch with a thud, making a show of being shocked.

The other man, Hispanic, spoke up.

"He was in a house with several Central Americans—and some men associated with the violent anti-abortion movement. They had enough explosives down in the basement to start a war. Funny, after all the problems with Moslem extremists, no one's been worrying about whether the Christian fundamentalists might act up. You have any idea how your cousin could have got himself involved with these people?"

I drew a blank. I'd never been particularly good at lying.

"Maybe it was mistaken identity," Benjy said. "They might have thought he was someone else. Dr. Miller, for instance. Was he a known abortionist?"

"Heavens, no!" I protested. "I knew Dr. Miller at Harvard. He'd never done anything that even resembled an abortion. He even refused to do fetal extractions from cows, he even—"

"Yeah," Benjy inserted. "He was almost a Christian. I mean for a Jew." Okay, I guess I was getting too carried away.

"I'm Detective Hernandez," the other dick said to us. "It seems like there's nothing really here for us. You guys were on your way out, dinner, maybe?"

I nodded. "Yes, sir."

"Can we see your ID," Roberts asked Benjy, who smiled casually, handing it to him.

He took down Benjy's license number.

"That's good enough," Roberts said coldly. "You guys can leave, just don't go too far. We're going to dust the place for prints; we might ask for yours later."

"Okay." I looked around the room casually one last time, and saw my own reflection in the big living room mirror. My eyes misted for a second. I was sure I saw Josh, too, wrapped in one of his fluffy acqua towels, with this line of golden light glowing all around him. We'd just made love. The light pulsed on his chest, then near his adorable mouth with those dime-sharp dimples on each side of it. He smiled. I blinked, then left with Benjy.

"Where did 'Milton' come from?" I asked in the elevator.

"*Paradise Lost.* I've been been reading it. Real heavy stuff, man. Once you've been driven out of the Garden, you know it. What'll we do now?"

"Can they trace the van to that house Henry Nathan was in, in Queens?"

"Nope. Cousin Anthony and I rented it. They can't trace it to anything except us."

"Good. Let's drive up back to my old apartment. It's near Columbia."

"All right. But I think I need some pizza first."

chapter ten

We found a place on Ninth Avenue that had very good pizza, and split a large pie that was almost as big as the table. Benjy ate most of it, with mushrooms, peppers, onions, extra cheese, and sausages, then paid for the pizza. I had another bankcard, I realized, in my desk drawer at home. My checking account still had several thousand dollars in it. It would probably be good another week or so, before the bank closed my account to withdrawals.

We went back to the garage next to Josh's building and Benjy paid the cashier for two day's parking, virtually cleaning him out. As we drove up Eighth Avenue to Broadway, I kept wondering why everything looked familiar; I had an unsettling feeling I'd never been there before. Bars and restaurants near Seventy-Second Street triggered little blocks of memory in me, yet it could not have been I who'd gotten drunk in one, maybe twenty years ago, or gone to a notorious back room for sex in another several years before that. It just didn't seem possible. It must have been someone else, but . . . if every single cell in your body is replaced every seven years, yet we keep the same memories, are they really the same? Or do they become vague copies whose imbedded images shift with these changes, creating new memories, our "histories," that become only little fictions we tell ourselves?

"What made you decide you loved me?" I asked, shifting to the present.

His eyes were glued to the traffic in the street.

"I dunno. Maybe if I was ever going to love a guy, he'd have to be as crazy as you. Besides, I'm a Christian—Christ was a resurrected Jew. Maybe you *are* Christ, in some way. Ever think about that?"

"I've thought about a lot of things. It's just that I don't have any answers. I could give myself up, come back, I mean, but that seems impossible. I can't explain it, but I'm afraid that who ever almost killed me once will try it again—and I may not be so lucky next time. That Mr. Nathan, the one in the car, he got Tillman to hire you. He and his crazy wife would do it—"

"I know. It makes me feel ashamed that Christians would do something like that to you. You're no abortionist, I know that."

"But you seem to be all right with the queer thing?"

"Yeah. I decided something, right after we met. I know this sounds funny, but we met pretty funny. Anyway, I decided God has got to be too big for this kind of shit. He made all of us, no matter what part of whose anatomy you put your mouth on." He scratched his head. "How far up do you live?"

"We're almost there. Usually you can find parking near a Hundred-and-Twentieth Street, near the School of Education. I live almost across the street from there, above Barnard."

I had been able to stay in my large apartment in Columbia housing due to a series of flukes—Columbia never likes to cut off its academic affiliations, and I had moved in right after graduate school, when I'd taught a freshman biochem lab at the college. The building had changed a lot in the last close-to thirty years. There were now yuppie couples living in it and a lot of snotty kids from the School of Business, who seemed to eat, drink, and breathe strictly money. I overheard one of them telling another in the elevator, "Only good management can save the world."

I found that idea, downright biblical in its conviction, frightening. I could see the Scriptures saying: "The sinners are they who cannot be managed. They are an abomination and shall surely die."

We got out of the van, locked it, and walked across Broadway. My hands shook as I unlocked the door to my building. Then, in the elevator, I saw Ellie Markowitz, a writer I'd known for about twenty-five years, coming up from the basement laundry. She had been married for ten years, divorced, and then had started dating again. She kept her body up, jogged, did yoga. She was wearing a pink leotard top, like a college girl, but she still looked good in it.

Twenty-some years ago, I had actually slept with her—and Blake, one of her boyfriends. They'd been having a party; I ambled in, we got stoned, the other guests left, and natural curiosity took over. In those days, that did seem natural. For months afterwards, she and I retained a conspiratorial, flirty embarrassment with one another, tiptoeing around the fact that I was more interested in Blake than in her. But since I was a hairy-chested,

Jewish scientist, people did not stamp the "Q" word hard on me; I was in "social" denial then. Socially, I never brought it up. Eventually, our flirting faded and we ended up talking a lot, usually agreeing with one another about liberal politics.

Holding a large plastic basket full of laundry, her face cast down, at first she didn't notice me in the dim light of the ancient elevator which always reminded me of something out of an old black-and-white prison movie. The condemned is taken up on one last ride. . . .

She looked up, making this little gasp. "For a moment . . . I thought you were—my friend Len Miller. But he's dead, right?"

"I'm his cousin. From Boston," I answered, putting on my thickest "Pahk ya cah in Hahvahd yawd" accent. "We ah-ways looked like twins when we wawh kids."

She smiled. "Like the old 'Patty Duke Show'?"

"Nevah saw it," I answered.

"Horrible what happened to him. Do they have any idea who did it? It was a break-in in his lab, right? We were all shocked. Just devastated!"

"Yeah," I answered. "A break-in. I think they wawh trying to steal somethin'. Drugs, maybe."

"You just don't think about that happening in New York now. Oh, we're at my floor. It's been nice meeting you. How long will you be around?"

"Not very long," Benjy answered.

She gave him a strained smile, then got out.

I was two more floors up. My heart began to flutter just being back in my building. But I felt human again, that was the only word for it. My apartment was in the back, at the end of the hall, where the overhead fluorescent lighting ended sharply in darkness. That used to bother me a lot. I was sure I'd get mugged trying to unlock the door one night, but it never happened. For years I carried a mace canister with me, then stopped doing that.

As my eyes got used to the dark, I saw that my door was swathed in plastic tape. It said: "DO NOT ENTER. POLICE CRIME SCENE."

All right. I might still be alive, if I'd kept that mace.

I pulled the tape down, balled it up, and handed it to Benjy. I unlocked the door and we walked in. The place was a mess. Drawers were pulled out, sofa cushions on the floor, dirty glasses left in the sink. The cops must have been there, looking for clues. The kitchen, like my lab, was the one place I was anal about keeping clean. Probably they'd gotten thirsty, raiding my refrigerator.

I immediately found my other bank card—and my spare pair of glasses—then looked through a stack of mail that the super must have brought up. It was strange looking through my mail. A lot of condolence cards had come in, mostly from old students, some lab workers, and various supply salesmen who came by and who knew me. They were addressed, "Family Of Dr. Leonard Miller," as if someone would appreciate the sympathy.

Certainly, I could.

I sat at the table in my kitchen, reading them, and began crying once more. I took off my glasses and wiped my eyes. My tears were futile, but simply facing my own death hurt me so much. Why would anyone want to kill Lenny Miller, a pretty darn-nice old guy, so violently? Benjy stroked my hair. I felt like I was at some old tear-jerker movie. You feel foolish crying, but do it anyway.

The phone rang. Benjy almost jumped out of his skin.

It kept ringing; I had to answer it. Putting the thick Boston accent back on, I picked up the receiver. "Yaw?"

Funny silence on the phone, then: "Lenny! Is that you? It's Alvin Jurrist. I'm calling from Turkey."

"Alvin? Alvin!"

"Yeah. Me. You got that tissue, I hope?"

"It came a few weeks ago. Shit! I didn't even get back to you. I was going to send you a telegram, but we had to keep everything a secret. I feel like an idiot. But Alvin—"

"What did you think of it?" he blurted out.

"Amazing. It's miraculous!"

"I thought so, Lenny. People would die for something like that. Or, maybe even because of it. I mean, there could be bugs in it, right? Viruses?"

"No, we didn't find any." Now I could talk on firm ground. "It was safe from that."

"It wasn't safe from my diggers. It scared the poop out of them. I saw it and went nuts! Every now and then, you luck out and find something. Then it's *boing!*"

I thought suddenly: if this phone's not tapped, why the hell wasn't it?

"Alvin, can you call me back in, say, ten minutes at another number? I'm having trouble with this line. I'll give you the number—"

"I need to speak with you, Lenny. You won't believe what else I've come up with. It's—"

"Wait, I can't hear you, Alvin. Call me at this number, in exactly fifteen minutes."

I gave him the number of the Pelican, a bar down the street. It had one of the last private phone booths left in New York, if not the world. The owner, Manny Tuchman, a hippie capitalist from the old Woodstock generation, used to lock himself in it, talk on the phone, and smoke weed. When New York Telephone tried to have it removed, he insisted on keeping it. Luckily, the number always stayed in my memory. Perhaps because the last four digits were "6970." Who could forget sixty-nine seventy?

I got off the phone.

"Who was that?" Benjy asked. He had disappeared into the kitchen, and now came back in, eating something from a small plate. He had raided my refrigerator and had found an almost-fresh jar of Manischewitz gefilte fish, a strange kind of yen I had every now and then. He was munching on one of the gelatin-covered spheres, dabbed with red horse radish.

"I had a roommate who was a total Jew," he announced. "He kept this stuff around. I used to make sandwiches out of it. It's tasty on white Wonder bread."

"Pardon me while I barf. I've got to go downstairs to take that call. It was from Turkey. The man who found the stuff the Nathans were going to kill me for just called. He never found out I was declared dead."

He swallowed some of the fish. "Want me to come with you?"

"Absolutely."

I hurried into my bedroom and pulled out a blue flannel shirt and a pair of jeans from my closet, glad to get out of Josh's clothes. I washed everything in a hyper-nonallergenic laundry powder that had no scent; Josh's posh closet reeked of synthetic floral. Putting on a dove-gray sweater I'd always liked, I looked at myself in my bedroom mirror.

Who the fuck was *he*? For a second, the sight of myself in my old clothes left me feeling deflated, like a refugee in my own body, exhausted by this war to keep me alive. I was grateful to be around, but couldn't I have come back a little more renewed, maybe better looking?

I wondered: does Warren Beatty go through this every morning?

Okay, probably not.

Out on the street, the full swirl of New York picked me up. A couple of people, barely nodding acquaintances, blinked when they saw me. Perhaps the *Times* had run a picture of me.

We got inside the Pelican and the warm rush of its scent—cheap rye and bourbon, toast in the back for sandwiches—hit me. Quiet drunks, nursing drinks by the hour, sat at the bar. The bartender, a slender young ex-Columbia student with the kind of wavy chestnut hair you wanted to walk barefoot through, looked briefly at me, then turned his head. There was a strictly mind-your-own-business attitude here that I'd always found close to enthralling.

Manny was in the phone booth smoking. I knocked on the door.

He cracked it. "What's ya hurry? One more minute!"

I looked at my watch. I should have said twenty minutes.

Manny opened the booth further, staring right at me. "That you?"

I nodded.

He got off the phone.

"I was speaking with my mother in Florida. She's got Alzheimer's. She's nuts. I thought you were dead. What's wrong? Am I a squirrel? Maybe I'm nuts, too?"

"It's a long story, Manny. But I need the phone. Talk to my friend here—just don't talk to anybody else, okay? Please."

"Whom I gonna talk to in this fuckin' dive, a bunch o' pissass drunks?"

His stomach proceeded him out of the booth. All hair, bloated stomach, beard stubble, broken teeth, Manny was like a crazy old Dostoevskian character, a holdover from the *ancien* petty gentry, the kind who drank fermented potato water and reclusively resided at his dilapidated dacha in the forest with his swaybacked horse. Somehow he had migrated close to Columbia and landed in a bar. I think his parents had originally owned it.

I got into the booth. There were a few joint roaches on the floor; Manny was getting sloppy. We were no longer in the generation of love, drugs, and student unrest. For a long time it seemed like the most militant protest we had was the march to get an MBA. I closed the accordion doors to the booth and a tiny ceiling fan, a vestige of another time, started.

The phone rang.

"Lenny?"

"Yeah. I'm here."

"I've found more of this stuff. A lot more."

"You did? Fully preserved?"

"Lenny, what I sent you was nothing. We're talking about three *whole* bodies."

"Wow!!!" Suddenly, I felt like I'd just been fucked by Apollo on a trapeze. That deflated feeling I'd had disappeared.

"That's how I felt. This is . . . unreal. They're fresh as daisies, Lenny. I mean, not daisies out of the florist, but anyway, they're not mummies. Still, they're gruesome. You've got to know that."

Gruesome? He didn't know from gruesome.

"A lot of people would have the crap freaked out of them," he continued. "But, hey, we're scientists, right?"

"Right." Alvin Jurrist was famous for being one weird dude. Weird, of course, never bothered me. How could it?

"They were just . . . *there*. Down about eight feet, in a new excavation. We were digging in another part of this old town. Gorgeous place. It was already old when the Greeks sailed in as tourists. It's a site close to Assos on the Aegean, filled with layers and layers of undisturbed history. Anyway, we came across this amazing structure. It was kind of like a refuge against invaders, an 'Ann Frank' house from two thousand years ago. Some horrifying struggle had taken place. We found three of them, lying together, hands touching. One's female. They're not wearing any clothes. I'm sure whatever they wore had rotted off, or been robbed from them—that was common then, right after death. Grave robbers. Maybe they killed themselves naked; it's hard to tell. But they're from the same generation as Christ; that's what's so amazing! These preserved humans could have known Jesus himself."

I grunted. There'd been fewer degrees of separation back then, but the Christ connection . . . anyway, why not? It didn't have to be that far-fetched, not if Benjy saw Christ even in me.

"I have no idea, Lenny, how they're preserved like this. Do you have any clues?"

"Clues?"

"Yeah. You're a microbiologist. You work with stuff like this, right?"

I almost dropped the phone from the sweaty palm of my hand. My heart was speeding. I went blank for a second in the middle of the adrenaline-rush of this: the excitement of this discovery was now mixed with pure, cold-sweat terror.

"You still there, Lenny? What do you think is keeping this . . . these people preserved?"

I managed to squeeze out: "Are they really . . . *dead*?"

"Lenny, I told you they're from the time of Christ! What else could they be? Don't get freaky on me. I want you to come over here and see 'em. You've got to do that for me. Will you, Lenny—and I mean soon?"

I tried to calm myself. Watching Manny gesticulating like a crazy street lady with Benjy, I knew I couldn't do this by myself. I needed Benjy to go with me to Turkey; for his sake, too. For the both of us, this would be life changing. I wanted him there, but what if Benjy chickened out?

"What do they feel like?" I asked Alvin, becoming a scientist again. "Is the flesh soft, kind of mushy, or is it still firm?"

"It's incredible, Lenny. It's like God touched these things and won't let go! You expect one to talk to you any second, their skin is so close to fresh." His voice almost cracked. "It's not like stuff we dig out of the ground. This is the greatest discovery of our lifetime! I haven't moved them."

"Good."

"Lenny, they're the way we found them. The diggers ran off. They said this place was sacred, close to *Tann*, that's God. 'Sorry, we will not touch it, Jurrist Bey.' You know how the Turks always keep that British formality. I'm just scared someone will leak it out, and this site'll get crazy. People can get hysterical—I'm close to it myself. I'm working to stay calm. How soon do you think you can get here? Do it fast, please? I'm not feeling so hot, maybe I got something from them—that's why I asked you about the bugs. You've just got to come see them, before anyone else disturbs them."

"I'll get there as fast as I can."

"Promise, Lenny?"

I felt slightly nauseated from sheer excitement. "I do."

"Thank you so much, Lenny. I'll last till you get here. I'm taking something for the fever."

"Good. If you go down and see those specimens again, wear a face mask."

"It may be too late for that. That's why I need you here as soon as you can come."

"Hold the phone a second, please."

I popped my head out of the booth, and got Benjy's attention. I wasn't sure if he had a passport. If he didn't, it would take three days for him to get one—you can do Super Quick service with more money. I'd lost mine once and got it back that way in two days.

He came over, martini in hand. "This is good. The boy put mint in it. I've never had a mint martini."

"Neither did Noel Coward. Listen, do you have a passport?"

"Of course, luv," he said, putting on a "Masterpiece Theatre" British accent. "What sort of rube do you think I am?" He dropped the Brit act. "All us kids got passports now. That's how you do spring break in places like Cancun or Prague. Why?"

"Just asked. I'll be right out."

I got back into the booth, and asked Alvin to give me explicit directions to his location. He was calling from the Turkish version of a convenience store, several miles away from the dig.

"They do a big trade in Alka-Seltzer, cigarettes, and donkey feed." He laughed. Alvin always kept his humor, no matter what. "You'll really like this place. It's kind of like being in Greece, but less spoiled. And, I have to tell you, there are some very handsome young men hanging around, too. Even though I'm a card-carrying hetero, I know what you like. You just have to be careful with them. They're very aware here of reputation, know what I mean?"

"Alvin, you don't have to entice me with the local fauna. I just want to know where you are, and how to get there."

"You'll come in through Istanbul. I'm about a day's drive out of it. You can take a car ferry over to a place called Bandirma, which cuts out a lot of driving, but the ferries don't run on the most regular schedules. So what you end up losing while waiting for the ferry, you can easily make up for in the drive, especially the way people drive here. You have to be careful on the road, but you don't need to poke around."

I took a pen and a scrap of paper from my pocket and jotted down his directions.

"There's no way to reach me directly at the site, but I can be reached by telegram. Direct it to 'Archeological Site Number Twelve, Assos.' Let me know when you get here. If you don't do the car ferry, then drive towards Bursa. It's an easy goal, with good roads, because it's a big metropolis and very industrialized. You might want to skirt around it. From Bursa, you'll be heading south and west. Can you remember all of this?

"Sure."

"Good. The rest any map of Turkey can show you. The roads are pretty good until Bursa, then they get kind of rural and bumpy after that. I'm counting on you, Lenny. Can you be here in two or three days?"

"You bet," I told him.

chapter eleven

*W*e were at the bar, and I was drinking a Manhattan with rye, a drink I only liked at the Pelican. Manny, who had taken instantly to Benjy, was staring at me.

"Want some pot? We can go back in the kitchen and smoke some."

I told him no.

"That's the problem. Too many people smoke alone now. It makes 'em tense and screws up their brains. I can't figure out how come you're alive."

"Maybe I'm not."

"Come on, cut the horseshit. You're right here. I been smoking wacky weed most of my life, but even I'm straight enough to know you're here in the flesh."

"That's true. Reports of my death have been greatly exaggerated. The truth is, some of those wacked-out fundamentalist types tried to kill me, but didn't finish the job—"

"The ones always going after you, because of your research?"

"Yeah. The Christian nutcases."

"Stop!" Benjy said, jumping off his barstool. "You're not going to bash Christians in front of me, you understand that?"

I nodded to him. "You're right. I'm sorry. I shouldn't bash Christians at all."

"Yeah," Manny said. "They're great guys. Charity, love, goodness. If you practice what you preach."

Benjy raised his second mint martini to Manny.

"Thanks for the drinks, Manny. You're right: *if* you practice. I used to think I knew all these things. Sunday school, stuff like that. We were taught gays were against God, and Jews—well, we weren't always nice to Jews. But I still believe in our Lord Jesus. I still want Him inside me."

I smiled warmly at Benjy. "I think you've got Him right there."

Once more I asked Manny not to mention that he had seen me, and he did a "mouth zipped" gesture. Before we left, I offered to pay him for the drinks, and he refused our money. I promised that we'd have lunch together soon, then Benjy and I walked back to my apartment.

He was a bit tipsy and all over me, kissing me with very minty martini breath. We were sitting on my bed.

"I need for you to get your passport," I said to him.

"Why, man? What's up?"

"I want you to go to Turkey with me. Would you, please?"

'Sure 'nuff, man. Turkey, isn't that someplace near Queens?" He hiccupped and smiled.

"No." I unbuttoned his shirt and stroked his chest, gently tweaking his dark little nipples. An instant quiver sped through me, like a shot of energy pulling me directly to him. "You said you wanted Jesus in you, right?"

"His Spirit. Sure. He's what love's all about, I know that. Love—gay or whatever the rest of it is. It's all too cool; I know it."

We got *big* naked, as in extremely fast.

Loopy from the martini, Benjy ended up knotting his shoes instead of untying them, so I just pulled them off him. The sweet rushy-gushiness of his lips and mine was pure heaven; his fingers, his nice cock, the squeezable mounds of his ass, the funny cork-screwy curls of his black pubes and hair. My bedroom light made his black curls sparkle. Taking the delectable, plummy head of his cock into my mouth for a moment, I felt that I could have searched through a slew of sex ads for him, and still not found anyone as good and loving as he was.

"Why don't you turn off the light?" he asked.

After I bounded out of bed, bending over to turn off the table lamp, my eyes spotted it: the lower part of my right calf. The area of the graft had changed. It was now swollen to about twice the thickness it had been only a few hours earlier, when we'd showered.

It was also a genuinely deep, reddish-orange now, like a chunk of smoked salmon, with sharply sunken pores resembling little craters. Such a pronounced change in its color and texture identified it as hostile territory: Insurrection. The invading renegades who'd arrived with a generous peace offering, were ready to shoot back. I attempted to wriggle my toes; they responded. Crouching over, I pinched them hard. There was still normal feeling in each little piggy.

Scared almost out of my wits, I pressed my fingers lightly into the orangey area. If something horrible were happening, a complete lack of response would mean that I was dying, once again. That the graft had stopped working; it was working against me, the little mother.

I could feel the pressure from my fingers, but not much. The same area on my other calf showed more sensitivity, though how much more, I couldn't really gauge. The graft was harder, definitely even more rubbery than when I'd first noticed it in the morgue. Maybe this was only part of its natural bio-cycle: what had become attached to me was now drawing away. In a few more hours, another day, perhaps, it might re-attach itself to its host and re-start the processes that were keeping me alive.

I wanted to believe that so much. Every hour, each day, now felt like a whole lifetime to me. So much had happened to me within the space of a few twenty-four hour periods. "Wait a second," I said.

"What's wrong, dude? I thought you were gonna—"

I hurried into my bathroom where the light was better, and closed the door. I flicked on the overhead light, turned down the toilet seat cover and sat on it. My bare rump shivered.

Bending over, I twisted my right heel up to look more closely at the area. An avalanche of despair hit me, as I saw that the magical things that had been handed to me could just as easily be taken away—Benjy. Those discoveries in Turkey. My own tenuous reappearance in life. Science. Love.

Joshua's face appeared to me from the basement floor. His small lips mouthed the words, mockingly: "Was it worth it, Dr. Len?"

I was dying again! The color and feel of the grafted area were testifying this. As a scientist you learn that only by reading signs meticulously and looking at the facts directly before you, can you know what's necessary to know. The graft was announcing my death with all the evident signs; it was happening in stages. But, which stage was I in? And how could I adjust to it?

In my jubilance over Alvin's discovery, I'd mislaid one valuable fact: I was supposed to be dead. Simple as that. So that "thing" that only happened to look like me, that was going through the motions of being Leonard Miller, was probably not fully alive, either.

A sob came out of me, rattling my body. Sliding to the cold tiles of the bathroom floor, I lay on my side, holding my knees and crying.

Benjy came in. "Need company?"

I couldn't answer him.

"What's wrong, Len?"

I showed him my lower calf, pointing out the hard texture and the strange color. I needed to tell him what this was all about, but I was scared. Suppose he, too, thought this was too weird, too unnatural, too "against God," and ran off? I—Lenny Miller, whoever, or whatever, I was—couldn't stand to lose this young man. I was crazy about him.

I had to pick my words well.

"When they tried to kill me, they injected this poison into me. This is what it looks like, Benjy. See, I have a feeling my reprieve is not going to last very long."

He looked at it closely, rubbing his chin. "I see."

"You do?" I exhaled.

"Sure, Lenny. When you're a black, Jewish, Christian—okay—*gay* kid like me, you understand about reprieves. All of life is a reprieve, really. It's the Lord's way of saying the dice are in your hands, though ultimately, He gets to keep them. Know what I mean?"

I nodded. He smiled, and I kissed him.

"It does feel kind of funny," he agreed. "Maybe we should take a better look at it, like scrape off a bit? I just finished my Intro to Bio course. It was a requirement, so I know something about this."

Golly!—this kid was thinking way ahead of me. If this had happened to anybody else, I would have immediately suggested the same thing. For a geneticist, a bio-researcher, I'd been going about this very unscientifically. Pursued by my own raw fear, all of my science had flown the coop.

"You got something like a microscope here?" he asked.

I still had my old junior high school biology lab set, with its forceps, scalpel, lances, old sterile-wrapped razor blades, glass slides, and a small Bell and Howel microscope. I remembered the first time I'd unzipped the set's leatherette case, pretending for my parents' sake to be excited, even though their super-bright, over-achieving little boy would have preferred a new Schwinn bike. The kit was still on top of a bookshelf in the living room, under an owl's nest of dust. Benjy held the back of a kitchen chair for me, as I stood on it and brought the things down.

I realized I didn't have any clothes on, but that no longer bothered me.

Before all of this had happened, I always needed some kick in the ass to jolt me out of my inhibitions—drugs; crazy sex. Now I felt shamelessly naked inside, too. What was there to hide, simple as that?

Back in the bathroom, Benjy looked at me, puzzled.

"I'm going to need your help," I said.

He shrugged. "Whatever."

I washed my entire calf with soap and let it dry on its own, before I sprayed the raised area with a little Bactine, a popular antiseptic with a mild topical painkiller in it. I kept the can around for poison ivy or mosquito bites. I had Benjy wash his hands, then carefully open one of the sterile blade wrappers and pop the blade into a lance handle. I propped my leg up on the toilet seat cover and pointed to the place in question.

"Just cut a small amount of flesh off from the top."

He looked at me in disbelief. "Huh?"

"You don't have to go in very deep. It's not going to hurt much. I don't think it will. I kind of wish it would hurt, but—"

His hands started to shake. "I've never done anything like this before. Not on a living person."

"That's okay, either did I, not on myself. I only need a little slice. Then we're going to stick it into this slide."

I had the slide ready, plus sterile gauze and some adhesive tape for a bandage. Nervous sweat started to collect on my forehead, more from not knowing what was going to happen than from fear of pain.

Benjy started.

Watching while he did it, I took refuge in the pure science part of it. He worked very cautiously. As I'd suspected, his first tiny incision did not produce a lot of sensitivity or blood. Was the grafting substance "sleeping"? It seemed so disconnected from me. Then, as he nervously pushed the blade all the way through, taking off about a fifteen millimeter slice, a quick, lurid shock of pain hit me, flashing straight up to my brain. I could even feel it stabbing into my eyes. I clenched them, screaming.

He almost dropped the lance. I opened my eyes. I was so happy, I wanted to kiss him. "It's still alive!" I shouted.

"You okay, man?"

"Yeah," I said, collecting myself.

There was enough material on the blade; we snapped it into the slide.

I put some peroxide on the cut, then taped gauze over it.

I had set up the microscope on the kitchen table and plugged the light in. When I flicked it on, I had that same sense I'd had as a kid, that I was on the verge of seeing something no one else had ever seen. I cleaned off the lens and peered in, gazing at myself.

Or, something close to it.

Even under the low, student magnification of my scope, my biopsy wasn't difficult to read. Cell membranes opened up; I could see the powerhouses of the mitochondria and the muscular fortified outlines of the nuclei. I'd become intimate with the anatomy of these structures under my digital equipment at the lab. For weeks I had watched these ancient cells interacting repeatedly among themselves, but it had remained an age-old dream to see living material like this do what it had done: completely revive something, especially a human, once dead. The cells, though retracting, were still obviously alive.

This left me with two questions. My first question was, what kind of bugle call would push my little soldiers forward to re-enter me, and would they keep me as alive as I needed to be? I blinked into the lens, my head shaking.

And the second question: did their retraction mean that they were "giving up" on me; that somehow this thing that had brought me back from death would soon return me to it—and neatly survive me by spitefully leaving me, Lenny Miller, their grateful but short-term host, to his own dust?

"It's not as bad as I thought," I lied. "I must have got some kind of infection in it. The peroxide will take care of that. I really want to thank you for helping me."

"Maybe you should use vinegar."

"Why?"

"Didn't they use that on Jesus? I've heard vinegar can be powerful stuff."

I shook my head. I wasn't exactly sure what vinegar had done for Jesus. I just knew what this strange, tricky substance had done for me.

"I'll be okay. But I want us to go to Turkey tomorrow."

"Tomorrow? I've got the van to return, I've got classes I need to start. My roommates don't know where I am, I—"

"But you'll go, right?"

His eyes brightened, with that sparkle that I loved dancing in them.

"Sure," he said.

I sighed, feeling more relieved than I had felt in—who could say? "Thank you."

We got back into bed. I reached out for him, kissing him. Who was doing this, I wondered—was it Leonard Miller, the scientist; Lenny Miller, the crazy queer who liked kinky sex from bar rag ads; or (really *strange*) this barely explainable, resurrected body that was probably dying again? What I did feel was porous with Benjy, as if he were kissing every cell and space within me as I kissed him. He was flowing into me.

About twenty years earlier, I'd had that exact feeling doing LSD on Fire Island, with the sun rising over the water after a whole night of dancing, sex, and drugs. In those days that was what the island was for: nights of dancing, sex, and drugs. I'm sure it's still the same for another generation of guys. I was "peaking," at that crest of the drug's wave, when you either enter into the full, dynamic curve of the Cosmos, or they have to pull you in and shoot you full of Thorazine to bring you down.

I sat on the beach naked, with this big man's hands softly around my shoulders. He was Daniel Ginsberg, a big, hairy, Jewish stud-accountant from Brooklyn, wigged out on grass and poppers. Sweet, loving, bearded. Deep-chested. Great thighs and dark, suntanned ass. His tongue was in my ear, exploding with each beat of the surf.

He became, at that moment, *All Men*, the great god of the Man-thing personified. I was sitting cross-legged and he knelt behind me, hands on my shoulders, his cock thick and densely alive with every beat of his heart; I reached around and touched it, held it. My brain went gratefully blank, stupid, giving up its contrary reason to the infinite roar of the moment, then its own quiet. We made love back in the dunes on the beach. I sucked him off. His cum was like *Hamlet*, I mean like the whole play was in it; and maybe even the General Theory of Relativity, too. I had memorized so much of all that. At seventeen, I was Hamlet, misunderstood, a *bissel* crazy. Hamlet thinks he sees his wronged, sainted, dead father, the King. Somehow, he had to become his father. But because the young Prince knows too much, is filled with too much secret information at one time, he dies; he's murdered.

Whole lines from *Hamlet* glimmered in front of me, traveling those vast linked neurons of my brain. I'd been just eating *it*—him Daniel

Ginsberg. And now Benjy, and now maybe the whole queer tribe. When it was over, and I "came down" on Fire Island, and later saw Dan on one of the sandy boardwalks, we smiled at one another, knowing way too much. I thought: thank the Universe for "straight people," whoever they are. They are the stalwart pillars of the great temple we must rob of its secrets.

Rob and escape . . . on spirited horses that are ourselves.

Now here I was with this beautiful dark man, making passionate love. I thought about how barely twenty-four hours earlier, he'd been a "practicing" Christian.

When I'd been roughly his age, in school at Harvard, I had gone to see a therapist, a wrinkled old lady from the Viennese school. She looked at my case, and said, "Are you a *practicing* homo*zeks*-sual?"

"No," I said.

"*No*? You mean you do not do *zeks* mit men?"

"No, I don't practice anymore. I'm really good at it."

She shook her head sadly. "Perhaps you vill not be able to take our vork zeriously, young man. This is not for the laughing matter, you know."

I told her she was right and left. I'd been depressed, worn to a ragged edge. People think that only neurotic concert pianists wig out and go berserk; they have no idea the emotional involvement in science. You feel as if you are placing your entire being on a slide, in a culture, in a research design that may be two percent off, and fails. Labs all over the world end up with these strange burn-outs, left over from a Bram Stoker novel, sucked in by the promise of a Nobel Prize and the cult of the Unknowable, offering little crumbs of wisdom as inducements. It's easy to become prideful. Arrogant. Then the truth hits you: You're no smarter than one of the clerks in your office. You've just been lucky not to fall apart.

I was determined not to become one of those, hence my descent into, and revelations from, wild sex. Today we can accept "Outsider Art," the art of the insane, the hoboes, the untaught. But we cannot, for the life of us, accept "outsider sex." Sex that's way out, unmapped, unexplainable. I liked big black men and Hispano-Asians from Brooklyn. One, named Jesús Pedro Dong, was a black belt with a reed-brown, hairless, muscular, violent poem of a body; he was very clean. I'd once eaten his lean, perfectly-sculpted ass, which fit beautifully in both my hands, for an hour. He would never call me anything except "Sir" and "Man." It was like receiving art, like going to the

Metropolitan Museum: you were just trembling from all that beauty.

But unlike the stuff at the Met, he was warm, touchable, and tastable. We pay billions for objects of Art, but let the inspiring, gorgeous beauty of men starve for lack of attention.

Benjy and I were sixty-nining, when I had this awful feeling that I had heard the phone ring.

I pulled away with difficulty, bolting up in bed.

Benjy shook his head. "I was just on the verge."

I smiled. The ringing continued, and I asked him to pick it up. He did. I listened close beside him.

"Dr. Miller?" a man's voice asked.

"He's not available. Who's calling?"

"I'm a friend of his. Who am I speaking with?"

Benjy put his hand on the receiver. "*Who?*"

"Tell him you're Josh."

"I'm Josh. A friend."

Uh . . . I thought Josh was dead."

(You *did*? How'd you know, you monster? You killed him. I made myself just listen.)

"Naw, I'm another Josh. He had two Joshes. Ever heard of that?"

Pause, then:

"Would you tell Dr. Miller—"

"The guy's dead. I was just at his funeral."

"Josh, you tell your friend Dr. Miller that we want that substance he's been working with."

"I told you he's dead, man."

"Josh. Wait a second. Listen, he's *not* insulting God by working with it. We know it now. We'll work with him—we'll help him—understand? See that, Josh? But we need that substance. We've got to have it."

I put my hand on the mouth of the phone, whispering, "Tell them I'll meet with them tomorrow night. Eight o' clock. We'll meet back at my lab. They know where it is. Hell, they tried to kill me there."

Benjy relayed the message, word for word. Then he hung up.

"You're really going to meet with them?"

"No," I whispered, and beckoned for Benjy to come with me. We tiptoed over to the door, and I looked through the peephole into the dark hallway. Was I being paranoid? Or just being followed? No one was there, not that I'd be able to see them. But I knew someone would find me. It was inevitable; like Henry Nathan had said, they were all over the place. I still had Tillman's pistol, in a bag I'd brought from Josh's. I made sure all three locks on the door were engaged, then the two of us crept back to the bedroom. I placed the pistol openly on the night table.

"We're going to be on a night flight to Istanbul by eight o' clock tomorrow," I told Benjy.

He looked at me, smiling. "Cool."

I turned off the light.

chapter twelve

The non-stop flight to Istanbul was fourteen hours, leaving at 7 p.m. from J.F.K. Airport. I spent much of the morning getting us visas and tickets through my travel agent, Amy, who worked near my apartment. I had sent a lot of business for the lab over to her, and she was not even surprised when I showed up at her office. She never read newspapers except to look at her horoscope. She'd told me that, being in the travel business, reading the news would scare her too much. Through her connections, she was able to get us two tourist visas to Turkey, without me having to show her Benjy's passport.

She also got us a good deal on the tickets; I put them on one of my credit cards that I never used, a Sears Discover card. As a struggling grad student I'd had to pay for everything with cash, so I had nine cards. It went through in a snap; Amy also got us one night in a hotel in Istanbul.

"You shouldn't have any problems," Amy informed me. "Travel is way down now, so once you get past security, things should be fine."

I had packed hastily earlier, after saying good-bye to Benjy, who had gone to return the van and get his things settled in Queens. I left my Columbia apartment as soon as I could, taking a taxi into Midtown to Grand Central, where I dropped off my suitcase in the checkroom. Due to security, the attendant, a nervous Indian man, asked for ID; when I showed him my passport, he didn't question it. Now that I was officially dead, I was sure that at some point all of my numbers, from my credit cards to my passport, would end up cancelled, but luckily that had not happened yet.

I had most of the day to kill, so I tried, like some movie character, to lose anyone who might be following me. I hurried over to the library on Forty-Second Street and walked through it, guardedly looking for any pair of eyes that might be settling on me. I left through the exit to Bryant Park, sat on a bench there, watched everything going on around me, then took a crowded subway down to Macy's. After rushing through several floors of the store, locking myself in dressing rooms, and concealing myself in quickly changing crowds of customers, I felt a little safer.

I took another taxi back up into Times Square, asking the driver to take me up through Tenth Avenue. When he dropped me off in the theater district, teeming with tourists, I was sure no one could have followed me after all of this. I was tired now, but still had several hours before I had to take a taxi for J.F.K. I decided then that what I needed was a drink at the Algonquin Hotel on West Forty-Fourth Street, with its wonderfully classy lobby, full of paneled oak nooks and deep comfortable chairs. I found a quiet nook away from everybody, and ordered a gin-and-tonic.

A young waiter in a white shirt and dark tie brought it to me, with a small bowl of cocktail pretzels. Really needing to relax, I dove into the drink, then looked around. The people in the lobby looked so nicely dressed and they all seemed to have something personal to do, some fulfilling engagement with life, while they sipped their chic cocktails. Except for Benjy, I felt terribly cut off. If by any chance I survived all of this, how was I going to come back? People might say I had faked my own death, but why would I do that—I wasn't getting any insurance?

I realized I needed to plan my next step, past my current "re-awakening." I was going to have to live off something and the longer I was dead, the harder it would be to come back. I could easily end up posing as a long-lost brother or cousin from somewhere, working at a small college in some place off the map. That is, if my past deeds didn't catch up with me and I weren't charged with those deaths in Queens. I was really floating now, somewhere out there beyond my actual self, the one who'd been previously killed. Like a lot of unattached gay men, I'd never even drawn up a will. I had remained HIV negative, and it just hadn't occurred to me to write one.

When I was "alive," I'd wanted to live my life to the fullest, to be fulfilled intellectually, and yet still have real emotional connections: something that wasn't easy for me. Even though I yearned for it, it was very hard for me to get outside the concrete, the clinical, and scientific. I desired some elevating transfusion of poetry in my life.

Instead, I didn't even own a dog.

At my own funeral, I'd had a bunch of tricks, colleagues, and strangers. My parents were dead; I had one older brother I'd never been close to, who didn't even come. He was three years my senior, and could never deal with my being gay. If I'd been hesitantly, tastefully, self-hatingly *Will & Grace* gay—really cute and castrated—maybe Stephen wouldn't have had such a problem with it. He could have allowed himself some tad of generosity to sympathize with me. It's amazing how many straight men want to sympathize with queers; it's when they don't sympathize with your "condition" that things get tacky.

Basically, they want you to be a stand-in for all their neuroses, sensitivities, and manly limitations. In other words, you're appreciated as long as you do your pansy Stepin Fetchit act. "Thank you so much, Massa, for toleratin' me and mah pathetic, uncoordinated, self-deprecatin', sissy-bitch queerness."

But I'd never apologized, and Stephen hated it. We hadn't said two words to one another in the last ten years. Steve had gone into the auto import business, high-end luxury Euro-cars, like Mercedes-Benz and Jaguar, no less. He'd made wads of "adult" money, lived in a big house in the suburbs of Tallahassee with a nice wife, Charlotte, and two girls, and religiously voted Bush Republican. My folks had had us fairly late, and died while we were still fairly young. I'd been a pretty radical grad student, while Steve quickly got hip to the faith that Yahweh was God and Capitalism was His religion. He was a Jew who kept a black yarmulke and a Smith and Wesson pistol in his glove compartment.

At Dad's funeral we'd had a brief "libertarian" conversation about the areas the government should stay out of. As usual with libertarians, the only liberties he was interested in were his own.

"It's the right to bear arms, Len. The Founding Fathers believed in it. If we have a Fascist take-over, like in Germany, I want my own weapons."

"All right. Then how about keeping the Government out of my bedroom? Isn't that a libertarian cause, too?"

"Len, give me a break! 'Spose I don't want kids like Lisa and Jennifer anywhere *near* your bedroom? I mean it's bad enough with the boys who come by—I've got to deal with them!"

"So you figure I should just keep that door locked?" I said. I hated the smugness on his self-righteous face. Suddenly I could imagine him, Joe Lieberman, and Bush Jr. in some kind of diabolical threesome, the three of them spitting half-chewed genitals out of their mouths.

"You got it," he said.

He was right: I got it. Just before going home, we gave each other one of those clenched-fist hugs straight men perform—no body contact at all—and I thought: blood may be thicker than water, but sometimes your relatives want too much blood. I felt closer to some of the men I'd met in the ads. Perhaps there'd been a time when we'd shared a bathtub and looked at one another's little peepees and smiled, but I knew I'd never see Stephen again.

After I came out, I wondered what my straight brother really thought about other men's dicks, feet, butts, faces. Was it just repugnance? Maybe it was childish, but I wondered what secrets he kept inside. I was a child still inside. Perhaps I'd truly been reborn again in this old body, and I was, now finishing my third, too-expensive gin-and-tonic, which the nice young waiter had been thoughtfully bringing me, still less than a year old at the moment.

It was time to get up and face my adversaries, even the ones I was born with.

I asked for the bill, put it on another credit card, scooped up some of the pretzels, and wobbled boozily through this little garden of cocktail chatter. Passing two genteel old ladies in hats with veils, I felt like I could have actually been on the Titanic, the one that finally made it to New York, if only in fantasy.

At the luggage check at Grand Central, I showed the Indian man my check, and he produced my luggage.

"Are you new to New York?" He'd forgotten completely that I had showed him my passport, with my address in the city.

"Yes. Very new."

"It is amazing, this city. Everything is here." He smiled.

I took my bags back into the huge busy main concourse, and made my way out onto Forty-Second Street, enjoying the slight, loopy drunkness I had. A buzz, as the kids called it. Everything was doing a jiggily, whirling dance, which didn't bother me as long as I didn't get too weirded out by it. Four people were ahead of me on the line for cabs. No one was looking at me; happy, hurrying crowds buzzed past me. I felt safe. The Indian man was right: everything was here.

"Are you going to the airport?" a man next to me inquired politely.

He had two suitcases with him. I nodded, then said, dropping all my paranoia and fear to the sidewalk, "I sure am! J.F.K.!"

He was neatly dressed, a visitor obviously from the more healthy hinterlands; he seemed slightly nervous, but decent, with the kind of ruddy, sun-brightened, soap-and-water freshness that New Yorkers instinctively, maybe stupidly, trust. He had boyish, hairless little ears and a neatly trimmed mustache, coppery light brown hair, and small but intensely bright blue eyes that glowed at me.

"Want to share a cab?" he asked.

Since he was ahead of me and very nice to look at, without another cautious thought I agreed. He quickly introduced himself.

"Ted Richards. From Salt Lake City. Ever been there? Beautiful country."

Shaking my head, I told him my name. When a cab approached, we stashed our bags in the trunk and got in. "J.F.K.," he told the driver, an ebony-colored young African man, perhaps from Senegal or Mali. The city had a set rate to the airports and it was posted in cabs, so there was nothing to do but settle back and relax.

Richards watched Grand Central disappear, then turned to me and smiled warmly. I looked at his clear outdoor skin and noticed how his head was held squarely upright by a strong neck, where a few pale sun-creases were etched into his tan. He wore jeans and loafers, a nice white business shirt and a navy blue blazer. He asked me what I did for a living. When I told him I was a microbiologist, he broke into a broader grin.

"Wow, great field! I deal in medical equipment. Salt Lake is a famous hospital town." He paused with his clear blue eyes on me. "Uhh, I guess you must know that?"

I nodded, not really caring.

Actually, thanks to three gin-and-tonics, I was wondering what he'd look like with all his clothes off. His shirt, unbuttoned at the neck, revealed a handful of silky, coppery hairs at the top of his broad chest; the big shoulders under his blazer promised a very attractive warmth. With his firm, apple-ripe cheeks, thin lips softly dimpling as he spoke, and strong, expressive hands, he had a genuinely tastable, almost creamy quality to him. I found myself not questioning at all the open, sweet friendliness in his face.

"My wife's a Mormon. I had to join the Church and it's kind of good, but, uhh"—he shrugged, then lowered his voice—"I don't believe in it."

I nodded mechanically, wondering if he knew I was undressing him in my mind.

"I mean, I believe in Jesus—who doesn't? But to tell you the truth, the Mormons get a little too crazy for me."

I looked directly into his cornflower-blue eyes. "Uh huh," I said softly.

"That eternal life business." He smiled sheepishly. "Do you believe in eternal life?"

I gazed out the window as we approached the Midtown Tunnel into Queens, with traffic swarming in like gnats. I believed in eternal traffic, the movement of all matter. It never stopped. One way or another.

I turned to him. "If it's really eternal," I offered, "you'd be doing the same thing over and over again. So whether you're there or not, what difference would that make to anyone, including yourself?"

"You mean heaven would be like a . . . big bore?"

He lowered his blue eyes, then they lit up, as if an out-of-the-way light in his brain had suddenly been switched on. "That sounds like the suburbs," he said. "One big strip mall that repeats itself over and over again. Dairy Queens, IHOPs, and Golden Arches forever. You have all those people who think they've just discovered something, but they don't know the same thing's up the road again, maybe five more miles, in the next mall."

"Exactly." I chuckled.

"That's why I like New York. You can cut loose here."

I nodded. "How loose do you cut?"

"Pretty loose. Want a drink?"

He fished a Tanqueray miniature out of a plastic shopping bag, emptied it into a lidded cup of ice, and offered it to me. I took it, and he made one for himself.

"Thank you. How'd you know I'd been drinking gin-and-tonics this afternoon?"

"Sixth sense, friend. I can't do this back home. But luckily, I'm not going back home."

"Where are you going?"

"Istanbul. There's a new hospital outside of town, and we're going to sell it everything!"

I smiled. Suddenly all anxieties left my head, taking with them all my persistent fears about the Big End coming. This man seemed like such a sweet chap; it was as if God Itself—the whole cooperative Universe—had put him there in that cab with me. Sipping his gin, he stretched out, his tanned hand accidentally brushing my neck; then he started casually, softly, massaging it, as if he were some angel sent to me.

"How'd you know how much I needed that?" I purred. I was tired and tense; I did need it, truly.

"I knew," he answered. "I'm a traveler, see? You New Yorkers are a tough bunch, but once you get to know 'em, you become pussycats. I like pussycats."

"Not just pussy?"

I turned red at my gauche question, and blamed it on the liquor, loosening my tongue. "Sorry, that was inappropriate," I said.

"No problem, friend. You're right. I don't just like pussy. But maybe you guessed that?"

Had I? All I could do was try not to smile too hard.

We were now going through Queens. Big cemeteries; little houses; apartment buildings. My fourth gin, straight over ice, had me smoothly sailing in the darkened theater of the cab, as the driver asked if we wanted some music. He put on a tape that sounded like it came out of an African tribal bazaar. Rhythmic drumming, a repeating wave of choral voices, exotic instruments.

"Hey, driver," Ted called. "Mind if we get *really* loose?"

"No, Monsieur. In my cab, you are the boss. *Oui?* Do what you want!"

"Gooooood!" He turned to me. "You asked how loose I got?"

Before I could answer, I felt him pulling up my shirt, then unzipping my pants. Was this some kind of drunken hallucination? Four stiff drinks and I was . . . totally unbent. My fingers ran through his thick reddish hair, onto his deliciously soft cheeks, his lips. I grabbed one of his hands and licked his palm. My head spun: we were on the parkway and cars were going straight through me, like every atom in me was splitting and splitting, and split—

"This is really crazy," he whispered. "I don't usually do such nutty things. But—would you mind if I gave you some head?"

"Mind?" I gasped, then managed to squeeze out, "Not a bit."

Angel? I definitely believed in the angel theory of gay men: When a good-looking man puts his mouth on your dick, he is, by any definition, an angel. He had my dick out and he pushed me back on the seat so he could suck it. I could smell pungent marijuana smoke coming in from the driver, as music boomed through the back.

"You guys gettin' jiggy back there?" he called.

I was bouncing through everything: time . . . those little corners of my mind where infinity came to visit . . . my own existence . . . as Ted's mouth worked on me. Then he pulled me over to him, guiding my lips onto his lavishly good cock: firm, silky, juicy with pre-orgasmic sweetness. I wanted him: but good. Approaching orgasm, he jerked himself a few times and in one fast shoot came in my mouth, his hands on my cheeks. Some thick, slightly salty cum leaked onto his fingers. I licked it off, feeling like a glistening tide of deep-space plasma had washed right through my brain.

As he pulled himself back together, I realized I was too drunk to stay hard. His face wobbled into a generous smile.

"You okay?" he asked.

I felt stone cold. My head was off my shoulders and now on a rollercoaster. I was afraid I was going to barf up half of Europe.

"You're going to be okay," he assured me, as he zipped me back up neatly. "New Yorkers don't drink the way they used to. It used to be a hard-drinking town, but you'll be okay." He placed his hand on my forehead. "Why don't you put your head down here on my lap?"

I did, and he started chattering in a very friendly manner to the driver, speaking in a foreign language I couldn't understand. "It's Ivory Coast French," he explained to me. "I picked it up there selling medical stuff. I guess you can say I pick up things fast."

"You could say that." I lifted my head. He brushed his fingers through my hair and we smiled at one another, like we'd been speaking a dialect of our own.

At the airport, we went to the Air Turkey terminal, and he paid the driver, without asking me for a nickel. A porter with a trolley helped us with our bags, and I managed to tip him. I was still feeling slightly out of it, so Ted kept his hand lightly on my upper arm all the way to the counter.

"I'm Mr. Richards and this is my friend Dr. Miller. We're both going to Istanbul, so we want to sit together."

Before I could even hunt for them, he pulled my ticket and passport out of his jacket. I was shocked for a second; he must have taken them when I was trying to keep half of Europe inside me. They were now in his hands. What was he doing? My eyes widened when I tried to answer this simple question for myself: *Who was he?*

"Wait a second!" I was out of breath, but trying to seem sober. "Look, I'm waiting for my friend Benjamin Rosenbaum. He's a student of mine. I have a ticket for him. I've got to wait for him."

Ted looked at me, and then at the Air Turkey clerk, a beautiful dark-featured woman whose hair was covered by a scarf.

"Lenny, come on." His mouth was at my ear, like we were sharing a secret. "Benjy's not around. He's found some other entertainments. Believe me, I know what I'm talking about. Why don't we just go to the gate?"

Panic set in. The booze wasn't helping. I tried to breathe deeply. "I've got to be—I know he's coming!"

"Lissen, Lenny. I've got Benjamin's ticket right here."

"How did you get it? How did you get—"

"Dear," he turned to the Air Turkey clerk. "I'm afraid my friend's a little out of it. He gave me the tickets, because—well, you know how some men get when they drink?"

She looked at us, puzzled.

"I'm alright." I was dead serious. I was going to pull myself together. "I just want to know how you—"

"Come on, Len. Relax. Chill out. I'm here to take care of you. You can rely on me. We'll leave the ticket with the lady here, and when your student appears with his passport, she can give it to him. Okay?"

I nodded. He was right—I *could* rely on him, with that trustable, kind face. I just didn't expect him to be there for me like that.

Ted showed her the ticket.

She frowned; her dark eyebrows knitted closer together. "Sir," she said. "I do not want to be responsible for this ticket."

"Then just have us paged. I travel all over the world, so I know how you guys work. Your job's not easy, especially now with so many problems in your part of the world."

She nodded. "Thank you, sir."

"When young Mr. Rosenbaum comes to this counter, you can give him a pass to go through security, and we'll be at the gate, waiting for him."

She smiled. "I can do that. I'll just call the gate and tell them that your friend has arrived. You still have two hours before take-off. You'll need it, because of heightened security."

She smiled at me, ripping our tickets, and gave us boarding passes. I still felt unsteady, but that feeling I had, the dizziness, the spinning, began to slow down.

In truth, I was glad Ted was there; he knew the ins-and-outs of security, the magic words which in my current state seemed as foreign as Ivory Coast French. His sample case was loaded with sharp surgical tools anyone would have thought were dangerous, but he got it through security, smiling, eagerly offering to lock it himself and hand it directly over to the cabin attendants. "I look trustable, don't I?"

"Yes, sir," they answered.

Shortly after, we were on the moving walkway, and then at the gate, sitting. I felt anxious. Benjy was trying to get to me, and I had no idea what was holding him up. Ted asked if I wanted another drink, and, dumb as it was, I took another Tanqueray miniature from his plastic bag just to calm down. As I slowly sipped it, he pressed his large, very reassuring hand over mine.

I looked at him. The clear face, the small teeth, the nice mouth that ached to be kissed. He seemed so frank and natural, a pole away from the guys I met through my ads. They were down-and-dirty and for the most part knew what they wanted, but they never seemed as frank, honest, and sweetly natural as this man.

"I want you to know," he said, licking his lips, "I've never done, uhh, with a guy what I did with you in that cab."

My eyes became blurry, making it hard for me to concentrate on him. I put my glasses on, then put them away again. As frank and nice as Ted seemed, all I wanted to do then was get on the plane with Benjy, and know that he was all right.

I squirmed. I wanted to believe Ted. "Never?"

"Yeah," he whispered. "That's the truth."

"Then why'd you do it with me?"

He shook his head. "I dunno. Sometimes you know something's going to happen before it does. I've traveled a hell of a lot, my friend, and I just *knew* I could trust you. Can I, buddy?"

"Sure, Ted. You can."

"Good." He squeezed my hand. "Don't worry. I'm going to get you to Istanbul, I mean that. With or without your friend."

I felt better. I could have kissed him right there, instead I only nodded and realized I had to use the john. That gin! I needed to pee pronto, and, if I had to, throw up, since I wasn't out of the woods totally in that direction. I got up.

"Where you going, Len?" he asked. I told him I needed to use the men's room, and he smiled. "I'll go with you. You need some company now."

As soon as I got up, I knew how right Ted was. My stomach was pole-vaulting straight up into my throat. I'd been dead a few days earlier. Now, half-alive, I was guzzling alcohol like a preppy school boy on a binge. Had I really drunk that much? Maybe the graft was speeding up again, pushing the alcohol, express, straight through me.

Once on my feet, I felt like I was strolling through a corridor of fun house mirrors and endless wobbling terminal aisles. Ted had to hold me up every few steps, since my knees kept buckling. What was that line about "depending upon the kindness of strangers"? Was Blanche DuBois going to catch that jet called Desire? Ted's fingers lightly danced through my hair.

"Peek-a-boo!" he whispered. I laughed some, and for a moment stopped noticing my stomach.

Finally, a men's room. Closed up tight. A portable sign outside announced, "Use Other Facility. Cleaning in Progress."

"Time for another men's room!" Ted joked, but suddenly nothing was funny. The whole terminal started to do insane loopy figure eights around me, and I was afraid I'd pee in my pants. Anxiously, I grabbed on to Ted as well-dressed people stared, hurrying past us. I felt like I was doing a constant U-turn through this place crawling with curious creatures from outer space, called business travelers.

We found another men's room, behind a little alcove. It was open.

"The magic door!" Ted proclaimed, opening it, then beckoning me in like a cartoon caterpillar with a wiggling index finger. "Peek-a-boo!"

For a terminal bathroom, it was small and empty, with only a few stalls and two urinals. Maybe it was used only when the main one was being serviced. Ted started laughing hysterically, like he could no longer control himself. He went over to a urinal and unzipped himself. I was all set to do the same thing.

"Peek-a-boo!" He took his cock all the way out of his pants and, joking, began waving it around. "Peek-a-boo! Peek-a-boo! Peek-a-boo!" I started to hate this. Why was he taking his dick out and "Peek-a-boo"-ing me with it? Was he going nuts, too? I felt weird. Too drunk. Certainly not myself, whoever Lenny Miller was.

I also knew I couldn't pee next to him, not with him waving his pecker around like that. Okay, so he had to make up for all those lost opportunities in Salt Lake City with the wife and kids, but this was too much. I stepped back away from him, but he snook up behind me, groped me, and unzipped my pants all the way.

He reached into my underwear, twirling my dick in his hands. I needed to pee, and he wasn't helping things. I tried to look behind me, scared someone might walk in any second. Officially, I was dead. If a cop had come in and found us both drunk, or having sex or—

I pulled his hand from me, zipped myself back up, then, very seriously, walked over to the last stall in the back. To feel more confident, I put my glasses back on.

"Hey!" he laughed. "Come back here right now! Where—"

I opened the door. My blood froze. The overhead lights throbbed, their feverish intensity assaulting my face.

Standing behind the toilet, roped to a water pipe, was Benjy. His head was slumped over, his mouth gagged, his arms tied tightly, and his throat cut. Blood oozed from it. I flinched, jerking violently away from the blood; my glasses crashed to the tile floor. They shattered, the sound echoing in my ears.

The ceiling fell in on me, and the floor zoomed up to my nose. I backed away, retching. Yellow drool with the stench of gin in it came out of me. Ted grabbed me.

"It's okay, baby. I'm holding you."

He shut the metal stall door. Its loud click reverbed into a bang, bang, bang . . . BANG. The house blew up once more. I started sobbing. Ted led me to the sink and splashed cold water on my face.

"You knew him?"

I nodded, choking the words out of me. "Benjy . . . Rosenbaum. What am I gonna do, Ted?"

"You didn't tell me he was colored. With a name like Rosenbaum?"

"I loved him. I really loved him."

"I know." He put his arms around me from behind. "I know you loved him. And you didn't really know him that long, did you? I can tell."

I coughed hard to clear my throat. I nodded, my eyes heavily filmed with tears. I had to shake the tears out of them. "How'd you know?"

"Like I said, when you've been traveling as long as I have, you know about these things. You pick up on stuff real fast. Maybe too fast."

"What should I do now?" I felt empty. Not scared, just empty. What was there to be scared of—I'd already been dead? I felt numb. I was delivering myself to Ted Richards, but what else could I—

"You and I are going to go to Istanbul," Ted announced, flashing that helpful smile. He grabbed a paper towel and dried my face. "That's what you're going to do, Len. I told you I'd never done anything like this with another man before. I meant that, buddy."

Next to the sink was a janitor's closet. Ted found another tripod-mounted sign that said, "Use Other Facility. Cleaning in Progress." He went out, positioned it quickly in front of the door, then took my arm and pulled me from the bathroom.

chapter thirteen

*W*e were seated back at the gate. People were boarding the plane. Our row would be called shortly.

My life was in Ted's hands. I realized that, walking back almost cold sober in silence from the men's room. I had to get on this plane.

Ted exhaled. "It's still hard to believe that was Benjamin Rosenbaum, your friend."

I nodded to him.

"Damn, I thought he was going to look like some kind of rabbi. Shows you what I know!" He was too loud, and must have seen the concern on my face. "Sorry. It's just . . . well, I thought they were going to page us before he got to the gate."

"Someone followed him. I feel responsible. I feel so—"

"You need to get yourself out of this *big* time, don't you?"

I looked at him. What could I tell him? Nothing. "Yes," I whispered.

"Good." He moved closer to me, lowering his voice. "Buddy, let me tell you. What the hell can *you* do about it? Nothing, right?"

Yes. I'd got Benjy into this. He'd been followed, all the way here. His killers could be anyplace, just as mine had been. And still could be. "Nothing." I squeezed out the word. "I can do nothing."

"Good, man." He shrugged his broad shoulders. "People are so damn funny! You think you know 'em, then you don't. These sort of young men are involved with drugs, illegal games, the wrong type of friends. Satanic cults. You name it—any number of things."

"Benjy wasn't."

He smiled at me with that warm friendliness that I wanted immediately to hide in. "Are you sure?"

My head hurt again, my eyes felt strained. "No."

Our row was called. Ted pulled me along by my elbow. "Then there's just no telling, is there?" We moved as if by magnetism toward the plane.

"They've got some great food on Air Turkey," he announced smiling. "Do you like shish kabob?"

I didn't answer. Another attractive woman with dark eyes and a head-scarf took our boarding passes, handing both stubs back to Ted. He smiled at her.

"See." He got close to my ear. "This is going to be easy. We'll eat. Maybe sleep some. Fool around. Do you ever fool around on planes?"

I shrugged. "Maybe," I said in a whisper that also seemed to come magnetically out on its own.

"Good, buddy. I live in a 'maybe' world myself."

We found our seats in the back of coach, in a two-seat row by a window. I had checked most of my stuff in my luggage, though I had some sleeping pills from my medicine cabinet on me. I thought about popping a few, but wasn't sure how they'd mix with all the gin I'd drunk. A lot of the people around us looked Moslem, but as soon as we were seated, the cabin attendants came by with a cart filled with alcoholic drinks.

Ted ordered a scotch. I had a Coke and some Extra Strength Tylenol, swallowing two for the pain in my head. The pain started to feel like an immense flashing sign announcing that I was entering Hell again. They gave out magazines. Ted took some copies of *Field and Stream*, *Sports Illustrated*, and a few others I would have had to have been paid to read. No *Scientific American*, nothing even remotely gay, like *Men's Health* or *Details*. I closed my eyes to rest them, trying to nap as we taxied for take-off.

I started going through several interesting formulas and equations in my head, things I had memorized ages ago in grad school, just to block that sight from my brain. I was wandering through them, but could still feel Benjy's rough hands on my face, my head. The way he would tender-ly touch me. I decided I needed to keep his hands on me, in my mind. I kissed them over and over, until somehow I fell asleep.

I must have napped for about an hour. We were up in the sky. Ted woke me, and we had dinner. It was shish kabob, not on skewers, but lamb, anyway, and good. Ted told me that he had called his wife on the plane phone, and she was doing okay in Salt Lake City. So were his kids.

The lights were now out. Some people were watching a movie, filled with cute young actors who looked like they came from a J. Crew catalogue.

"You ever been married?" he asked me.

"Not to a woman."

He got closer to me. "Gay marriage?"

"I guess you could say that."

"What's that like? One of you does the housework and the other one works, something like that?"

I shook my head slowly. "That doesn't even work with the straights, does it?"

"Naw. Not much, except with the Mormons. They're still back in that. You ever fooled around with a married guy?"

"I've fooled around with everybody."

"You don't seem the type, Len. You seem very serious—like you'd want some kind of guy who'd mean everything, heaven and earth to you. That sort of stuff."

"We're not always what we seem. I guess you can attest to that."

He nodded, his eyes brightening, like another one of those little-used lights had turned on.

"When I was a kid," he said, "I did everything. Twelve, thirteen, fourteen. You know how kids are. They don't put stuff into little compartments. If the kids weren't preached that what we adults disapproved of was wrong, they'd never know it. I love my wife because she's a woman and she's my wife and we have these kids, but sometimes I've thought if she wasn't a woman, I'd be bored to death with her. I mean, if she ever became, like, a man. Know what I mean?"

"No," I answered, then admitted, "Yeah. I know what you mean. I've had lots of sex with guys I couldn't have had half a conversation with. Not that it made a difference. We didn't need to talk. We didn't need anything in common really. All of the new gay marriage stuff loses out on those old nitty-gritty connections that men used to have. Back then, you didn't want to marry a guy, you just wanted to have fun with him and"—I wanted to say "lose yourself for a while," but I didn't. "Of course," I added, "some of those nitty-gritty connections could turn violent sometimes."

A short while later I managed to drop off to sleep again, despite that image in my brain of Benjy tied up to the pipe. There was now that image and Josh on the concrete floor. I kept trying to wipe both images away, but didn't have enough old rags and mental Windex to do it. Finally I decided to make a kind of peace with both of them. Why fight it? They wanted me to remember them. They were counting on it. Both of them were smiling at me, especially Benjy.

I realized how beautiful Benjy had been. I hoped he forgave me. He'd been in love with Christ. And with me—of all things—and he'd been crucified trying to reach me. He'd had such a genuine purity of spirit, something I'd been looking for all my life, in my own convoluted, never-smart-enough-to-know-it way.

A tide of welcome sleep overcame me as I thought about the people who must love him. How unjust the world would seem to them. Still, God, the old fashioned one, the big fatherly *He*, would carry them through that. Perhaps you might say that Benjy had found himself at last. He had taken on the Christhood he was in love with; he had found it.

It had all happened so fast: meeting Ted. Benjy dead.

In one of my philosophy classes at Harvard we had discussed what would happen if we discovered that all of waking life were only a dream. The answer, of course, was nothing. Nothing would happen. You would only continue with the dream.

Something tickling in my pants woke me up. The plane was dark; Ted had thrown a blanket over both of us. His hand was exploring the inside of my underwear.

"Thought I'd surprise you," he whispered.

"You did."

"Wanna fool around?"

"Here?" I was still groggy.

"Sure, buddy. Hey, wait. Suppose we try one of the johns? No one's up now."

He peered over towards the galley area in the back of the plane. The cabin attendants were all seated, there was no line for the bathrooms, and a lot of darkly bearded men and women in head scarves were either sleeping or reading quietly.

He got up and motioned for me to follow. I zipped myself up and obeyed, like a puppet on a string. Drifting past snoring sleepers and a few readers, I let the outside of me follow Ted until he pulled me into the bathroom, locking the door as a bright light turned on.

My mouth was a tar pit of sleep and the retching I'd done, but he stuck his tongue into it, then pushed his pants and boxer undershorts down around his ankles. His flag was at full attention. Jumping up on the sink basin, he pushed up his shirt and started playing with himself. His dick was fully ready, perky, a bit stubby. Puppyish, like he was. It was slightly less than mid-sized, exuding an All American-boy freshness; it just happened to be on an adult male.

The shaft of it kept flicking back and forth, like Tinkerbelle's wand, collecting all the glow and sparkle in the light of his peach and coppery pubic hairs. They darkened into a more concentrated narrow trail that traveled up his stomach, sinking into his navel. He was insatiably horny, reaching for my head for me to suck him. I did that, falling onto auto-pilot. It wasn't difficult. He wasn't so big that doing it was a struggle; he was easily satisfied.

His equipment quickly started to shake, rattle, and then spurt again. Some of it went down my throat and some of it got on my face. After he'd come, he jumped down. I washed off in the sink.

"That was great!"

"Shhhh," I warned him.

He lowered his voice. "Len, you're a Grade-A cocksucker."

I nodded. A thought came to me: Was being a Grade-A cocksucker a genuine accomplishment? Or was it more in the line of getting your job done on time and doing what was basically necessary without any complaints?

He asked me how I was doing: in short, did I want to do anything else for myself? I still felt like an anvil had been dropped on my head. Pulling his pants up, he gave me a quick kiss on the cheek.

I wondered, did he do this with girls? In Salt Lake, did girls suck him off and did he give them a quick, sporty, gentlemanly peck on the cheek? I was sure other straight guys believed Ted was cool, a gentleman, a regular sport. The kind of guy you could depend on, always there in a pinch for you.

I cracked the door open. Two people were waiting to use the john. I told him to go out first. He did, then I slipped out.

Next in line was an elderly lady in a headscarf, wearing a very shapeless dress. She was ready to push the door open as I got out. She looked shocked.

"Saves water," I said. "If two people use it."

She looked blankly at me. I walked past her. An older gentleman, perhaps her husband, came up to her. They started speaking Turkish, and I realized that she might not have understood a word of English.

Ted was back at our seats. When I sat down, he threw the blanket back over us.

"I feel like the dam burst, Len."

"Huh?"

He took my hand under the thin airline blanket and held it.

"Yep, the dam's burst and it's taken me to this precipice. Now I've got to jump off it. Know what I mean?"

"Nope."

"Okay, maybe you don't." He took a deep breath, then let it out. "Len, you can't imagine what it's like to live with a strict Mormon girl. Every appetite and pleasure known to humankind, they disapprove of, except having babies and Little League baseball. My wife thinks that when *Sports Illustrated* started putting girls in bathing suits in it, it became pornography." He licked his lips and announced, "I'd really love another drink"

"You would?"

"Shit yeah!"

I couldn't help smiling.

"Listen, buddy, she knows some gals who're involved in polygamous relationships. That's not too goofy for her. But we can't even have Maxwell House Instant Coffee at home. My two kids are brainwashed. The boy can't wait to go out and do missionary work. He's nineteen, and it starts in a year. June's so happy she can't stand it. He's such a beautiful kid, he's already got a body that won't quit. I keep wanting to ask him, 'Son, ever eat pussy?' 'Do you enjoy jerking off?' 'Do you know how nice a good blow job feels?' But he really belongs to her. She's got him by the balls already."

He jumped up, like he had come to the end of his *spiel* and there was nothing left but an anger he could not control. He went to the back and returned with two Dewers miniatures and two plastic cups of ice.

"Thought you'd like this."

I nodded, though I wasn't in the mood to drink.

He got into his seat and poured me about a half of one of the scotches, then poured himself a full one and what was left of mine.

"I had to bribe the purser, but he was easily bribed. I've done a lot of traveling in these countries. You can break every law in the world, but you've got to make sure they never feel a loss of face when you do it. I mean, you can do everything—and I mean *everything*—as long as you keep up the fairy tale about appearances. They don't think it's hypocrisy; it's just their culture."

I thanked him for my Dewars, sipping it slowly while he gulped his. "How's that different from us?"

He looked at me blank for a second, then said, "Yeah. We whitewash the outside and brainwash the inside."

I gazed at him. His small blue eyes were no longer glowing. They looked tired and heavy.

What had he meant about the dam breaking? What about me seemed to attract men like this? I thought about Benjy. Maybe he and Ted hadn't become "professional" queers yet; they hadn't swallowed all the rules of what's possible, what really makes a man attractive. I hated vacuous, professional queers, the kind who erected tight, stylish little fences of bitchiness around themselves, destroying that natural sense of curiosity I loved. "What drew you to me, Ted? In the cab, I mean?"

He took another big hit of the scotch. "It's crazy, but I knew you were there at the edge of something. Something strange, some destiny."

"Pretty sharp edge, wasn't it?" I took a deep breath. "I mean about Benjy; right there with the razor."

"I'm sorry about him. What a shock! But what can you do about it? You've got to go to Turkey, right?"

I nodded to him.

"Okay, I figured that." He took another swallow of scotch. "You've got a face that pulls people in, Len. Its wise. It's not just a fun-and-games face. You've seen a lot and yet you're still approachable. I could see that. I've learned how to read faces well. Do you read faces?"

"No. I'm not used to that."

I wasn't. Except in sex, I'd never thought of myself as a great connector with people. Sex was the great common denominator: Once it started, you didn't have to worry about the latest look, line, or hip bit of crap you'd be judged by. Now I felt grateful for Ted, for his clear suntanned skin. If he were really reading my face, did he know how naked I felt, as naked, really, as I had been at my "awakening" in the morgue? I felt utterly tender towards him, but vulnerable. I would need to protect myself. Could I?

"It's okay," he said, his small eyes darting around, taking in the passengers across the aisle from us. Then he kissed me on my cheek again, not a quick peck, but a long, lovely, soft kiss. I could have slept nicely in that lullaby of a kiss, where his lips met my cheek.

He drew away. "It's okay," he repeated. "Who needs to read faces? I'll do it for the both of us. Get some more rest, I can tell you need it."

I did: rest from my own brain. I kept trying to make some sense out of it. Why did Benjy, my beautiful friend, have to die senselessly for me? I could feel his presence there, touching me. The hardness of his hands, the softness of his touch. And Ted, he was a strange angel. How did he arrive suddenly? As Ted said, I was at the edge; but was he aware it was the edge of my very life, and I had no idea how long I had to live? Maybe that had drawn both of them towards me.

I looked over at Ted. His scotch was gone. He was now asleep, his head tossed back, his mouth open.

I hoped Benjy's spirit was finally released and he got to be with the other queer saints: Da Vinci, Whitman, Jesus, and certainly himself. Benjy was a saint, in his own way; as was Josh. But I—I was no saint; I wasn't even worthy of them. I was just an obsessive scientist who reverted to his animal self to crash the strong fences of his own intellect. The fences seemed to be getting higher again; were they protecting the animal deep inside me—or just goading him?

Writing on the fences: I needed something that would chalk a relationship between my coming back into being, my tragic adventures with Josh and Benjy, and what had happened in the airplane john with Ted, the non-stop Energizer bunny of sexual performance. Not too long ago, I would have reveled in that scene, but I never could have initiated it as he did, hopping up on the sink with his stubby dick out, hard and twitching. I was a good cocksucker, but *he,* all that energy! In school I'd learned: "A spring, forced back as far as it can go, when released will exert all the power of its repression."

BANG! It must have come from years of Ted staying locked in the dark. After my recent spell at Bellevue, I could understand that. I'd been hungry, too; ravenous for life. For sex; for knowing; for living. But maybe I'd been that way even before I'd been killed. It was just that due to my own repression, I could hardly admit my yearnings to release my appetites. Now I was . . . releasing them. I'd been through a lot in the last forty-eight hours of my life.

If this *really* was my life. And not just some dream of it.

My eyes no longer hurt so much. My head felt better. Showing mercy for me, Benjy and Josh decided it was time for me to sleep again. They left me in the dark, and I did.

chapter fourteen

We arrived in Istanbul about three in the afternoon, their time. It was like landing in Oz, just not quite so colorful. The colors were more muted, and the men had this kind of baleful quality, wearing dingy suits, right out of a 1930s black-and-white Italian movie. Ted got us through customs in a wink, which was lucky because I was still tired. Jet lag? Or too much chaos, organic and psychological, still going on in my body?

Despite the hotel reservation I had made for me and Benjy, Ted insisted he already had a room reserved for us in a new, charmless American-tourist hotel near the Bosperus. Our room, on the sixth floor, was spacious, complete with a very luxurious, American marble bathroom and golden views of the sunset over the black waters of the harbor. I went out onto the tiny narrow balcony and watched swarms of little boats like toys. The distant sounds of diesel engines and the shouts of the men working on the boats rose up to me.

Some sounds came also from street vendors, among the crowds hurrying through the streets, then streaming into alleys, archways, and arcades. An amplified call to prayer came from mosques, but most women did not wear veils or the long, sack-like Islamic coverings. Istanbul was like a Western city that had somehow been robbed of its place in our "modern" era. It was flash-frozen into a chunk of early twentieth century time.

I went back into the room, just as Ted had finished making a call to his wife. "How you like the place?"

"It's fine. The view from the balcony's beautiful. How's your wife? You call her a lot, don't you?"

"She wants to make sure I'm not screwing some young girl."

"You're definitely not doing that."

I stretched out on one of the two large double beds. He joined me.

"I did that once," he confessed. "I met her in Salt Lake. She wasn't a Mormon, either. She was a neat little thing. Very pretty with a nice young body. Bright, a marketing student. I met her wandering around a mall. We fucked like rabbits for a week, every time I could squeeze in a chance."

"What happened?"

"She started doing the 'marry me' business and I knew I couldn't. I had a family, and she was too young. I wasn't going to exchange one set of problems for another."

"I won't ask you to marry me. I might ask you to travel with me, though."

"Where to?"

"An archeological site near a place called Assos, on the Aegean coast. I need to leave tomorrow."

"What time?"

"Is that all you're going to ask, 'what time'?"

"Yeah. I have a meeting at noon. It'll be over with in a few hours. We can take off then."

I smiled, a bit puzzled. I had hoped he'd be able to leave in two days, not the very next day. "Don't you want to know any more details?"

He was kissing my ear with his soft mouth, blowing into it, then sticking his tongue into it. "Sure."

"Assos is . . . supposed to be nice," I said, purring.

"It's nice."

"But it's a long drive. Are you still up to it?"

"Why not?" he asked softly, his lips brushing over my cheek. "I love Turkey. I get paid to fly over here, but they don't need to know how I spend every minute. I'll arrange for my other meetings to take place at the end of my week. This way I'll get to have some real tourism as well. The archeology will be something to tell June about when I get back. She likes for me to fill her in on the details, as long as I don't give her the wrong ones. How do we get to your site?"

I read him the instructions and told him what Alvin had said about taking the car ferry.

"Yeah," he agreed. "The ferries here scare me worse than the roads. They overload the hell out of them, and every couple of years one disappears and goes bye-bye. Let me look at the map."

He pulled out a map of Turkey and traced the route to Assos, along with its tourist interests. "This looks great! There are some spectacular Greek and Roman ruins near it. And a good beach, what else could I want?"

"How about dinner?" I asked.

The dining room of the hotel was done up in what you might call "International Visa Card Modern." Plaid table cloths; fresh bottles of Heinz ketchup nearby; bread and butter. It could have been a steak-and-ale house in Des Moines, which suited Ted, a steak-and-baked potato eater. He ordered something that looked like a full rump of a cow, well-done.

"One thing I don't take a lot of chances on is food," he announced, his mouth full of meat. "After you've had your third case of food poisoning in two weeks, like I did once in Africa, you know how to be careful. I won't eat fish unless I see it jumping out of the water. Speaking of water, it's not a bad idea to drink only bottled here, although Turkey, I found out, has good water. France, strangely enough, can kill you, but Turkey is pretty much all right."

I smiled. I had roast pigeon—a local specialty the menu said, with pan-fried potatoes cooked with cubes of eggplant, raisins and nuts, and seasoned with hints of cinnamon and cardamom. There were very sweet carrots cooked on the side. I liked it, but Ted refused to try any of it. I had no idea how he'd do traveling through the country, but I was sure he'd find a way. He asked me if I wanted to go to a bath later.

I lowered my eyes to the potatoes on the plate and wondered about the back of my calf, which he hadn't seen. "A bath?"

"Yeah, buddy. Come on. They're a tradition in Turkey. The men go, soak and relax. We can get a private room, if we want."

I brought my eyes up to his small blue ones. They twinkled at me.

"All right," I said.

After dinner, we went down to the desk captain to ask if he could recommend a bath, a *hamam*, as they were called. He was a big man with a shaved head and a very big coal-black mustache.

"What kind of services would you like?"

"Gee." Ted shrugged. "Just something two men traveling together would like."

The captain cocked his head to one side, giving us a questioning look. "*Peki.* Two . . . regular American guys, right?"

"Yes, sir."

His big mustache curled up into a smile. Taking out a city tourist map, he wrote down the name of the bath on a slip of paper, then told us how much the taxi fare would be. He went out with us, got us a taxi, and Ted tipped him.

In the cab, the driver gave us a quick look back and asked if we were sure we wanted that *hamam*.

"Why not?" Ted asked.

"Is only for tourists. Like your hotel. Maybe you men would like something *different*."

I could see part of his smile in the rearview mirror.

"Sure," I said, smiling back. "Let's *be* different."

"Good. I have something for two men like you. Something more like Turkey. Yes?"

"Okay," I agreed.

"*Iyi!* Is close to Sultanahmet Square, where the old Hippodrome was. You know it?"

"I know the Square," Ted said. "But not the *hamam*."

"Very old, but many young men go. Very *hosh*. Nice."

"And the young men?" Ted asked.

"Very *hosh* also, Sir."

The *hamam* turned out to be up a hill, in a section of Istanbul that, as Constantinople, the Romans had walked through, and later the Crusaders. We passed the large Sultanahmet Square with its towering obelisks and monuments, then several smaller squares teeming with cafes. Men spilled out of them, smoking, talking, playing cards and dominos at outside tables, drinking tea. Little colored lights were strung through them and the air was alive with Eastern music, loud talk, hands clapping, and the joy of being out at night. I wanted to get out and walk as we drove on for eight or nine more long blocks, until we had passed the last lighted square.

At an unmarked doorway on a dark corner, the driver stopped. The street was empty, littered with a slime of discarded wet papers, and the gutters were oily with black sewer water. The shuttered buildings looked as inviting as a slum in the Bronx.

"Maybe we should go back to the bath the desk captain told us about," I whispered.

Ted shook his head, quietly handing the driver the Turkish lira that he had asked for, which turned out to be less than the captain had suggested.

After Ted knocked on the door, a slim young man, dressed in a long, high-collared blue robe, opened it, bowed, and led us down a short passageway.

We came to a office, marked "Interdit." He motioned for us to remain, then ducked into it and opened up an iron window grill.

"Now, *efendim*, what can I do for you?"

Ted asked for a private room. The young man nodded, offering to hold our valuables in a safe. We checked our passports and some money, and he gave us two large towels and a very old filigreed key.

As he led us down several broken limestone stairs into a high cavernous atrium, clouds of cedar incense mixed with fragrant oils drifted up through twinkling lights and groves of darkness, from which half-naked limbs suddenly appeared. My eyes followed four tiers of walkways climbing up above me, to a lofty black-domed ceiling, shining with gold-leafed stars.

On the first floor, an ancient rocky pool was fed by a bubbling stream. Private rooms, hidden by ornately carved wooden screens, lined the inner court on three sides. Under the railings and around the pool, strings of colored light bulbs glowed like footlights. The fourth wall was pierced by a shower of triangular, leaded-glass window panes which brought in wedges of light sneaking in from the outside. Some of the panes were tinted deep ruby, amber, and green, while others were clear but mottled by age.

Men in thin white cotton robes or draped only with towels glanced out from the rooms or promenaded around the balconies. The young clerk led us to our room on the second tier, opened it with the key, and snapped on a light bulb barely bright enough to make a difference. The room contained a small closet for our clothes and a narrow platform with a pillow on it.

"If you would like a massage, gentlemen, I can arrange for a man to come into the room and do it for you both. Or you can have one down by the pool."

"Why don't we try it down by the pool?" I said, too dazzled by the place to want to stay in the small room.

"That will not be so private, sir. You can have a very nice young man in your room, if you'd like."

"That sounds good to me," Ted said.

"No," I insisted. "Why don't we try the pool?"

Ted shrugged and the clerk left.

"Why didn't you want him in here?" Ted asked as he rushed to get his clothes off.

I sat on the bed and took my time. Despite the low light, I wanted to get a quick look at what was happening on my leg. "I guess you've never been to a place like this before."

"No, pal. Too busy working. Besides, sometimes I have co-workers with me and I've got to play the Mormon husband. Anyway, up until now I wasn't ready. But this sure feels okay."

I watched him amble barefoot and naked around the room. Peering through the notched openings in the window screen, he lost himself in what the balconies and the court below offered. I got up, undressed, then sat down to examine my lower calf. The welt felt thicker, but in what light was available, the color no longer appeared to be quite so red. Relieved, I watched Ted gazing through the screen.

We had never seen each other naked before. I broke into a Cheshire-cat grin at how good he looked from the rear with his muscular round, moon-white butt against his tanned legs. He turned back towards me, smiling. "This is some place. Kind of like out of a story, isn't it?"

"I think so."

He returned to me, leaned over and kissed my forehead, like he was offering me a reward for this new-found bit of freedom. I pulled him closer, feeling the warmth from his navel. His lower belly was flaxed with coppery hair; his crotch, silky and tan-lined, was much lighter than the rest of him. I gave the short shaft of his cock a quick kiss, as his fingers roamed through my hair.

He spotted the welt on the back of my calf. "What's that?"

I hesitated. "Nothing."

"Wait a second. Let me look at it."

He dropped down on one knee to inspect it. "It doesn't look good to me, Len. Maybe we should have that massage in here."

"It's just a burn," I said. "I got it a while ago in my lab. Things like that happen all the time."

"Your lab? Are you sure? It looks brand new to me."

"How can you tell?"

"I'm around hospitals all the time, buddy. So I see a lot of burns and injuries. This one looks serious." He got back up. "Are you sure you don't need a doctor to look at it?"

"Naw." I shook my head and got up also. "Come on. Let's see what the locals are like, before we get a professional in the room."

We wrapped the towels around our waists, hung our clothes on pegs in the small closet, and locked the door. The lock was flimsy, and being a New Yorker, I felt insecure about it. Then I quickly lost all my fear as soon as we got out onto the balcony and I saw what had kept Ted glued to the screen.

Young men like egrets flocked around us in white towels and robes. Some were incredibly beautiful with fine features, coal-black hair, and skin as fresh and clear as the winners of a California male beauty contest. Most amazingly, they had an open curiosity and physical candor about them, with no reticence about touching others, that in America would have seemed outrageous if not impossible. I felt as if I had stumbled upon a piece of paradise, as they softly ran their hands over our necks, shoulders, and chests, smiling, laughing, nodding and winking.

chapter fifteen

$\mathcal{B}$ y the time I had made it down to the pool, I'd lost all my fear about the welt on the back of my calf. I felt as if I had been accepted at the *hamam*, merely on the sight of my smile and by my accepting the gentle charms of the men around me. The pool was warm and had a high mineral content, though I was not sure how clean it was. Taking off my towel, I eased into it's murky rocky bubbles, as Ted settled on the edge, watching the men who appeared in groups of two or three, but rarely alone.

A young man I'd noticed on one of the balconies, barefoot and barechested in a pair of sheer white drawstring pants, approached Ted, squatting at his shoulders. He had a wrestler's beefy, muscular body with a swirl of onyx-black hair on his dark chest that narrowed into an enticing trail down his tight, rippling stomach into his white pants.

"Would you like a massage, Sir?" His voice was soft and friendly. "I would be happy to do that."

Ted turned and looked up at him. "What's your name?"

"Sulieman. I'm a very good masseur."

Ted looked around him at the young men who were now at a distance, and perhaps less approachable in this strange place than he had thought. "All right."

I waded over to him, and asked him if he wanted the key to our room, which I had on a string around my neck. He took it and he and Sulieman went back up the stairs. I stayed waist-deep in the water, watching groups of men who appeared to be in their twenties or thirties, a few in their forties, come down from the tiers in robes, towels, or blue boxer shorts, and walk around the pool. Unlike in American bathhouses, where a cold war of rejection, stiff attitude, and hard cruising was customarily waged, these men touched each other in the same natural affectionate way. I watched as if I were looking at a ballet, although I still had no idea what went on in the rooms.

Then, without any warning, two very strong hands touched my shoulders; I turned to see a young man in the water, perhaps in his mid-twenties, smiling at me. He was clear-skinned with a very light silky complexion, but sparkling black curly hair. He had a thin, but beautifully defined chest with small aubergine-dark, shiny-wet nipples rising slightly from its surface. His arms were very muscular, and he had a long neck with a pronounced Adam's apple. He was perched comfortably on a rock, half-submerged in the pool's bubbles, and I wondered how tall he was.

Of course, I smiled back.

"Are you American?" he asked.

"Yes. From New York."

"Aw, New York! Very big place, right?" I told him it was. "I've never been. Do you have *hamams* in New York?"

I nodded. "Something like them, but nothing like this."

"Why is that?"

"People here are so friendly."

"*Friendly?*"

"Yes. They seem friendly."

"Sometimes yes; sometimes not."

"Why not?"

He raised his black brows and shrugged. "I don't know. They can be cruel. The world is not always good."

"That's true," I said. "But you are."

He broke into a big grin. I touched his downy cheek, and he closed his eyes, still smiling.

I waded over to the side of the pool, and sat down. He paddled towards me, but stayed in the water and started massaging my feet. His touch was gentle, yet strong.

"That's wonderful," I said. "You're very good at that."

"Thank you. What is your name?"

I told him. He told me his name was Akbar.

"That's a nice name."

He frowned. "Not everyone likes it."

"Why would that be?"

"It's hard to say why. But I like Istanbul. It's very good for me to be here."

I leaned over and stroked his chest. His small silky nipples became more pointed under the touch of my fingers. He smiled.

"I'd like to massage your feet, too." I said.

"You cannot," he answered.

"Why not? If you get out of the water, I'll massage your feet."

He looked at me puzzled. I decided to lead the way and got out of the water, grabbing my towel. I wrapped it back around me, self-conscious being naked out in the open. Although the Turks seemed comfortable about touching each other, they did not appear unclothed publicly.

Akbar dogpaddled away from me. Still in the water, he was talking to a young, towel-wrapped friend who was sitting at the edge of the other side of the pool. I walked around to them.

"Hello," I greeted the other boy, who looked like he was eighteen or nineteen, shorter in appearance and darker than Akbar, with more of a soft, adolescent stomach.

"Hello," the boy said, looking at Akbar.

"My friend," Akbar said, "speaks only a few words of English. 'Hello,' 'Yes,' 'No.' That's all. We speak Arabic together."

"Where's he from?"

"From where I'm from. Bosnia. He lost everyone at home, but he has two uncles here from his mother. They take care of him."

"What's his name?"

"His name is M'met."

"Tell him I'm glad to meet him."

Akbar said something to him. I got closer to M'met and he placed his hands on my lower legs, running them lightly over them, stopping only for a moment at the welt. When he turned his head to me, I saw that he was blind.

Akbar and M'met spoke more together. I crouched closer to M'met and he touched me softly on my chest and shoulders. I kissed his cheek.

"You are very good," Akbar said. "Would you come back into the water with me?"

I wasn't sure I wanted to go back into the water, but decided to anyway. Some other men started to descend from the tiers, and I noticed among them Ted and his masseur, Sulieman. Ted had a big grin on his face.

"These guys certainly know their business!" he announced and then discreetly handed Sulieman some money.

"Perhaps I can massage your friend, too."

I looked at Sulieman. Although he was impressive, I wasn't interested. "I want to swim some more," I said.

"We'll get coffee or tea, maybe chat," Sulieman said to Ted. "Tell me more about yourself. I want to know!"

Ted smiled, slightly embarrassed. He handed me the key, then they walked out towards the office.

I put my towel down again, and went back into the water. Akbar joined me and started touching me on my chest and stomach. I was now completely hard; I couldn't help it. It seemed impossible for me to be so casual, but neither did I want to play at hiding it. I guided his hand to my cock.

He stopped smiling. "I did not know you wanted that."

"Is that bad?"

"Sometimes. Would you like to touch me on my feet?"

"Sure."

He leaned back so that most of his slim torso was out of the water. His hips were now close to me. I put one supporting hand under his firm back, and touched him with the other. I did not touch his cock, but stroked his thighs, traveling with my hand down to his knees.

Quickly, then, I realized that below them, he had no legs. Both of his limbs were gone past his knees.

"Do you still want to touch me?"

"Yes, Akbar. Very much."

He put his arms around me. "Can we go to your room? We'll talk."

"Sure."

"M'met will help me."

We went over to the edge of the pool where M'met waited, and I helped Akbar out of the water, although he really didn't need my help. M'met had a robe for him and his two prosthetic legs, made of very light plastic.

"These legs are very good. The International Red Cross got them for me. After I lost mine, it took a long time, but I got these."

Sitting on the stone floor at the edge of the pool, he quickly attached the legs using two small padded belts on each of them. Getting up wasn't easy, since he was down flat on the floor with his legs splayed out. Both M'met and I helped him. He had a moment of slight unbalance, but he overcame that.

"Was it hard learning to walk with these?" I asked.

He nodded, pointing to his head.

"It's mostly up here. You have no idea how much our balance is in the brain, and not the feet."

He seemed to have no problems walking up the slippery stairs to our room. He was careful and his prosthetics were helpfully fitted with rubber-soled shoes. "I'm lucky. Years ago they would fit you with these wooden pegs that made you look like a horror movie monster!" He laughed and so did M'met, who laughed even more after Akbar translated it for him.

"He likes to laugh," Akbar explained.

As I unlocked the door to the room, I saw more men coming down to the pool, while others lay on the tables in the shadows, getting massaged. Soft strains of Turkish string music floated up, mixing with clouds of incense and the moans of the men half-hidden on the tables and the muscular rubbing sounds of the masseurs, applying oil to various exposed parts of the men.

I felt lost. Akbar touched my face.

"You like it here?" he asked.

"Yes," I said.

I unlocked the door, and Akbar gently guided M'met's bare shoulders to come in. It was dark in the room, until the dim overhead light suddenly made the room glow. M'met felt his way around to learn where things were.

Still in his towel, M'met sat on the narrow bed platform. I sat down next to him and Akbar sat with me. "I lived in Cincinnati for three years," he said. "Before the war. I mean the one in Bosnia—then I went home. My parents needed me. I did not question going back."

"So that's where you learned English?"

"Some. I was in college in Ohio. Computer science. Everything in computers is in English, so you must know it."

"How did you like Cincinnati?"

"It was alright. Different. A lot more choices than you have here."

"Choices?"

"Yes." He smiled and shrugged. "You know, Coke and Pepsi. K.F.C. McDonald's. Ford and Honda. Choices like that. I felt very alone."

"But you don't now?"

"No."

He took his robe off. I turned to him. He was now naked, except for the prosthetic legs which did not really seem like a part of him. I dropped my towel, kissing him on his mouth.

"That was very nice. Islam says that love returns you to the Garden of Eden. All love."

"Even with men?"

"Yes, even with men."

I felt a great warmth coming from behind me; M'met was touching my shoulders and kissing my neck. I turned and kissed him, too. He had also removed his towel. He stroked my face and chest and smiled.

The soft strumming music drifted languidly into the room, as they both touched me with delicate, seeking fingers, followed by their soft lips on every part of me, first on my face, then down my neck, shoulders, and chest, then lower to my stomach and groin. M'met's fingers delicately explored the folds of my scrotum, then the underside of my penis and the blooming head of it.

Lowering my mouth to the blind boy's cock that was half hard and circumcised, I took it, as both of them caressed me. I got off the narrow bed onto my knees, and sucked each of them, experiencing this warm sensitive moment, surrendering fully to it.

I got up. Akbar stood and we kissed, with me embracing him, touching and stroking him, while M'met sat on the bed, his face in a garden of genitals, stroking, licking, and tasting both of ours to his delight.

Then Akbar sat back down. "I'd like to take these off. I never feel like I'm undressed with them."

I helped him with the straps, and he let them go on the side. I could now hold him fully to me, touching the stumps of his legs, kissing them softly.

He moaned. I could hear him release a sob.

"You have no fear of me, do you?" he whispered, tears falling from his eyes. "So many *gey* men cannot stand to see me. I hate it."

"You're beautiful the way you are, Akbar. I'm only happy that you're alive."

I kissed both of them, and the three of us embraced on the narrow bed. I had them both in my arms while they kissed me and one another, with my face next to them. Then they stopped for a moment, while Akbar stroked the hair on M'met's head, letting his fingers trace the boy's face.

"I want to tell you how it happened," Akbar said softly, with one hand on my chest and the other on M'met. "I was walking through a field, taking a short cut to our house. How stupid! I was wrapped up in my own thoughts; I should have known better. I thought no one had been there. A land mine exploded under me. My only memory was like I'd been hit by a truck. Or a tornado. That's what it was like. In Ohio once I'd seen a tornado. Funny, they sound alike—'Ohio,' 'tornado.'

"Suddenly I woke up, maybe three or four meters from the explosion. I was alone, and then—lucky for me—a woman from my village came by. She started screaming and help came. They put a blanket on my legs, they didn't want me to look at it. But I knew. I kept asking God to help me—I wanted Him to grow the legs back. Not to let me die."

I listened to his words, they were so honest. He was right about only being completely naked without his legs. He was that way now, with me. I remembered the way the house exploded. I could feel it; then softly, I kissed his face, his eyelids, his mouth. "I feel that you know what I'm talking about," he said.

"Yes. I also know what it's like to die, and then come back. Some power—"

"God?"

"Yes. God—kept me from dying also."

"I could tell. You were chosen, I felt it. When you've been through what I have, you feel things very much."

I pulled them closer to me, feeling that complete helplessness of love that overtakes you at such moments, when so many barriers have been lowered. Or do we really, desperately, want to lower them, but find the way so difficult? For a brief moment, I felt that I was going into that "state" when "God" opened Itself up and I became a fleeting part of *It*. There was just a hint of that, a rip in reality that exposed itself—and I wanted so much to take both of them with me, but . . . what I really wanted was to come back from that "state" with them.

But they were there already.

Akbar spoke to M'met in Arabic. "I told him that you understood. That you have also come back from death."

M'met smiled and the three of us kissed some more, holding, and caressing each other, until sex bloomed forth again, with me bending forward to suck Akbar while M'met pressed himself into me from the rear, until his cock found entrance into me. I was in pure heaven, but knew this was not the safest thing to do and pulled M'met from me, just before he came. He managed to do this in the palms of my hands, while I continued with my mouth on Akbar.

A knock on the door interrupted us. Through the window screens, I could see Ted with two other men in towels.

"Len?" he said softly.

I pulled a towel around me and went over, opening the door halfway. "Hi."

"You with those boys?" he asked.

"Yeah."

"Is this place crazy or what? I wish they had a branch in Salt Lake City! Want us to join you?"

"No, I don't. I'll be out in a minute. Maybe two minutes."

"How 'bout a half hour?"

"Sounds better."

"I've already had two massages. I feel like butter. You should get one. My friends here want to meet you."

They nodded at me. They were big and impressively handsome, with arms and chests like Russian weight lifters, but at the moment I wasn't sure about anything else. I had this deep sense of satisfaction that I did not want to have changed.

"Are you with M'met and Akbar?" one asked. He had a Mongolian steppe of unruly black hair all over his broad chest, a short black beard and huge eyebrows.

"Yes."

He smiled. "Good. I am Ezekial. I'm a Turkish Christian"—he pointed to his friend—"but he's a Moslem!"

I nodded, not sure what a Jewish, formerly devout-atheist was supposed to say.

"It's good," he said smiling, "the three of you. Sometimes that is the way God works. He says, 'When one does not have enough, three is better!'"

He let out a hearty laugh, then the three of them left.

I shut the door. Akbar had his legs back on, and his robe. He was standing up, with M'met.

"I think we should leave," he announced.

"Why?"

"They were making fun of me. They think God did this to me, so I have to suffer."

"That's crazy. They were just laughing about three men being together."

"Are you sure? I heard what he said about not having enough. Sometimes people do not always say what they mean."

He had a point.

"It still hurts to hear people laugh. I feel ashamed. I love you and don't want to feel ashamed."

"Then spend ten more minutes with me, please. And"—I felt bad about this, but wanted him alone—"ask M'met to wait outside."

He spoke to M'met, who left us. I drew him back to the bed, helping him remove his legs, and we made love again, only the two of us, but I felt that others were present: all the men I'd ever attempted to love, as I surrendered to his skin, his lips, the music, and those tender, fragile feelings I could previously only allow myself to release after exhausting myself in the wildest kinds of sex. In the midst of this, he pressed my cock into his asshole. I slowly fucked him, but pulled out before I came and sucked him, until he came in my mouth. I climaxed on his chest, and we kissed for a long time. Then I helped him put on his legs again and we sat on the bed, with him in his robe.

I stroked his neck.

"That man with you—"

"Ted?" I said.

"Yes. He's different from you. I can see that. Be careful."

"Why do you say that? I mean, he *is* different, but—"

"It's the way he talks," he warned. "I think he doesn't say what he means, either. You need to watch out."

I nodded. Suddenly energyless, what I really needed to do was lie down. I did and propped my right leg up. Even in the low light, his eyes found the place where the tissue was evidently moving away from my flesh.

"M'met noticed that," he said. "His hands knew it. Did they re-attach your leg there?"

"No. This re-attached *me*. I was dead once. I've come back to life."

He looked into my eyes. "Then we do understand each other!"

I turned slightly from him. "I don't know how long I'm going to live, Akbar."

"I was afraid of that," he said.

"Can you see it?"

He kissed me softly on my cheek.

"Yes. I think even M'met can."

I got up and put the towel around me, and opened the door. Ted and M'met were waiting outside, separately.

"We need to get outta here!" Ted said. "This place is nuts. Those two big dudes wanted to fuck me in the worst way. It'd be like getting plowed by a truck!"

I smiled at him, then said good-bye to Akbar and M'met. The two of them embraced me, then I watched them descend the stairs, passing men who nodded silently to them.

"I feel like I've just been in one of those old Bob Hope-Bing Crosby 'Road' movies," Ted said as he got back into his clothes. "I'm not sure if this is like a lot of other places here, but I think I could really start to love Turkey."

"We should thank that cab driver, if we ever see him again."

He was dressed. He sat down next to me, as I finished tying my shoes. "I want to thank you for being here with me." He ran his hand over my head. "I never would have done something crazy like this without you."

"But you're the one who wanted to go."

"I'm a salesman, Len. Sometimes I have to talk *myself* into things."

At the desk, we retrieved our money and passports from the clerk. Sulieman appeared. He shook Ted's hand very formally, then he handed me a slip of paper.

"What's this?" I asked.

"From your friend Akbar, sir. He wants you to have it. You have made a good friend in him."

I nodded, and took the paper. On it, in very neat handwriting, he had given me his name and address, his phone number, and also three words: "Remember. Watch out."

hen we got back to the hotel room, I showered while Ted had a drink and made another call to his wife. Not being married with kids, I had no way to judge these things, but it seemed strange to me that he called her so often.

While toweling off, I came back into the room.

"How's June?"

"Mormon as ever," he said, sighing. "She asked me if I'm drinking, smoking, having coffee. I told her no. I'd never do that, right? She didn't ask me about sucking dick or almost getting fucked by big Turks, or anything like that. Funny how Mormons never ask about that. The kids are fine. I love the hell out of them. When do you want to take your trip tomorrow?"

"As soon as we can. Are you still up for it? I mean, I'm not sure if it's going to be steak-and-potatoes all along the way."

"Hell, you saw me at the Garden of Allah tonight. I can go native as well as the next guy."

"I guess you can."

"Renting a car shouldn't be a problem. Last time I was in Istanbul, I got one with a driver, but, heck, I can drive here. You just have to watch out for the nutcase drivers. Ever drive in one of these countries?"

"No. I don't even drive in New York."

"Listen. Greece, Turkey, they make New York look like a bunch of little old ladies from Pasadena. The only rule of traffic is you don't get yourself killed." He unbuckled his belt.

"That sounds like a good rule no matter what."

I liked the way he took his clothes off, stripping with no self-consciousness at all. As a kid, I used to watch teen-age boys, out of the corner of my eye, take their clothes off in the locker room of the local "Y." Joking, popping towels, laughing, punching one another, the boys walked around as if they weren't totally bare-assed. They were clothed in a buddyish denial of being naked that I already knew I couldn't be a part of without knowing it was an act.

He smiled and paced around the room a bit, as he'd done in the *hamam*, passing the mirror without looking at himself. He crouched, fished a black toiletry kit out of his suitcase, let out a loud fart, then got up, shut the door to the bathroom, and the shower started.

In the bright light from the bedtable reading lamps, I could really observe the back of my calf; it did look markedly less reddish, but it no longer felt as if the graft were a part of me. Now it was more like a secret cargo I was carrying, like a rubber filled with heroin that drug "mules" swallowed and took across borders. I was taking this across another border . . . between life and death.

Was I being paranoid?

One tiny problem—a microscopic tear or cut—in one of those rubbers and it was all over with. The heroin leaked out into your intestines, and you died. But what about a problem with this thing? This substance was doing . . . only *God* knew what.

I couldn't figure it out; but unlike Akbar, I didn't know what God was: I had no real way of approaching It, or *Him*, as some people called God. But love in some form kept hitting me. I was aware that I wasn't worthy of all this love, but maybe *it*, this strange substance itself, knew that my own particular miracle had a tight boundary of death around it, and this impossible, unexpected miracle was inviting love, urging it, directly into it.

Ted's shower was still going. I rolled off the bed and spotted his sample case. I opened it and glanced at what was in it. Lots of catalogues and sales forms for surgical products—stainless steel tools, appliances for sterilizing, bandages, dozens of kinds of tapes. I pulled out a routine-enough expense form. My eyes shot to the top of it.

In very simple lettering it declared:

World Wide Christian Medical Missions.
Christ Is the Only Language We Speak.

The shower stopped. I clicked shut the briefcase, rushed into bed, then turned out both of the bedside lights.

Ted got in with me. One of his knees accidentally nudged the back of my right calf, further up, near the knee, but close enough to the substance to remind me of it.

I froze.

"You sleepy, buddy?"

I grunted.

"Come on, Len." He put his arms around me, pulling me to him. I still couldn't face him.

"Tell me. What d' you think of married men now?"

"They're okay."

"Just okay?"

I turned to him. The smartest thing would be to try to kill him. But could I? How did Akbar have him pegged so fast? Or was I only being crazy? Lots of Christian groups were doing good things. They weren't all blowing up family planning clinics and murdering doctors who just happened to be doing abortions. "Happened to be": a strange term. In Bosnia, some people just "happened to be" Serbian Moslems, so they were thrown into starvation camps or had their legs blown off. The innocent just *happened to be* something, or did they? "Happened to be" robbed a stark tragedy of an actual face. I didn't just happen to be in my lab. I was there; just had Josh had actually been there for me, just as Benjy had been.

"I think married men are wonderful," I answered. I kissed him, putting both my hands around his neck as I did it. I pushed my tongue as far down his throat as I could, while my hands tightened around his neck so hard that my thumbs could feel the jump of blood inside his veins and pressure from the big carotid arteries themselves.

I kept kissing him and squeezing my fingers, tightening and tightening them. He struggled. His legs bounced and his hands sprang up to mine. He bit down hard on my tongue.

I let go, looking into his eyes. I couldn't do it. Damn it! I'd stopped breathing.

"Wow!" He got his breath back, turning his face back from me. "That was way hot!" he shouted. "My dick's hard as a rock!"

I tried to breathe again. I felt as if I had forgotten how.

"Sorry 'bout your tongue, buddy. I heard about guys who jerk off and try to hang themselves. Is that what you tried on me?"

I could only look at him. Then the air blew itself out of me. "Yeah . . .

you could say that."

"You are kinksville, man! You are—I can't believe you! I guess you get carried away sometimes."

"Sure." I was trying not to cry. I felt like I was smeared in shit all over: I couldn't kill him, not even for Josh and Benjy. I could see them in the room with me, disappointed. They had turned their backs to me, ashamed probably of my cowardice. Josh's shoulders were hunched, his head down. The glowing light I'd seen on them, out. "I hope I didn't scare you."

"Scare? Man, the only one who scares me is June. Buddy, you are sex itself!"

I felt something in my mouth. I jumped up, rushed into the bathroom, shut the door, flicked the light on, and spit a small wad of saliva mixed with blood from my tongue out into the sink.

"You okay?"

"Yeah," I said as clearly as I could, then asked if he had any gauze. He said he did in his sample case. I opened the door and he handed me some and I stuck it into my mouth.

"Sorry. I bit the hell outta your tongue, didn't I?"

I did not say anything else, but let the gauze absorb the blood, then put it into the garbage. Mouth wounds healed quickly, I knew. As long as I watched out for pepper, there would be little pain. I got back into bed with him, feeling really bad. I wanted to ask him, flat out: "Do you intend to kill me? Why don't we get it out in the open—"

But I couldn't.

First because he'd lie. And second because if he didn't do it, someone else would. And it would be someone I didn't like as much as Ted. Of that, I was positive.

We went back to bed, turning off both lights. I turned to him, and guided his head to my chest. He kissed my chest sweetly. He was crying openly now.

"You make me feel like a fool," he sobbed.

"Why?" I whispered.

"Because you've got this whole sex thing down right. You're gay. You can be gay. It's no big deal for you. You don't know what it's like for me. I'm nothing. Neither fish nor fowl. I'm in love with my kids, but not my wife. June keeps me grounded that's all; without her, I'd get so far out that they'd have to go back in for me with a net."

"What do you mean?"

"Drugs. Booze. I'd fuck and suck my life all the way to hell. I'm compulsive about wrecking things."

"She keeps you from that?"

"Yeah. My family delivered me to her years ago. After I was about two doors down from skid row and they'd picked me up again. I couldn't fight it anymore. I realized it. I was trapped."

"By June?"

"By June. By me. The leopard can't change his spots, so you find someone who'll change it for him nicely. That's where June came in. She's sweet, really. I needed the Lord Jesus . . . and my family got me June."

"I see." I leaned over and kissed him. "So, that's where all that . . . Christianity comes from?"

"I gotta believe in something, Len. We all do. Everybody's desperate to hold on to something, buddy. If you only knew—there are about a hundred million guys like me. We come in every shape and color, with all sorts of brains. Smart ones. Dumb ones. Cute ones. Ugly ones. We don't hate cocksuckers, because that's what we are. We just can't be what we are. We hate ourselves really. There's no place for us. You got any idea what that's like?"

"No. I don't." I put my hand on his face; his eyes were wet with tears. "You're pretty strange to me, maybe as strange as I am to you. Or to myself."

He lifted his head from my chest and kissed me on the cheek, very softly.

"I need to do something for you, Len. I need to take you where you've got to go. And I need to do that for myself as much as for you. Then I'm going to have to come back here to Istanbul, do my business, and go back to my wife in Salt Lake City."

"Have you ever thought about leaving June?"

"About once a day; around the same time I think about killing myself. The two ideas seem to go together. Facing myself alone, my old demons, and death. Without June, I'm scared of what I'd sink into. And what would I leave her for? I have nothing else. She's got nothing. She doesn't have a career or anything. She's just a Mormon housewife who married a non-Mormon she knows nothing about. Plus, she'd take the kids away—and I hardly have them as it is. Do you have *any* idea what that would do to me?"

"I can guess."

"How's your tongue?"

"Better."

"Let me see."

He put his lips on mine and rolled his tongue into my mouth.

"I can't taste anything," he said. "I'm really sorry about biting you. I'd really like it if you just blew me a little bit, you know. How'd you feel about that?"

"That could be arranged."

"Good. Those guys at the *hamam* were swell on the massage, but not much on the real action. I think you got more than I did, though your friends were kind of peculiar."

"They were."

I slid down and put his cock in my mouth. His stubby dick was hard and very hot. I hardly did anything, just gave him a few deepthroated thrusts and he squirted right away. A real jiz blast. He tasted more zincy and bitter than he had the night before. Maybe it was all that held-back anger or sadness coming up.

He was already asleep, when I got back up to him. Watching him snore away, I felt kind of dumb, useless for anything except a good blowjob. This man wasn't going to kill me, not in any ordinary way. No, he'd more break my heart probably than anything else; that is, if there were anything left of it after Josh and Benjy. They both passed before me, nodding sweetly, their beautiful lights back on. Benjy touched my head; Josh smiled. They'd forgiven me. I was glad.

The next morning Ted got up early and went to his sales meeting. I slept late. Around eleven, I wrote out a telegram and took it down to the front desk.

"You did not go to the *hamam* I directed you to," said the same desk captain who had directed us the night before. "I called to look after your welfare."

I wondered if he'd been looking for some kind of kickback. "We went to another one," I said, smiling. "It was fine."

"You must be careful. There are all sorts of delights here in Istanbul, but dangers as well. What can I do for you, Sir?"

I asked him the directions to the closest telegram office, and he gave them to me. The office was only about five blocks away, but it was around a corner, through a passageway, and up a hill. He looked straight at me, as if asking, "Are you sure you want to do this simple task alone?"

Once outside, I felt as if I were leaving the modern world and going back in time again. As I walked away from the harbor and into a warren of streets, shops, small cafes, and outdoor stalls, people thrust everything at me—flashlight batteries, carpets, fez hats, a cat. Was I supposed to buy a cat? If the cat wouldn't do, I was shown a canary. I passed a pile of birds in cages, mostly racing pigeons, with a few others twittering and calling behind their bars. Thousands of pigeons flashed rainbows of iridescence above me, swooping into dark feathered arcs from the top of one tower to the next, like the pigeons circling Venice's famous Piazza San Marco. Istanbul, when it was Constantinople, had been like Venice's cousin: two dangerously beautiful, powerful goddesses of the sea.

I made it through the passageway, then up the steep hill. Trudging up, I noticed several Western-attired women smiling openly at me, as if they wanted me, a stranger, to be happy here. I started to feel tired again from so many competing sensations. People on top of me, birds, animals, smells. Since my "come-back," my mind filled up quickly, overwhelming me with a rush of images. My eyes felt weaker, I missed having glasses. I slowed down as the exhausting rush of images hit me.

Finally, a sign in about seven languages outside a small shop announced phone and telegraph services. I walked in and a white-haired clerk handed me a form. I wrote to Alvin: "I'm in Istanbul, leaving this afternoon to see you. I hope you are well. Looking forward, Lenny."

The clerk took my form inside a small office. He came out and told me how much it would be, only a few dollars, and I handed it to him in Turkish lira. Stamping something on the form in Turkish, he gave me a copy of it.

"Do you want an answer, sir?"

"Always," I joked. Then said seriously, "No."

Going back, down hill, was much easier; but now fatigued, I decided to rest at a small outdoor cafe. A very pretty girl of about twenty, her dress a bright red silk with a wide skirt, sat near me. She leaned towards me, smiling.

"May I read your palm?" She spoke perfect English. She reached for my hand, and motioned for me to sit closer to her.

I was tired, but figured why not? It would give me some relaxing diversion and I had some lira on me; how much could she ask?

"Would you like a coffee?"

I told her no, I'd wanted a Coke, but she insisted I have some tea. A very handsome waiter came out. With his fine features, light brown eyes, and very nice teeth, he looked more Italian than Turkish. He brought me some mint tea. I took some money out for him; he thanked me, and she looked at my palm.

"*Hosh*. You have good hands." I looked into her dark, mascared eyes, which reminded me of one of those piercingly real, Greek mummy portraits from the Egypt of the Ptolemies; I wondered what she could see about me. Impishly, she smiled. "You're not from here."

"Shut up!"

"No, I'm only joking. Let me be serious." She turned my hand in hers, as if it were a fish she was thinking about buying. Her smile dropped. "No, no, no."

"What?"

She looked into my eyes. "You were very close to death. Several times."

"Yes?"

"You beat it every time. But—"

"What?"

Suddenly, two ragged boys rushed up to me out of nowhere. They were about twelve or thirteen years old, and dressed in once colorful but faded T-shirts and dirty torn jeans.

"Mister?" one said. "You like company?" He wrapped his bare arm around my left shoulder. I shrugged and felt the other boy's hand reach into my right rear pocket. I grabbed it and pulled him away from me.

"*Toz ol! Toz ol!*" the girl shouted. "They're pests! Like rats! *Toz ol!* Get out, you two!!"

They disappeared; I felt safer. At least I didn't keep any money in my right rear pocket. It was on my left, in my front pocket. "You were saying, but . . . *what*?"

"It's not important." Her face became sternly serious. "Why don't you go? Please, I'll give you the reading for free."

"Free? Why?"

She got up and hurried away from me.

I ran after her, and grabbed her upper arm.

"What did you see?"

She shook her head. Up close, under the mask of her make up, she looked older than I'd thought, maybe thirty at least.

"Let go of me! What can I say? Your hand told me you won't escape again, sir. It's true. God knows this!"

I dropped my arm.

"I'm sorry, sir," she said, lowering her gaze.

As she walked away into an arcade filled with little shops, one of the two street boys came out the shadows to meet her. I drifted back towards the hotel, feeling really spent, like a cheap tire after a blow-out. Perhaps the graft was actually bigger and more alive than I was. I was just attached to it, hanging on for dear life.

"Everything okay, Sir?" the desk captain asked, smiling. "You find the office?"

I told him I had, and he told me that Ted was not back yet.

"The other gentleman checked you out already. You can leave when he returns. No hurry. Maybe you want to shower before you go, you look a little—?"

I thanked him. He was right; I looked wilted. And, truthfully, he could have helped me with the telegram. Why'd I try to go there on my own? And why was I believing that woman? I was a scientist. I believed in rationalism—I felt completely foolish.

In the elevator up, I checked my left front pocket. Empty.

I couldn't help laughing. The joke was on me! All of the woman's seriousness had just been a ruse to get my mind off being tricked. The boys were like lightning, one hand in my right back pocket only a decoy for another hand in my left front one. The woman must have seen me pay the waiter and put my money in my front pocket. She probably gave them some kind of signal while my eyes were on her. Luckily, I'd had almost no money on me.

I'd been tricked before, tricked into death. But I couldn't trick "God," whatever It was. No scientist—atheist or total believer—ever believes he can, because "God" is always what lies just up ahead. It's bigger than you, it's what you can't control. In the room, I sat on the side of the bed. I removed my shoes and pants, then gave it a look: I decided, immediately, that the place on my calf was getting better. It was looking exactly like normal, regular flesh. A little reddish and lumpy, maybe, that was all. But *normal*.

Whatever was going to happen, I could deal with it.

I put my shoes and pants back on; then put my head in my hands and started crying, weeping loudly for Josh, Benjy, but most of all, for me. For the Leonard Miller whose body someone—or something else—was now residing in.

Or, had it always been that way? Flashback: my childhood, realizing that to survive I had to wear the mask—like the woman's made-up face at the cafe—of a "regular boy." Baseball. Rough-and-tumble football. That kind of tough, mush-brained talk regular boys knew how to do. All foreign to me: more foreign than Turkey. By nine, though, I could do a regular-enough imitation of a regular boy. It's just that I could also see right through me doing it.

Strangest, though, were those moments when, for some reason, my mask dropped. I was then my real self, and could see very clearly that the other "regular" boys were wearing masks of their own. Hard, impenetrable masks, stuck on their faces like concrete.

A knock on the door. Ted came in. "Didn't want to startle you," he said. "I rented a car. It's a real beaut—an old Chevy. Turkey is where the old American cars go to retire. Americans don't, just our cars."

"Sounds good."

He came over to me and sat down on the bed. "You okay? You look like you've had a hard day."

I nodded. "I'm okay."

"You look kind of," he hesitated, then said, "Wilted. I know that feeling. Sometimes things just don't add up the way they should. Want a shower?"

I nodded, and went into the bathroom. He was calling his wife again. I'd stopped caring, I didn't even want to listen. If he were calling someone else, who cared? I wanted to get to Alvin Jurrist, and after that—well, I wasn't exactly sure I'd be part of an "after that."

After my shower, I got into my pants quickly, not wanting to deal with the welt in front of him again.

"My boy hurt his arm rollerblading downhill," he reported. "Luckily, he didn't break it, but he's got to wear a sling. Kids! You try to keep 'em alive until they figure out that they don't need you anymore."

I finished dressing. "Then what happens?"

He came over and kissed me. "Then you try to figure out who does."

Downstairs, Ted paid the bill, without asking me about sharing it. "It's all on the company. Don't worry. How was your morning?"

I didn't tell him about getting pickpocketed, being set up like a dumb American; nor about the girl's warning, which seemed like a set-up, too. No wonder she didn't want to charge me for the reading. I would have reached for my money and known I'd been robbed.

A uniformed valet, who looked like he was left over from a Hollywood Bengal Lancers movie, brought up the car with our bags from the hotel's underground garage. After I tipped him, he did a little bow.

"We hope you come back to Istanbul soon and see us, sir," he said as Ted got into the driver's seat and opened the passenger side door for me.

"We will," Ted said. "I always stay with you."

I had been in enough cities in Italy and Greece to know that the secret to driving there was patience, stamina, and having at least another pair of eyes with you. I was the other pair of eyes, though they weren't very strong. Mostly Ted looked straight ahead, and ignored what was happening on either side—cars swerving onto the sidewalk; small kids dashing into traffic. I would have been a nervous wreck, but Ted could have been calmly driving through the countryside in Iowa, the effect on him was about the same.

The old Chevy sailed from one expressway to another. The highways looked like they were left over from the time of Napoleon, and for all I knew might have been. Along the water, the views were picturesque and tawdry at the same time, a combination of slums and monuments. We turned onto some smaller roads, then got out of the city sprawl completely.

We were on a two-lane blacktop with no traffic around us, except for cars occasionally speeding past us at about ninety miles an hour.

"They have one rule of traffic here," Ted explained. "You don't get killed. After that, everything's okay."

I had a map out and managed to navigate with it. We would have to skirt through about five larger towns, including the sprawl of Bursa, and maybe a dozen or so villages to get to Alvin. Going through Bursa, we had a showdown with a speeding eighteen-wheeler and a horn-crazy trucker who was going to kill us, until Ted pulled over for him to pass. Afterwards the countryside turned beautiful, not lushly green but a rippling olive-gray, with distant brighter fields of beans and clover. Farmers plowed with donkeys and women in long dresses carried earthenware jugs on their heads. I had been to Greece, but not Turkey, which felt more foreign and farther back in time.

I noticed a dark cloud traveling over us. We could not get away from it. Then around seven o' clock, the whole sky became the color of that cloud and it poured.

chapter seventeen

*W*e could see almost nothing in front of us, only glimpses of rain-lashed countryside through the side windows. Ted found a place off the road and parked. He turned on the inside car light and looked at his map. "I hate this," he growled.

"Rain?"

"No! Being parked out like this. Turkey is famous for bandits, you know that?"

"No, I didn't know. Are you scared?"

"Sure, a little but—" Reaching across me, he flicked open the glove compartment and fished out a nickel-plated pistol. Heavy and clumsy-looking, its tarnished surface was deeply scarred. The weight of it looked far more lethal than its accuracy. "I told my guys at the hospital what I was up to. So they lent me this."

He held it out for me like a waiter holding a merlot bottle. I touched it cautiously; it had probably survived several guerilla wars already.

"It makes me feel a hundred percent better," I said.

"Your ultimate strength comes from the Lord, but He never said anything bad about using one of these."

"You're not going to get all-Jesus on me now, Ted, are you?"

"Not a bit, buddy." He made sure the safety was on, then tucked the gun into the waistband of his pants. He gave me a quick kiss and I clicked the glove compartment shut.

"I hate like hell not having a shoulder holster. I should have asked my friends for one."

The rain let up; everything looked black outside. Ted switched off the inside car light. I'd put the map away. I asked him if he knew where we were.

"No place famous, I'd say. There're some towns around us. The question is, which one to go to and try to find a place for the night. How far off is your friend, you think?"

I unfolded the map, and he turned the light on again. "Probably about six or seven more hours."

The deluge resumed, and the car started to leak from the roof.

"Let's get out of here," he said, trying the motor. It would not even turn over. My imagination raced through every catastrophe that could happen to us: robbed, kidnapped, murdered . . . of course I'd been through all that before; but this time I'd have to give up my life for Ted, of all things. I wasn't sure really why I felt that way, but I did.

Suddenly, the motor turned over.

As soon as we got back on the road, the rain stopped and the sky cleared. The moon came out. Three-quarters full, made of bright silver, it appeared so sharply brilliant in the black sky that it could have been cut out by a razor blade.

"We could drive all night," Ted announced, "but I'm getting tired."

I offered to drive, but he said that was ridiculous. He was right, it was; but I could have tried to make some foolish attempt at it. After another hour, we reached the outlying reaches of Balikisir, which our map identified as the fairly ragged capital of a province. Basically a way-station for travelers on the way up to Ankara or over to the coast, it had a plaza for buses and a moderate-sized railway station, but almost no street lights and no open shops or cafes.

Despite the clear moonlight, it was dark, deserted, and unsettling. The buildings were decrepit, featuring old signs in Turkish with a few in German and French. Then a big circular cherry-red sign proclaimed "Coca-Cola!" in Turkish, next to a huge billboard displaying the classically-Anglo features of the Marlboro man in a spotless Stetson hat and clean white cowboy shirt. Beside him was a simple three-story frame structure with some small lettering in English on the front that said: "Rooms. Tourists. Warm Showers."

"Thank you, Jesus!" Ted cried, as he eased the big Chevrolet to the curb.

The comfortable-looking lobby was cheaply furnished, but clean and well lit. A woman who, despite her impossibly short, blue sleeveless sun dress, was probably leaving the vicinity of sixty, quickly emerged from an office. Her deeply-lined face was caked with pale make-up. Thick, waxy black mascara outlined her eyes, contrasting with the long bleached straw-blond curls of her hair. She smiled coquettishly, shrugging her wrinkled freckled shoulders.

"*Efendim! Iyi akshamlac!*" We looked at her dumbly. "*Guten Abend*. I am Freulein Gutschnitt, but please, call me Inga. Your host. What can I do for you?"

"We'd like a room for the night, Ma'am," Ted said, smiling back at her. "And a shower. We'd really like that. Is it possible to have anything to eat?"

She showed her yellowed teeth and dimples.

"And why not? We are civilized here. Can I see your passports?"

We handed them to her. She studied our faces and places of origin. "New York?" she said to me. "There, I have been! I have some distant Turkish cousins who live in Brooklyn, by Atlantic Avenue. They sell cars and rugs. I like all the—" Her hands fluttered in the air; I guessed she meant craziness. She lit a long thin cigarette that smelled of cloves and let its smoke drift around her. She blew out the match. "—but for me, it's impossible. All so busy, busy, busy!"

She put our passports in a desk drawer and told us the price of the room, about forty-five dollars. She showed Ted a guest book to sign. "Now, would you gentlemen like anything else? Some company perhaps?"

Ted turned back to me, letting out a questioning sigh. "Want company?"

I was not sure what to say.

"We have some very nice young people for companionship, gentlemen. Girls, or . . . ?"

"You are tempting us, lady," Ted admitted. "Why don't we see the room, and shower. What can you get us to eat?"

"For *essen—ja*." She thought for a moment. "I can make you some eggs. With cheese, bread, a little meat, potatoes, some olives. And I have a wonderful cake for dessert. Very tall, with cherries and chocolate. How does that sound?"

"Sounds neat to me," he said.

"Neat?" She grinned. "I'm afraid I'm not familiar with your *neat*."

"It's, you know, *good*. We'll take it. Len, she's going to make us dinner. And then—"

"And then, you can tell me what you'd like," she said and led us up a short flight of stairs to the second floor. Popular-sounding Turkish music, like Middle Eastern disco, came in softly from the floor above it; perhaps her young companions were kept there. Our room was small, with a low ceiling, a ceiling fan, and one bed that was only wide enough for two very close people.

"Dinner will be ready in perhaps thirty minutes. The shower is down the hall." She handed Ted an old key with a fancy scroll at the end that looked perfect for Bluebeard's castle, then left us.

"It's a brothel," I said.

"No shit, Shakespeare. But I like the dame at the desk. She must have been a looker at one time."

"You're not going to go hetero on me, are you?" The bed was lumpy and sagged a bit, but I was too tired to care.

Taking off his shirt, with the pistol still crammed next to his ribs, Ted splashed some water onto his face from a small room sink. He used a thread-bare towel hanging by it to dry himself. "That's the problem with you guys. You don't realize some men go for young pussy, too."

"What happens when it's not so young?"

"That's called my wife." He smiled, devilishly. "Speaking of which, I wish I could call her, but I don't think my cell phone'll work around here."

I tried not to stare at it, but could not keep my eyes off that nickel-plated gun. "You don't seem to be able to do without talking to her."

"I'm married to her. I *like* being married. Sometimes."

"And what about the other times?"

"That's why I travel, friend. And why we have Turkey and other such adventures. Let's see what the Freulein's offering up in the way of food."

We found a small dining area off the lobby. It had three cafe tables and she had set one for us. The food was simple, but tasty and fresh. The cake was heavenly. She smiled as she cut it, obviously proud.

"Can I offer you one more piece?" Her blackened eyelashes fluttered. I demurred, but Ted was all for it. He dove into it, licking the chocolate icing off his fingers.

Three men in dark suits came in as we finished the cake. She greeted them in Turkish, then left us.

"They must be locals," Ted said. "That's a good sign. Repeat business shows you're in a reputable concern, even if the concern is of ill-repute."

After we'd had coffee, a pretty young woman carefully cleared the table. She was about twenty-five, dressed in jeans, backless shoes, and a tight black blouse, which she had partially unbuttoned to reveal her cleavage.

She smiled at us. "You're from America?"

Ted nodded.

"You like dinner?"

"It was fine." He smiled directly at her.

"Can I bring something up to your room?"

"Maybe."

She disappeared behind a door into the kitchen. We got up.

"The help here sure is friendly," he said, stretching. We were both so tired that just climbing up the stairs took some effort. He managed to jiggle the door unlocked with the key, and I crawled onto the bed whose mattress felt like it was filled with old corn cobs.

Ted took off his shirt, shoes, socks, and pants, and in his boxer undershorts carefully folded his trousers and put them on a chair. He put the gun on the chair, then picked it back up again and knotted the thin towel around his waist, with the weapon secured inside the waistband of his shorts.

He opened the door. "Shower!"

After he was gone, I thought how easy it would be for him to come back in and shoot me. He could work out something with that old whore downstairs and then . . . what? Whatever it was, I didn't want to die in this shabby little room, even though I was buried already—somewhere in New York, there was a tombstone with my name on it.

But even if Ted had been picked to kill me, I didn't want him to do it. Truthfully, I liked him. He wasn't that much different than I was: Both of us were just fronts for something deeper, something missing in both of us that we painfully lacked.

What? The answer scared me so much that I couldn't even imagine it; but I knew that after I saw Alvin, I wanted to go back to Istanbul and see Akbar and make love with him again. I wanted to show him that I could love him, even if he had no legs; even if I'd only been taken with the antique splendor of that Arabian Nights setting that had brought us together, and which had allowed me, finally, to glimpse the possibility of really being loved.

I had wanted that so much, because I wasn't sure if I could love Lenny Miller—that sad old dead guy—ever again.

He'd only been a shadow, all work; kinky sex, as anonymous as possible, for escape. It had been impossible for him really to connect with anyone; to feel that raw, tender simplicity of connection I'd felt with Akbar that had been so real and yet so exciting. I felt like I could touch the very substance of that connection; its tenderness. Its crying wants. I could feel that—and it brought me back, almost against my will, to one early evening in my early teens, in the jock-itch-ridden showers at summer camp. I was tired after a whole day of bluffing through team sports, while doing my arduous, imperfect masquerade as a regular kid. That's when I saw Skip.

Skip was this other cute Jewish kid I couldn't keep my eyes off of. Brown-eyed, sun-darkened, freckled, spidery-skinny; all legs, elbows, ribs, and soft little nipples that poked out with a fine crease in each one. Picked-on sometimes; sometimes defiant. At about five-foot-seven—not quite his full height—he was one of the outermost sparkly planets in the cluster of quietly smart-ass brainy kids with whom I hung around. I had a . . . thing for Skippy I couldn't name, and there he was, smiling at me at another end of the showers.

We were alone. Everyone else had left to go to dinner, and I kept edging toward him in the steam, with that lump-in-your-throat desire that directs you toward someone. I was aware, though, distantly, of trying not to get aroused. The taunting ghost of desire, that big iridescent soap bubble of sexual longing, was just hanging up there, and I kept trying to blow this forbidden excitement someplace else, even though it and Skip's smile were engaging me gently by the short hairs.

And, although Skippy had definitely perfected that Jew-kid dorkiness that protected boys like us from our deeper feelings, his smile was glowing now. It was dancing right there at the surface, even more naked and inviting than he was. It appeared so spontaneously: it was as if it had traveled all the way up from his almost hairless, admittedly prematurely large testicles into his small stomach, then through his slender chest and neck and out his chiseled soft lips to caress the very air at his face which had become . . . beautiful. He was luscious; I was shocked.

I wanted to touch him; I kept trying to find some "excuse" for this attraction, some reason for it. I mean, okay, both of us had neurotic, controlling Jewish parents, and we were both smarter than most campers: two things that could, under the right conditions, drive two horny young teenage boys to experiment. On top of which, there were those top-secret practices of adolescent males no one could talk about; but there we were now alone. And I could see all of those "inducements" loosely scribbled on his young lean face, which was at once both goofy and seductive.

Something "adhesive," as Walt Whitman used to describe male attraction, was drawing me closer to him. I came within an inch of him, though my heart was hammering. He bent his head towards the shower. There, right next to my hands, were his bony tanned shoulders, his silky back, his little butt; my heart ached.

Suddenly, he emerged from the water, facing me, his little dick twitching. It was almost hard, Sephardic brown, hairless, slightly thick. He laughed—"Miller!" then peed right there at my feet. A foamy yellow whirlpool, it bubbled like beer down the open shower drain.

I became made out of stone. Cute little Skippy was way too far ahead of me, or was I just too far behind? He looked me in the eye, and that dumbly seductive, fresh-as-dawn smile of his stopped. Then he brought up this cute little girl we knew at camp, and his mouth, all wise-ass again, slammed like a door on anything between us. He resumed being a dork. It was over. We finished showering separately. I let the water run onto my face, getting into my nose and mouth; I wanted to choke on it. He left. I felt immeasurably stupid, painfully alone. I was waiting . . . maybe for Akbar.

Lying on the springless bed, I could smell the recent rain mixing with dust and that smell that I called *Turkey*: slightly spicy, salty. Raisins. Whiffs of oregano. The sea. Me. I could smell me, authentically. I took off my shirt. I was sweating. It was close in the room, like in summer at camp. Ted knocked lightly on the door and came back in, freshly showered and once again wrapped in his towel. The only-too obvious bulge beneath it came either from the old pistol, or a new very appealing, nineteen-year-old girl who came in with him.

Dressed in jeans and a tiny tight white tank top that outlined her appealing breasts and small waist, she bounced into the room.

"Hello! I am Kaila!"

Ted was beaming. "Isn't she a doll? The old girl downstairs brought her to me in the shower." His eyes appeared wide open, quite guileless, yet predatory at the same time.

"So, would you like a party with me?" she asked, all smiling. Kaila was attractive, like a dark-eyed colt, but her insistence reminded me of the young woman who had read my palm.

"I don't know," I said.

"Come on, Len. Two guys and this cute chick? You don't know what that can be like!"

Before I could answer him, he switched off the light, unknotted his towel and carefully put it aside with the pistol under it. As he lifted her tank top off, she stepped out of her backless shoes, but kept her jeans on. He sat on the bed and she stroked him, then went down and kissed his cock. He leaned back while she sucked him, then he sat back up, unzipped her jeans, and peeled them off her.

She wiggled out of them. She had a nice firm stomach and very sweet young breasts, but her hips were wide and already a bit jiggly, reminding me of those love-handles I couldn't lose. I watched little bits of light in the room bounce around the girl and Ted; I was fascinated, as if I were watching an amateur Turkish porn movie. Now Ted wanted me in it. He leaned back again on the bed and grabbed me, pulling me towards him, kissing me hungrily on the lips.

He drew my hand to his cock. It was hard, hot, and wet from her mouth. I still had on my jeans and Ted struggled to unzip them with one hand. Finally he got to my cock and pulled it out. I wasn't ramrod stiff the way he was. I felt suddenly nuts. Out of place, uncertain. I was attracted to him in this scene, but it reminded me painfully of Skippy. There was just no telling when Skip's door would slam shut again. Unlike Ted, I wasn't a repressed Christian on one hand and a sex-starved, porno-ape on the other, with a greased switch that jumped back and forth between Straight and Queer.

He wanted me in the middle of that switch. "I think I'm going to shower," I announced.

"Okay, buddy. Come back when you want to." He dove into her breasts, sucking at her nipples.

I put my equipment back into my jeans, rezipped, grabbed a towel, and left the room. The hallway seemed very bright. A man wearing thick glasses in a shabby-looking business suit, somewhere in his forties, appeared from the stairway, smiling.

"You like it here? From America, right?" His glasses twinkled at me. I nodded. "America is all right. You can buy anything there, right? Tell me, are you interested in poppies?"

"No," I answered firmly.

He put his hand on my bare shoulders and let it run quickly down my bare chest.

"Very interesting flowers, poppies. I can get everything for you. We process—clean, all white, know what I mean?" He smiled suggestively. After the palm reader, how stupid was I supposed to be?

The bathroom, down the hall, was empty. I really needed a shower. Barefoot, I slipped out of my pants. The water started off freezing cold and then got warmer. I used a bar of green soap that smelled like olives and lathered up. There was a knock at the door.

I thought it was Ted, and answered, "Yeah?" I hadn't locked the door, and realized that whatever I had in my jeans pockets could be stolen.

I peeked out the shower curtain into the small, dimly lit room to see a young bearded man of slightly above average height. Maybe twenty-six, he was dark and leanly handsome, with wide angular shoulders, wearing only jeans unbuttoned at the top and a pair of rubber shower sandals. Suddenly, I thought: God! It's Skippy. All grown up.

He smiled at me genuinely. "How is the shower?"

"Fine. I'll let you have it in a minute."

"No, sir. Would you like me to shampoo your hair?"

I did not think twice. "All right."

He took off his jeans. The young forest of black hair on his lean chest thinned out at his navel, then reappeared as a sparkle of anthracite curls at his groin. From that appeared this thick, flowering stem of a circumcised penis, bouncing suggestively over the short hairs on his big, high scrotum. He got into the shower, and his hands were soon all over me, starting with my back and shoulders.

"You like your back rubbed, Sir?"

"Yes, I do."

"And your head, too?"

"Yes."

"And other parts?"

He was now in front of me. I smiled, kissing him.

"You kiss? Men here do not kiss like that."

"How do they kiss?"

He kissed me very softly on my cheeks. I thought I'd pass out from the sheer soft loveliness of his lips on my cheeks.

I smiled. "Very nice, the way they kiss here."

Kneeling in the shower, he massaged my calves and thighs. His hands went to my cock, which was hard. He soaped it and then stroked it.

He got up. "Let me do your hair, Sir."

"All right."

He took some shampoo from a plastic bottle he had brought with him, poured a bit in his hands, then ran it through my hair, softly kneading my scalp. I put my head on his chest and kissed his nipples as he did it. He sighed.

"You are very friendly," he whispered.

I closed my eyes and felt everything pouring through my senses: his hands on my head, the ripples of his chest, my arms around his waist, then my hands on his firm hairy stomach, then down into the rich, wet curls of his pubic area. I wanted to suck him so much that my brain was going *boing*, but I was not sure about it. I had to hold back, I—

Okay. I didn't hold back. I got down and put the sweet head of his cock in my mouth, cupping my fingers around his firm ass, that felt like fine, taut silk and young muscles.

He pulled me up. "Let me finish with your hair, Sir. Then we will do more in my room."

He ran his fingers all over me, getting the soap and shampoo off me, then he turned off the shower and we got out, drying off with more towels that he had brought with him. We put our pants back on. He told me his name was Ahmet, and that he had lived in Istanbul, but his family was from this area.

"It is hard to find a job now. I am studying geology. I want to be an ocean geologist." He spoke slowly, with a soft voice.

His room in the back on the third floor, lit by only one tiny red light bulb, was hardly more than a pantry with a small bed and a place for his clothes. I wondered how he knew that we couldn't go back into my room with Ted. He helped me unzip and get out of my jeans, as if I were a child.

"Lie down," he said. "I'll massage your back."

I did and he took some oil and worked it into my back muscles, then further down, kneading my buttocks until I was whimpering from relief and excitement. I could feel electricity running through the air, from his hands and body to me.

I turned around. His jeans were still on. Flipping over, I unzipped them.

"I am not sure I should do this. I am only to massage you."

"I won't tell anyone."

"Okay."

He got out of his jeans, completely hard and very beautiful. As he leaned over the bed, I knelt on it, kissing his neck and his chest. He guided my mouth gently to his stomach and then lower. I licked the head of his cock, then got its stiff, beautiful shaft down into my throat until my lips were at the base, nuzzling his small curls.

As I did this, he stroked my cock skillfully, then had me lie down. We merged, sixty-nining. He was very good at sucking me and I felt completely drawn into a circle of sensuous power, spinning through a space where my brain was gorging on air, on the sheer driving, satisfying perfection of doing this.

His mouth, his fingers, drew me into him, closer and closer, until all the nerves and muscles in my groin and hips, all of me, reached that pinnacle and released my own white thickness into him.

He stopped and pulled his penis from me.

I kept my hand on his dick, until slowly it became flaccid again.

He turned to me.

"I am sorry," he whispered, his voice strained with embarrassment. "My girlfriend does not like it if I come with a man."

"I see."

"You think that strange?"

I didn't know what to say, or even if I should destroy something by saying anything. He clicked on another small light, then lit a very aromatic cigarette, offering me a drag from it that I declined. "It's Turkey. Americans don't understand us."

I sat up. "Have you been there?"

"No. I've been to France once. I can speak French. I have heard America is not very good to Turkish people."

"I don't know. It's a big place. It's hard to say."

I got up and put my jeans back on. I needed rest, and wasn't sure if sleeping in Ahmet's room was an item offered on Freulein Gutschnitt's menu. He stood up and I kissed him on his cheeks.

"Will you be here tomorrow?" he asked.

I told him no.

"I would like to shampoo you again."

"No. I have to leave. We are going close to the Aegean coast, where I have business to do."

"It is nice there. I hope your business is good and without problems."

I thanked him and went back downstairs to our room.

I knocked on the door and Ted let me in. He was alone, wearing his boxer underwear.

"Some place, ain't it? You must be great luck, Len. Who'd think we'd get out of a storm and run into a place like this? I guess you found some company of your own?"

"Yeah. How much do you think all of this entertainment is going to cost us?"

He got some water from the sink and began brushing his teeth. After spitting some toothpaste foam into the sink, he said, "Don't worry. It's usually much less than you think." He gave his teeth a few more strokes, then spat again. "I've been through this sort of thing before, just not here. I'm sorry you didn't want to play with the girl. You remember her name?"

"Kaila?"

"Yeah. Pretty thing, wasn't she?" He got into bed. "I guess girls just aren't your thing. What is it, that pussy fear? Some gay guys I know have a stark fear of it. Hell, it's just another opening. You ever tasted young pussy before?"

"Sure," I said, smiling broadly. "I've tasted it before. It tastes just like chicken."

"It does not! It tastes like . . . anyway, why *do* you gay guys find pussy so funny?"

"We don't find it *funny*, Ted. We just prefer eating the outie parts of men to the innie parts of women."

I took out my toothbrush, then went over the sink.

"Seems like only a fucking prejudice to me," he said.

"Prejudice?" I squeezed some toothpaste onto my brush, then caught his eyes in the mirror over the sink. They had that same twinkling glow he'd had in the line for taxis at Grand Central.

I smiled into the mirror at him.

"Isn't *prejudice* kind of a . . . funny word to use, Ted, for a man with a Mormon wife?"

The room got quiet. I lowered my head, brushed my teeth, spat out into the sink, and then turned back to him. He was already fast asleep.

chapter eighteen

The next morning we had breakfast in the little dining area. Two cops came in, spoke to Freulein Guttschnitt, and looked over at us.

One, a slender good-looking man in his early thirties, with hawk-like features and a short beard, was obviously an officer. He strode over to us and asked to see our passports. I had forgotten that Inga had them, and had a moment of panic.

The officer smiled. "Not good," he said, "when people ask for what you don't have. Right?"

"I have their passports," the Freulein offered. She got them out of her desk. Keeping one eye on us, the officer scanned them, making me feel as if I were being stripped completely naked—and not nicely this time.

His obsidian eyes never looked directly at me; he turned slightly from us, licking his dry lips. "You tourists?"

"Yes, Sir," Ted answered. "Tourists, that's all."

"And you look for local color, true?"

Ted looked directly at him, his face totally serious. "Yes, Sir."

The officer broke into a huge smile, as Inga Guttschnitt brought him a cup of morning coffee and offered him a cigarette. "*Iyi!* You got the right place!" He gulped the coffee, then lit the cigarette, blowing its smoke up to the planked ceiling.

He said good-bye to the Freulein, who grinned proudly at him as if he were, at the same time, both an adored son and one of the more sexually appealing friends *of* an adored son; then the two cops left.

"I am friendly with the police," Inga explained, a new cigarette in her hand. "It helps things. I will have a bill for you gentlemen when you are ready."

Back in the room, we packed. Ted put his pistol back in his suitcase. "Glad I didn't have to use that. Those cops scared me. I was afraid they were going to try to shake us down. I guess the old girl's on good terms with them, like she said."

We went back downstairs and Inga did have a bill for us. It was whopping, about triple what we thought we'd pay, but like any other modern innkeeper, she took credit cards and Ted pulled out his Visa. Back in the car, I offered to pay my half of it.

He shrugged, saying we could do it back in Istanbul. "The bill included a 'local gratuity.' I guess that must mean money for the cops. Funny, the way they actually put it in the bill."

"I liked the part about my shampoo."

We were now on what was actually a good road, with more fields around us. I could feel that we were getting closer to the coast—the sky was bluer and the countryside had a kind of Mediterranean radiance.

"When did you have a shampoo?"

"In the shower. When you were having what you were having with the girl."

"And was the shampoo nice?"

"Very nice."

"Funny place, isn't it? People are so nice and yet—"

"Yes," I said. "There's an 'and yet,' isn't there?"

Looking straight ahead at the road, Ted said, "Maybe there always is."

We stopped off for lunch in the first small village we found on the coast. It was really lovely, with beige stone buildings against the brilliantly blue sky. I thought about asking if we should go for a swim, but decided not to. I needed to get to Alvin, and there was no telling what the rest of the road would be like.

My fears proved correct: what seemed like a normal highway suddenly gave out, and we were on twisting, hilly country roads gutted with holes big enough to wreck the car. We stopped constantly for sheep and wagons, for local buses that took up both sides of the road and made us wait, and a few daredevils who were either going to pass us or run us off the road into a ditch. One kid gave us the finger as he passed us.

"He must have figured out we were Americans," Ted said, swallowing his anger. "You carry a lot of baggage with you when you travel now, don't you?"

We got into Alvin's camp just as the evening was darkening the hills and a fresh breeze had started to gather the light scent of wild thyme and clover on it. With a folded umbrella at his side, Alvin was sitting on a fence, still as a statue, waiting at that part of the road that led to his site. He was stone white. His once-dark hair had turned gray, and his skin was colorless.

I looked into his brown eyes, so pale they looked amber yellow.

"I'm so glad to see you, Len." Tears came down his cheeks. "I wasn't sure I could hold out much longer. I think I picked up some kind of weird bug—hepatitis, maybe. It's hard to tell. All of this is just so damn strange. You lose all the science and brains you've got."

I introduced him to Ted Richards, who shook his hand. "Is there anything we can do for you?" Ted asked.

"I just want Len to see this, and then I'm going straight back to the States. I'm frightened. I've got to tell you, I *am* frightened."

He got into our car and we drove over to the camp, which would have been about a fifteen minute walk. His field office hut was close to a group of two-man tents. He offered us one to sleep in, after we got out.

"The men left. They couldn't take it anymore. Some of them got sick, too. I don't know what it is—if it's the things we found, some disease they carried, or something in the atmosphere. There's no telling. That's why we need to see this fast. I want you to see it, Len, before anything gets disturbed."

"You mean the whole bodies?" I asked. "Perfectly preserved?"

"Yeah. Whole bodies. And they are *perfectly* preserved."

"Like mummies?" Ted asked. "I didn't think they had mummies in Turkey. I'm no archeologist, but I didn't—"

"Oh, they had mummies here," Alvin said. "But these are not mummies, actually—" Sinking wearily into a camp chair outside his field hut, he drank some water from a canteen, losing his train of thought. "We've got good water here. It comes from a safe well. I've tested it. I'd love some ice right now. Just ice and some Coca Cola from a fountain. When I was a kid back in Omaha, that was one of the great things of summer. Going over to a drug store with real fountain Cokes and a marble counter. Kids today think Coke was invented by McDonald's, but no—"

He stopped talking and mopped his forehead. Was he delirious? I put the back of my hand on his forehead. It was blazing.

"That sure feels cool," he said. "Ice. Coca Cola. Pie. Real American pies with apples and whipped cream—"

"What about the mummies, or whatever you call them?" I asked.

"They scared the crap out of my diggers. The first time we found that thing that I sent you, that was bad enough. I mean, to find a fresh piece of a foot like that. Wow! Then we dug into another direction. There was a town there. Houses. Stables. Workshops. The Romans must have finally put it all to the sword, sometime towards the end of Caesars. This was a great port before that, filled with galley ships and traders from all over. Lots of intrigue. Religion was the big question then. It was like belonging to a political party today."

I closed my eyes. "Nothing's changed. People still kill for religion." For a moment, I was afraid to open my eyes; afraid I was going to break down and cry. I felt bad for Alvin. He'd been sucked into this situation like I had been. All he had wanted to do was know more, like any scientist would.

"Some of our religious extremists now are just as bad," he said. "In those days you wanted to make sure your god was Top Boy. When your god was, then that put you on top with him."

"Wait a second!" Ted said. "Isn't that trivializing it? You think Jesus Christ came along and—what did you call it?—just wanted to be 'Top Boy'? Is that what you're saying?"

Alvin closed his burning eyes, took some more water, then lowered his head into his hands. "Sorry. I didn't mean to offend you."

Ted stared at the last rays of sunlight seeping into the distance hills. "You can't talk about Jesus like that, sir. 'Top Boy?' God Almighty, that's where guys like you get into trouble. You don't know just how much the world needed Jesus Christ. He came for all of us, he spoke for—"

"Ted," I said. "Alvin's sick. Let's try to do what we can for him." I put my cool palm back on his forehead and asked him if we could help him get over to his tent.

He shook his head.

"You need to see those things first, guys. The place. The site and what's in it. It'll get too dark soon, and my strength's giving out. Heck, it's getting dark for me already."

Ted nodded, a streak of shame colored him. "I'm sorry. Why don't we do this in the morning?"

"Ted, I may be dead by then. I've been waiting for you guys. I got Len's telegram and I was so happy I cried. You don't know what that was like. I kept thinking, maybe I should leave all this. It's too—" he stood up, finishing his sentence "—too full of impossible questions. I can't answer 'em. The truth is: I don't know who can."

"Then let's don't waste another moment," Ted said.

Weak-legged and stumbling, Alvin led us over to the site. We had to climb up for about half a mile through a steep, rocky, roadless terrain of grass and bush, passing between two huge crumbling sandstone cliffs that stood guard over the area like sentries. Once past them, we ended up on a great plateau, like a meadow in the air, once good, undoubtedly, for defense, with a view that unrolled for miles, stopping just short of the shore. We could not view the sea, but we could smell it: on the evening wind, a phantom, tantalizing whiff of salt water mingled with the blowing scents of clover and wild flowers.

Sniffing the fresh air, allowing my nose to inhale fully the aroma, I felt like I had been there before, in that very place. The feeling took over my body like a wine drunk at dinner, and I felt a relaxation that was hard to shake off. I wanted only to lie down in this meadow and drink from the lowering sky, as its deep purple color intensified to darkness; but I couldn't.

"It's there!" Alvin shouted. We were at the edge of the plateau, heading down into a narrow valley between hills. With his large paraffin lantern and our bright flashlights, we could see a town that had been lost and buried for close to two millennia. I could see the rotting roof beams of partially excavated structures, and the beginnings of old brick and stone pathways; it was like discovering something new, yet very old.

Ted's face was tense with excitement and barely contained jubilance. His eyes took on a purple depth in the reflected light, though his mouth was clamped shut. What impulse was he holding down, I wondered, that was racing through him?

"Look," Alvin said hoarsely. "Jesus, the historic Jesus himself, could have walked on these bricks. He could have taken a boat here from Galilee. There was trade from there all the time. He might have come during those twenty-odd years that we've lost from his life. No one knows what he did then. He could have had a family here. Anything."

"Why not, Lord!" Ted screamed. "A family! The family of Jesus. But we're all His family. He accepted us with all of our sins. He gave us Life. Hope! He was greater than our ability to know Him! Even I—" He stopped talking and looked away from us.

Alvin tried to smile weakly. "Ted, I just meant that historically—"

"That's all right," I said. "Let's go on. You're too exhausted to explain more."

Alvin directed us with his free arm. "Around that bend there's the place that causes the trouble. I hope you two are not given to fear, are you?"

I smiled. Fear? Was he joking?

Ted turned back to look at him. "Alvin, keep your pep talk, man. Are we going in now, or what?"

"Ted, I need to warn you. This is not something you're going to be prepared for. I've been to Peru, Egypt. I've seen whole cities of the dead. But I think I lost several of my marbles down there."

I smiled and took Alvin's arm, offering him some water from the canteen. Even with the cool evening winds whistling through the valley, he was sweating. He dribbled some of the water down his khaki jacket and offered Ted the canteen. Ted took it and drank quickly, wiping his mouth with the back of his hand.

We continued walking on the old, broken pathway in the last glimpse of light. "Sometimes," Ted said, staring around him, "the real cities of the dead are the ones filled with live folks. I know that. I've been close to dead myself. That's why my heart is in this place, too."

"Good," Alvin said. "Just don't lose it here."

We followed him deeper into the site on a narrow roadway paved with closely fitted stones that had been partially exposed, until we hit what looked like the entrance of a large structure, some kind of house. Alvin's crew had placed a protective tarp on the protruding entrance. He drew the tarp apart.

My flashlight lit what looked like an entrance hall. A narrow, descending passageway veered sharply from this, then dropped into nowhere. I could see no farther. There was only this swallowing blackness.

"I told you this was scary," Alvin warned. "Are you up for this?"

"What do you mean?" I asked.

"I mean this is the last refuge of people who met their deaths here. I firmly believe that. There's horror and violence down there, but there's also—"

"I've got to go," Ted interrupted. "My life is down there. I want to go in there in the worst sort of way."

"You'll go," I promised him. I tried to grab his arm, but he wrenched it from me and pushed in ahead of us by himself, led by his light.

"Wait!" I shouted. "Why do you want to go in there alone?"

I wanted to run after him, but he disappeared, sucked into the waiting darkness. Alvin took my arm anxiously.

"I need you here," he said. "Your friend's not scared of anything, but you need to see this. No matter what, we'll meet up with him later because there are only so many ways you can go down there."

The two of us went in, stepping down onto ground that was soft and powdery. I shot the beam of my flashlight up to the ceiling, revealing stone columns with rotting, age-blackened wooden beams across them.

"Are you sure those beams can hold up?"

"No," he answered, his voice close to cracking. "I tried to get my men to reinforce them, but they left. All I know is that they've held up for two thousand years. So one more day shouldn't kill 'em, unless your friend does something crazy."

"Like what?"

He shrugged. We walked slowly and carefully down the slope of the cramped passageway, which was only about two inches taller than our heads. "People go crazy down here," he explained, almost whispering. "They freak out. You're alone in the dark. You can get lost and hit the wrong thing, an old post, the supports could go, and—"

"I see what you mean."

The ceiling closed in on us until we had to stoop. I had forgotten how small people were at the time of Christ; a six-footer was almost unheard of. As the way got narrower, the faint light that had seeped in from the distant opening gradually disappeared. I kept hoping we would see Ted's light, but all we saw were rotting beams and piles of dirt and plaster. There were no freshly cleaned frescoes or sparkling mosaics, the kind of attractions you found at tourist sites after all the excavating had been done. I saw almost nothing, but heard strange burrowing sounds.

"It's the rats, down here in the passageway," Alvin explained. "Don't worry, rats can be a good sign. It means there's air and everything's healthy."

I chuckled. "They say that about rats in the New York subway system."

Just when my knees were starting to ache, a thick rounded stone wall abruptly ended our descent through the beamed passageway. Closely tracing the wall's bowed surface, we stepped through an entranceway cut into it, only big enough for one man at a time, into total darkness. Alvin's lantern was the only light. I kept hoping I'd see Ted's light at some distance, but didn't.

Past the wall, I realized we were not inside a structure anymore, but were following the ruined walls of underground buildings, and a passageway whose ceiling appeared composed of the floorings of even older structures, making it already ancient at the time of Christ. Such a way would have been completely secret and unknown to outsiders.

"This is the cool thing," Alvin said, "that we stumbled onto this. A lot of people living here two thousand years ago might not have known about these underground passages down here."

"What will we do about Ted? Suppose he's really lost?"

"He won't be the first one. But like I said, only so many passages have been excavated and at some point he should be able to see our light."

We continued on, carefully making our way farther down, with stone walls that seemed more secure than the previous passageway on both sides of us. I was starting to feel almost comfortable, except for a thick cloud of dust that had settled in on us, caking our shoes and clothes, clogging my nose. Its slightly decayed smell reminded me of the vaulted spaces of a poultry market and its fine, almost unseeable feather dust floating endlessly through the air. I remembered that close-to-nauseating smell from childhood, when I was dragged to a big kosher butcher in the Bronx.The smell disappeared as the passageway took on a noticeably upward grade and we approached another low portal cut into a wall. When we stooped to walk through it, a trickle of fresh air hit me. My eyes had been squinting against the dust. Now I opened them fully to what felt like a fairly spacious room.

"We're almost there," Alvin said. "We're at the doorway to the beginning. Or is it the ending?"

"What do you mean?"

He shook his head and shrugged wearily. "I don't know. There are so many questions and mysteries here. But I think this was that last refuge against destiny. You'll see what I mean."

The room's amazingly white plaster walls and ceiling glowed with the light from Alvin's lantern and my flashlight. The wall opposite the opening was pierced with a tiny window, no bigger than a handkerchief, through which some real fresh air seeped in. I had a strange feeling that at some point I had belonged in this place, that some part of my own physical presence had been there. Again, a genuine relaxation spread through me. I started walking through it, looking around. As I touched the walls, getting some of the flaky plaster dust on my fingers, I forgot about Ted, and Alvin.

Twenty or so large earthenware jars, some broken, almost all waist tall, stood in various places to store provisions. There was also a pile of heavy circular stone bowls. I counted eight of them, close to two feet in diameter, weighing about forty pounds each. They had probably been used with a pestle for grinding grain or spices. A clay seal or insignia was stamped on some of the jars. With my flashlight, I looked closer at the seal.

"It's Greek, the most popular international language of the period, mixed with some Hebrew and Latin script," Alvin explained. "It tells us where the jars came from. Some from Greece, others from Judea, Persia, and parts of Turkey. It also tells us that they'd already been taxed. It seems that the Romans, like any good government, never let you get away from taxes."

At the other side of the room, several of the big jars stood by a table of rotting planks that was barely holding up.

"They must have been eating over there," Alvin whispered. "I bet you'll find a last meal somewhere." He looked around and suddenly asked, "Where's your friend? I thought we'd find him waiting here."

I shook my head.

Alvin directed his lantern towards the table. "Maybe he's with them already."

"*Them?*"

"Yep. In the floor opposite this table's a hole. It's only so wide." He moved his palms out to slightly more than the width of his chest. "He must have found it. I guess nothing was going to stop him. Most people would be afraid."

"Should he be?"

He shook his head. "Wait. You'll see, Len."

We approached the other wall. By it was an entry hole cut into the floor, covered for all those centuries by one of the big jars. You could see an impression of its weight on the floor timbers, around the circumference of the hole. The jar, once half-filled with sand, lay broken near it.

"A really lucky accident," Alvin said. "One of my men tried to move it. The jar was heavier than he thought and it tumped over. You should have heard that sound! Somebody—maybe other secret followers, there's no telling when—had put sand in it to stabilize it and keep it there. So the hole remained a secret."

I noticed a very heavy wooden plank nearby, which had been turned over on its side, not an easy thing to do.

"I was afraid of rats getting down there, so I had my men put that on top of the hole. How your friend knew to move it, I don't know, but he did. I guess he couldn't wait for a rope."

I stared down into the hole. It was so dark that I couldn't see the floor below it, or any light from Ted's flashlight.

"Ted!!" I shouted.

Alvin put his finger to my lips. "Wait. We'll be down there in a few minutes."

Alvin took a coil of braided nylon rope from deep inside his jacket pocket; I helped him lash one end of it securely around the plank. Then, lifting them together, we brought the big stone bowls over to weigh down the plank as securely as we could.

Winded, Alvin sank down onto the floor.

"Boy-o-boy! When I did this before, I had several men with me, and I wasn't so damn sick. Now, Len, I warn you—don't be shocked by what you see down there."

I helped him up. His body was shaking from over-exertion. Leaning on me, he crouched down, holding on to a fistful of the rope with both hands, then letting the rest of it dangle into the hole. I sank to both of my knees and grabbed his shoulders to steady him. I wasn't sure Alvin would make it in, but, still shaking, he edged his way through the narrow opening, gripping the rope as hard as he could; then he lowered himself, cautiously, into the space below.

"I made it!" he called. There was a soft thud, then he disappeared into the darkness, calling for his lantern.

As I lowered the lantern with the rope, all I could see was the top of Alvin's head.

"Be careful," he warned. "This drop here can fool you!"

He wasn't joking. From the narrow opening, it would have been easy to misjudge the distance to the floor below and possibly break a leg. I began to lower myself slowly, hand-under-hand on the rope. I certainly wasn't as muscular as Ted, and it took every ounce of upper body strength I had. Several painful handfuls of rope later, gritting my teeth, I dropped the last two feet to the floor, without breaking anything.

The ceiling of this small hidden refuge was barely six feet in height; the floor, worn brick or stone, was brushed with a fine layer of white lime over it. Still brilliantly white, it reflected the beams from Alvin's lantern, blinding me for an instant as I turned to him after being in the dark.

"There's your friend," Alvin announced.

I forced my eyes open. Ted was on the floor, unconscious.

He was lying on his side, curled up like a caterpillar, his knees pulled up and his hands clasped under them. Three completely preserved human beings lay next to him. One of them, a man whose gaunt, weary face I might have seen on a subway, so alive in death he appeared, had his darkened, slender hand resting fully opened on the back of Ted's head.

chapter nineteen

"They move," Alvin whispered. "That's why the men got so freaked out. They were terrified. I was afraid the place'd become a side show, or condemned by some of the local religious fanatics who might have tried to kill me. It's hard enough for me to take, Len. Even now it sends chills straight up me."

There were two men and a woman, completely naked.

A shudder went through Alvin. "Watch."

Almost imperceptibly, they moved like dried twigs dancing in a puff of wind. Their flesh was rearranging itself, their limbs settling into variations of a pattern that had been established over a span of two thousands years. Their faces showed no expression; but no pain, either.

I couldn't turn away from them; I felt as if the breath had been punched out of my lungs. I was transfixed, trembling, but still had to approach them. Crouching, I extended my hands, then cautiously ran them over ridges and valleys of skin wrinkled like the meat of a walnut. My fingers skimmed the closest man's right forearm. An inky swirl of rigid ligaments and veins ran down the inside of his arm all the way to where his hand rested on Ted, who, even unconscious, seemed abnormally alive next to this unnatural calm.

Suddenly, my initial nervousness gave way to excitement, as I drew closer, bringing my face next to each of theirs. They were not breathing, yet were not cold either. An insect's degree of warmth came from them, as proof of some continuing discernible activity. Their eyes were lightly closed; their teeth visible beneath slightly parted lips.

The woman's face, with its arched nose and firm mouth, had once been beautiful. It still looked young, even stretched tight from time, her cheeks sucked in. Her small collapsed breasts were sunken under empty pouches of skin. As she shifted slightly, the bodies of the two men on the floor moved into more upright positions. I watched mesmerized, my hands still on them, feeling every small shift in their movements.

Perhaps responding to my presence, the man whose hand rested on Ted grimaced violently, withdrawing his arm as if he were in the siege of a nightmare. He hunched his shoulders, tightened his neck, and appeared to break from the dreamless sleep the others remained in. As if to console him, I knelt over him, placing my palm softly on the flat plane of his leathery chest. I remembered what it was like to emerge from that condition others call death, and felt an immediate closeness to him. One of his nipples, hard as a small peach stone, rolled beneath my fingers. Something—a breath?—swelled through him like a wave. It seemed impossible, yet there; at the very distant, pale edge of life.

He reached for my hand. I let him take it, and he relaxed his grip on my wrist. That feeling I'd had of the breath being knocked out of me stopped; instead, I felt a flawless peace. My body was now his, exactly as the substance grafted on my calf surely must have recognized that it had returned to the source of its origin.

I lay down prone on the white powdery floor, propped up slightly on my elbows, and invited his blind touch to explore me clothed.

"I can't watch!" Alvin cried. "This is *too* weird. You're not scared of them at all! What are you, some kind of—"

He stopped talking—how could I answer him? What could I say, that I only wanted to be there at that moment with them—whatever they were? I was one of them, I knew it; a part of their own flesh, a part of them. Only my brain was mine, and for once it was trusting me, without taking me outside of myself, without sending me into one of my "states" that ultimately terrified me.

"I'm alright," I called to him. "Can you leave me alone here for a moment?"

"You're—" Alvin stopped himself, before calling me insane. He turned, walking sullenly away from me, the bright beams from his lantern wavering under the dark opening. I could hear him pushing his breath as he jumped, shoving his lantern up into the hole. How he had done that, I wasn't sure. Probably pure rageful anger got him to do it on his first try. I clicked off my flashlight, listening to Alvin mutter to himself and breathe hard in the darkness, as he pulled himself up on the rope.

When he was gone, I felt actually less afraid. Nothing was forbidden,

I was alone with these . . . my fellow creatures. I lay there with the man's hand on my wrist. I turned my body to touch him with my other hand, exploring his face and neck and then down, all the way, to the firm, muscular ripple of his thighs and loins.

He moved towards me slightly. I exhaled deeply. All of my breath gathered warmly outside of myself, drifting towards him.

I could feel my own breath like a dense cloud in the air, and all I wanted to do was be clothed in it. I got up, undressed completely, and lay down again with my knees slightly raised on the cool lime floor. I had never felt so free in my life, sublimely happy, like a flower recognizing its own fragrance, exposing itself to the night. Darkness was now the element of my creation, as nurturing as the liquors of the womb.

I placed myself within their reach and their hands came to me, blindly finding that place on my right calf. Cradling my leg, they touched me with their hands and lips, as the substance drew itself towards them. For a moment, I was convinced that it had separated itself from me, and they had reclaimed it as their own.

I was willing, absolutely, to let them have it.

I would die again, and remain with them in this dimension that seemed larger than either life or death. If they desired, they could reclaim this tissue that had been separated from them. After the horrible deaths of Josh and Benjy, I was ready to relinquish this gift that had resulted in so much violence.

But *it* was not ready to leave the host it had brought back to life. The substance was left on me, and they blessed me, the two young men and the young woman, blessed me with their hands and lips. With their closeness. With the unwritten prayers of the dark on my face and arms. On my chest, stomach, and legs. On my groin. On my sensitive places. The penis. The scrotum. The navel. The mind.

Their whole presence, ravaged by time, held me.

The slack, empty sacks of her breasts covered my face, then parting, like clouds, invited drifts of light to cascade slowly through the room. In their wake, the elements of time stopped for me and I saw the three of them alive once more. Beautiful beyond my hopes, but wracked with the horrors of fear. Young, running, pursued by a mob and the drawn swords of Roman soldiers who beat on every door. They had crossed the sea, but their identities had been revealed in this town that had provided one last fickle refuge. The handsome young men were Essenes, deep-thinking mystics from the seaside caves of Judea; the three were cousins, and would find themselves witnesses to a man who had been crucified in Jerusalem. His torture had lasted into that stormy night, until it ended when his lifeless body was brought down from the cross.

Then the three of them, in a frenzy of grief, extracted one of the blood-stained nails crudely hammered into his flesh, and marked their feet and palms with it. With the sharp point of the nail, the girl gouged a deep cruciform "X" into the callused heel of her right foot. Years later she stumbled by a stream just beyond this place, and lost that part of her foot to a centurion's sword. With his orders to kill, his eyes blind with fury as his horse charged into the crowd, he hacked at her over and over again. I screamed as his razor-sharp blade cut her; her blood flowing like my own wounded head.

In the noise and turmoil, she managed to crawl into a nearby stable. At night, her cousins came for her, lifted her, and brought her through the underground passages to this hidden room, where they prayed one last time to the God they had embraced.

"What happened?" I cried. They answered with silent kisses on my body. I felt as weightless as that light had been—those pale drifts of light falling and falling, slowly, then extinguished into darkness. I was with them. But now would drown in this sea of time. I cried. I made what noise could come from the air leaving my lungs as I tried to clothe myself once more only in the essence of myself, my own breath.

But it was no longer enough. I felt alone. Cut off. Frightened. No longer self-contained and happy. I wanted to reach out, to beg.

Please, *please*.

And He—that great *He* coming out of that thing I only knew as *It*—was there, someplace; I was sure.

God would hear me crying, and would come to deliver me with His mouth on my lips. Who else could reach this tormented place and bring sweet life to this death? I knew as much as I knew anything that He would come and make love to me in that great, celestial way, and I, like a comet traveling outside of my former self, would this time invite Him to me without any of my usual resistance.

A mouth, warm and giving, kissed me. Powerful, endless arms

embraced me. Lips, moist, open, flowering, explored my very self.

I had desired all of this. All of my strange, kinky, unsettled past had led to it, all of my experiments; my explorations. I had to capitulate. Surrender. There were no more excuses of the burdens of consciousness for me. I was releasing consciousness, and with it myself. God, this thing we invent until *It* invents us, was embracing me. Making love to me, and I could release myself to Him—but only when the ultimate time came.

And it did, throwing me into that painless escape from coarse humanity that humans desire all their lives. The Great "O." The Zero . . . the sea at its silver dawn after the great storm. Light emerged, the light of the cosmos. Of the infinite orgasm. Of the deliverance, and the reprieve.

Of the blessed, longed-for reprieve.

And the light as I beheld it, as I made myself see with eyes wide open, the light . . . was Ted.

I saw him in the dark and knew. The lips and willing mouth had been his. Alive at that moment as I had not been. Nothing had held him back, no sin, no fear. Nothing. Nothing from his past, or future.

His face was beautiful, lit with a warmth that came from him whole, and from behind him. From the three of them, as I saw it: the end of them. Barricaded into this basement room, where they prayed one last time, then ended their struggle on earth with a poison so secret that its original formula went back to Creation itself.

Who were they? The cousins no one had claimed in history, not named in any text? Archangels? Wisdom taking the guise of young flesh? Or some form of an ancient blood and substance that belonged only to God?

They held on to each other, rocking in the throes of death, lit by a light that I could not know even down here. The light of hope and faith, so alien to me. I had shared their flesh, but their essence, their pure spirit, their love, was something I drew towards, but, like a comet's flare, could only distantly glimpse.

The glow I'd seen on Ted's face vanished, leaving me alone now in my own darkness, with all of its threatening horror. Terrified, I drew myself up, rocking back and forth, holding my knees, sobbing out loud. I cried for everyone who had died around me. But worst, I cried for myself, for the real, *dead* Leonard Miller I would not be allowed to embrace.

Finally, I could take this no more.

I had to shake this emptiness off me. I could no longer expose myself to it. No longer was I the flower that knew its own fragrance and was happy; no longer did the dark feed me. Because now, I knew more than I was capable of knowing.

I found my flashlight and snapped it on, feeling colder, more afraid, deader than I'd ever felt. This was worse than my re-awakening in the morgue. I was afraid I'd throw my guts up, but what guts did I really have? I should have stayed dead in the morgue. I hated the thing that was on my leg. Why didn't *it* return to them, and leave me dead at last, and in peace?

I struggled to get my clothes back on as fast as I could, then flashed the light's beam directly on Ted.

His eyes were fully open, but there was nothing behind them. The light hit the silvery whites of them and its reflection bounced violently back at me. My wrist holding the light shook so hard I had to steady it with my other hand. He was like some pale, drowned, half-submerged corpse, as it was being raised to the surface in its waterlogged shroud of clothes.

Turning away, I waved the light over the three bodies. They lay like inert figures of wax, with no movement in them at all. They looked shrunken and horrifying; they were simply hideous curiosities, somehow preserved—but why?

I could no longer take my freezing, cut off, shaken feeling. No wonder Alvin was sick! I hated being down there. He was right: I should have been afraid of the place. Trying to make myself breathe deeply and slowly, I steadied myself. I crouched over Ted and shook him several times, as hard as I could.

His eyes blinked rapidly. "Am I alive?"

"Yes, you are, Ted."

"Is the Lord Jesus with us? I saw the Lord Jesus, I tell you I saw Him."

My heart was pounding so hard I could barely hear myself.

"You saw him, Ted. You saw what you needed to see. Now we've got to leave. But I swear, if he's anyplace, he was here. As close to you as I am. Even I know that."

Ted got up, then started retching loudly. Was he sick, too, like Alvin? Trying to calm him, I held him close to me, putting my hands on his face, then I kissed him

He turned from me to avoid my lips, chanting between convulsions:

"I praise You, I praise You. Be with me, Lord, and I shall walk forever in Your path and accept death. Be with me, Lord, and I shall accept Your commandments."

We'd seen too much. I wanted to revert back to my old self, the scientist, with my own skeptical limits. Putting my light back on them, I seriously studied the bodies to see if they'd move again. None of them moved; not a twitch, not anything.

"Which one do you think is Jesus, Len? I want to kneel and pray for Him to take me. To take me back to Him."

"He's not here, Ted."

"You told me He was!"

"He was here in some form, but he's gone now. He's definitely gone."

"Then you saw Him, too?"

My pulse was still pounding. "I'm afraid so. I did see him. When I saw my own death."

"Your *death*? *Your* dumb death! SHIT! I'm willing to die for Jesus! I will be *resurrected* with Him! And all you saw was your own dumb death?"

"Please, Ted. We've got to go. We need to get out of here!"

I took his arm, but he jerked away from me. I took him again and pulled him harder, managing to get him over to the hatch opening. Alvin was waiting above us with his lantern. He raised it high above his head, and I stared up at him. His face was even more drawn and feverish-looking than it had been before. But the lantern's golden light gave him the appearance that he had been transformed, simply from being down there once more.

I placed Ted's hand forcefully on the rope and started to shove him up, forcing him to understand that I would not let him stay down there any longer; it was too dangerous. It took all the strength I had, but I wouldn't allow him a moment longer there. As fit as he was, he ran out of energy suddenly.

"I can't do this. I can't make it up on this rope," he cried.

"You've got to."

He sank to the floor in the dark. Shining my flashlight's beam directly in his eyes, I yelled at him to get up, grabbing him by the shoulders when he resisted. It took Alvin at the top and me at the bottom to get him up the rope and through that narrow opening. I threatened him several times and he screamed his protests, but he made it up.

Then with Alvin's help, I got myself up. Amazingly, getting up the rope was easier than getting down it. I knew that I had to leave that room, and despite everything I'd been through, something had given me the strength to escape.

Alvin was worn out as we trudged back in the moonlight towards the tents. If he'd been bothered about my staying down there without him and asking him to climb out alone, he didn't show it.

Ted was sobbing. "Damn you! Damn you! Damn you! Why wouldn't you let me stay in the presence of Jesus?"

I could only shake my head while he screamed at me.

"You bastard! I'm a sinner! I know I'm a sinner. You led me into temptation over and over again. That's why I need to go back to Jesus! *Why?* Why wouldn't you let me do it?" He screamed until his voice became hoarse.

Alvin tried to calm him, whispering softly, "It's okay, man. You're freaked, that's all. The things down there transform you. They do what lightning does to animals. There's nothing rational about it. In all my years in archeology, I've never seen anything like it. Even my diggers split. They're simple guys from around here, no schooling. They split like scared animals; I've never had diggers run out on me like that!"

We arrived back at the tents. Alvin went to his, and we went over to ours. Ted seemed a bit calmer. He sat on the edge of his cot with his hands rubbing his face. It was hard for me to talk, but I knew I had to say something.

"Something happened to you down there, Ted. And to me. We can't fool ourselves. I know I'm going to die soon."

He looked directly at me. "No shit, Shakespeare."

"I didn't mean it like we're *all* going to die, I meant—"

"Sorry. I knew what you meant."

"You're going to kill me, aren't you?"

"I am NOT!" He turned away. Then he looked at me with all the bitterness draining from his face. "I saw Jesus down there, Len. I know it. I touched Him. That's the only thing I know."

I nodded, and put my hand in his.

"You did. You saw the *real* Jesus. That's why I was afraid. I was afraid you'd stay down there and never come back up."

chapter twenty

There was a narrow shower stall with a couple of gallons of tepid water above it and both of us managed to shower off. Ted dried himself, shivering all over, but not simply from the night air.

There were two cots in the tent with the tent pole between them, that I managed to pull together as close as I could. Getting into my cot, I pulled a sheet over me, with a light blanket over my feet, and clicked off both our flashlights. In the dark, I could see the glow of the moon outside, like the dim nimbus of a halo, through the light gray covering of the tent opening.

Ted lay face-up in his boxer shorts, on top of his cot.

"I wish I had a drink," he whispered. "I wish I had anything."

I nodded. "Uh huh."

"I don't know what got into me, Len. It was like something was moving through me. It was so powerful, it was like being inside a hurricane. You have no idea what it felt like."

"Why do you say that? I mean, that I have no idea?"

"Because you don't accept Jesus. You don't know what it's like to love Him and to need to join Him."

I sat up slightly. "Doesn't that sound . . . queer to you?"

He turned towards me, his eyes filled with anger.

"Don't give me that! You fags turn everything into all that queer-gay shit! Let me tell you, Jesus is BIG. He's huge. He's all the love in the world that you always wanted—that you screamed out for. Have you ever screamed out for love? Have you? Do you know what that's like? You scream out and scream out and nobody answers. Then, just when you're ready to die, Jesus answers. He does. He answers you." He sighed, lowering his voice. "I know. He answered me when I was ready to kill myself, 'cause I couldn't take my own sins anymore."

He started crying again. I could only hear it and felt this icy distance between us, between me and his own self-loathing and pain. I could not—

would not—comfort him. Because all I could feel was the pain of my own death. It hurt to reconnect with that. First, my death in the lab, and then my death again in that underground room. That room was the last refuge before death; or was that what death was, really?

I remembered that sense of gratefulness I'd had in my lab; grateful that the pain and fear was over, and only death remained. I took a deep breath, trying to come out of that awful feeling of hurt that separated me so much from Ted.

"When did you want to kill yourself," I asked softly.

"When I realized I couldn't control my own urges. When I knew that I wanted to be a good Christian, but couldn't."

"I would think Jesus would know that."

His voice cracked with anger. "Are you making fun of me?" He sat straight up. "I can't be what I need to be, devoted to Jesus, and you're making fun of me, Len. I know it. I thought you were better than that. I thought you were chosen for something great. That's why I brought you here."

"You did?" I asked, barely able to pull the words out of me.

"Sure, buddy. That's exactly why I did it."

My eyes closed. I wanted so much to believe him, and so badly to make sense out of all this. It was my downfall: needing to make sense out of everything that had happened to me. I still couldn't do it. My headache returned to me, even worse than when I'd awakened in the morgue. With my eyes still shut, I tried to massage the pain away, pressing my fingers lightly over my scalp and forehead.

Ted came over and sat on the edge of my cot, placing his hand very softly over my eyes. "You were chosen. Weren't you, buddy?"

He kissed my mouth.

I lowered my head with his lips still on mine. He took them away. "Why, Lord," he asked, "did You choose this man? And why me, your undeserving servant, for Your work?"

I opened my eyes, looking directly at him.

"Tell me the truth, Ted. Were you sent to kill me? You know what I'm talking about."

"No, Len. I swear, I was sent to love you. I know that. The Lord sent me. I'm a sinner, a fornicator, a—"

"You sucked me off in that room, Ted."

"I *what?*"

"You heard me. You took me in your mouth and I shot my gay-as-all-get-up jiz right into you. So, is that queer or what? You're straight, married, like to suck cock, hate the shit out of fags, love Jesus—the truth is you want to kill me, don't you? You want to blow me away, and I don't mean with your mouth. Right?"

He looked away from me, but put his hand lightly on the sheet covering my chest. "I did that down there?"

"You did."

"In the presence of God?"

"Yep."

A flash of a smile passed across his face. "Holy shit! I don't remember it."

"It was something," I admitted. "It was as close to God as I think I'm ever going to get on this earth. That's why I thought you did see Jesus—in me."

He looked at me seriously. In the moon light coming through the tent, I could see the curious, deep expression on his face, now only inches away from mine.

"I *was* with Jesus when that happened. I was so far away from the life we call this life. But, Len, if that's what I did, I'm condemned. I can't help myself. That's all I can say."

He rested his head on my chest. I raked my fingers gently through his soft hair, and leaned over to kiss the back of his neck.

"I am condemned, but I can live with my condemnation, Len. Do you know what I mean?"

"Why are *you* condemned? I haven't condemned you at all."

He sat back up.

"I know, and for that I love you, buddy, with all my heart. I can't help the way I feel about you, despite all the hurt and fear that's in there. I've tried to go straight so many times. I tried one of those Ex-Gay, back-to-Jesus groups. I was cruising parks in Salt Lake and scared my wife was going to find out. I wanted to belong to Jesus. I think I was in love with Jesus, just like He was a man."

"He was, wasn't he?"

"He was God. God that took the form of a man. I wanted to belong to Him. Instead, I was sucking all the cock I could get my hands on."

"What happened?"

"What do you think?"

I shook my head.

"There was this other guy there. Good-looking, strapping-husband type. Two boys in Little League baseball. He and I started getting together for prayers—and, I admit, beers—and one day when my wife was out of town, we couldn't hold it back anymore. So we got into bed. In my house, where I wanted Jesus so much. And he fucked the crap out of me, and I loved it, buddy. I felt totally screwed every which-a-way, but couldn't help the fact that I loved getting fucked—something no normal, moral guy s'posed to like—and I was crazy about this man, and I was in my bedroom in my Mormon wife's house, and it just killed me. The guilt. The hurt inside me. It just ate me. I had to tighten up so hard inside, I thought I'd crack. You don't know what it's like for people like me to feel so torn and conflicted. You don't have any of those sort of conflicts, do you?"

I was really worn out. My head had stopped hurting somewhat, and now I wanted him close to me. I knew that if he just got close to me and held me, I'd feel better. I lifted the sheet up a bit from me.

"Would you like to lie with me for a while, Ted, until I fall asleep?"

He stared at me, then said, "You didn't answer my question. Do you have conflicts, too?"

I nodded.

"Mine are past conflicts," I confessed. "They're fucking battles. Some are easier than others, but you probably have those. For instance, I like kinky anonymous sex with wild guys. But I still want warmth and romance. That's a fairly easy conflict, really."

"Sure. That's like me with my Mormon wife, right? So what's your other conflict, buddy?"

"Okay: I believe in goodness. Yet I want that *goodness* to have all the knowledge of the world in it, in the old biblical sense that knowledge comes straight from your body as well as your mind. How's that for a conflict?

He smiled. "You're getting closer."

"But the worst one," I said, admitting this even to myself for the first time, "is that I really want to know what God is. I want to know God; but I don't really believe in *it*—God—as a separate, knowable *thing*. Something you can call on when you need it. Or Him, or whatever you call God. Can you see what that must do to me?"

He pulled me close to him. I was crying and he kissed the tears off my face and got into the narrow cot with me. He slipped off his boxer shorts and we were naked together. He held me and kissed me, and I kissed him. There was something hard about his lips. They were like the rough, tight lips of one of those butch action movie stars like Mel Gibson or Bruce Willis, lips too defensive for casual intimacy, inviting only explosive connections.

It was like kissing the bull in a bullfight, something the matador does sometimes, right after the bull's head's been cut off.

He had an erection. I could feel it, and he wanted me to relieve that. I could feel that, too. But I felt immobilized in my own fatigue, which had grabbed any desire I'd had and turned it to dust. Fatigue is a thief, like aging. It sneaks up, demanding what it wants: your energy, even your will.

I fell asleep, holding the impression of his tight rough lips on mine. The lips gave way to a dream, which I wish I could remember as precisely as I could his lips, but I can't. But what I can remember is what counts.

I was with Josh, and we were on this beautiful, clean white beach at dawn. Maybe it was the beach at Fire Island. The light rising up from the water had that feeling you get after a full night of dancing, sex, and craziness: a spreading light filled with a fresh, longed-for softness; clear, perfect. It was that light of dawn's returning innocence that I admit I love. We were swimming in the surf, wearing those tiny Lycra Speedo bathing suits they like to wear on the island. We came out of the water, which was warm with little rippling waves, and suddenly the beach was crowded with men. They looked like "bears," big, hairy-chested guys, all naked, cavorting, free and happy.

They were pawing us, touching us all over, saying about our Speedos, "Take it off! Take it off!" and I had this intoxicating feeling you have when you're young and there's nothing at all between you and insane happiness. Every part of me was smiling, my chest and stomach, groin, even my rear end. My heart was smiling, too, and it was ready to lift me into that pure clear blue air, so that I could feel a happiness that defied gravity, a limitless happiness bouncing with energy.

Then, suddenly, marching to a loud samba beat out of the dunes onto the beach, came this group of outrageous Carmen Miranda queens: big shoulders, towering tutti-frutti hats, stacked wedgie sandals. Right out of Carnival in Rio. Heavily made-up, with giant false eyelashes, they smiled intensely like beauty queens as they tried to keep from tripping in their heels.

Now that innocent glow of dawn switched to intense disco spotlights, aimed directly into my eyes, almost blinding me. I'd been ready to fly, to bounce up into the air and whisk my suit off, wanting to be as naked as the bear guys. Instead, the queens surrounded me, screaming in a loud dialect of Spanglish-Jewish, "*Mu-chachka! Boychick!* Come weet' us! We want-*chu* now!"

They circled me, doing a punchy, aggressive conga, with clanging bells, whistles, disco tambourines, and Cuban drums, and started throwing various pieces of drag clothing on me, piles of them, so I could never be naked. The clothes landed right on my head, and the queens yanked them down on me, screeching with laughter as I started showing, against my will, heavy foam-stuffed boobs and huge padded shoulders.

"Who're your new friends?" Josh teased, smiling.

I had no answer for him, but the queens kept getting bigger until they were like linebackers, in ever-higher platform shoes and more outrageous outfits. Then, grabbing me by the heavy clothes thrown over me, they dragged me into the low surf.

"We've got to get out of here!" I screamed to Josh as I tried to push them off me, resisting as much as I could.

Josh shrugged his smooth, nicely freckled shoulders. He was still naked, except for his shiny black Speedo and he looked so beautiful in it with his perfect tan and slim waist. He had wandered back into the water up to his ankles, and was carelessly kicking little sprays of it into the air, flinging it around through the disco lights.

"What's wrong, baby?" Josh asked, "You always want to leave the party when the fun's happening! You never want to have any fun!"

Coming out of the water now, he smiled complacently, as if he were sharing a secret with the girls I couldn't possibly understand. I was too "dumb," stuck forever in science; and now I was completely out of my depth. I'd drown in that shallow water, weighed down by all the heavy drag clothes on me.

The clanging and drumming only got louder as the queens pushed me down again into the water, in my straitjacket of brassieres, skirts, and dresses. Choking on salt water, I managed to get back up to the surface.

I had to get out of the water, and over to Josh. Then, out of nowhere, a solution came to me: in order to to save myself, I realized I'd have to offer Josh *to* the queens. It was my only recourse. I'd pull him into the surf, and throw him at them. He would divert their attention, and that was all they were looking for. The noise around me made me feel as if I were in some huge washing machine with colorful rags swirling around me. Plunging into deeper water, I dove under, managing to pull all the sopping *schmatas* off, until I was naked now. Even the Speedo was gone.

Feeling safe for a moment, I re-emerged and tried to spot Josh. I had to get out of the water before all the Carmens could get to me again, and then get them Josh. He was really theirs; what else could I do? He had all the drag clothes. He knew just what to say at those smart parties with his bitchy clever gay friends. I would sit there silent. He could cut and maneuver through everything, in a way that I never could—I was an outsider, an outsider among outsiders; an outsider with everyone, even myself.

As I started swimming naked farther out into the water, that happy, buoyant feeling returned to me. I felt as if Benjy were there suddenly. Both of us were naked and just giggling with happiness. I could feel him smiling next to me in the foaming surf. The garish colors and disco lights disappeared. They queens were gone. Maybe their heavy hats and wigs couldn't make it into the deeper water, but I was free. Then Benjy disappeared, under the water.

I looked for him, dove under, came back up, then turned and looked back toward the beach.

It was empty. The bears were gone; so was Josh. And all the Carmen Miranda queens. As in most dreams, leaving the water and stepping onto the shoreline happened instantly. But I felt that I had gained this immeasurable weight as soon as I did it. No longer a kid inside, no longer buoyant and free, I was only naked, heavy, exhausted, and wandering by myself on a deserted beach.

I woke up feeling old and tired, alone, in the tent. I pulled on a pair of shorts and went out. The thin line of a fresh dawn hung over the horizon, but it was nothing like the freshness of the dawn in the dream on Fire Island. I was young for a while in my dream. And there was no smoke on the island, but there was smoke in the air now. It came from the direction of the site, stinging my eyes.

Hurrying back into the tent, I put on a pair of sneakers and a T-shirt and rushed out, stumbling, scraping my legs badly on the long upward path to the site. The entrance that Alvin's diggers had covered with a tarpaulin was now in ashes. Ted was sitting on the ground near it, wearing his T-shirt flopped over a pair of gym shorts, covered with sweat and grime, breathing hard. I knelt next to him.

"What happened?"

He looked away for a minute, then turned to me, his face full of despair. "Alvin went nuts."

"What?"

"He got me up in the middle of the night. I was sleeping with you, remember? He told me to be quiet and put something on, so I jumped into what I could grab. He waited outside the tent, then told me we had to torch the place."

"The room with the three people in it?"

"That's it, buddy."

"He must have been delirious. He's been so sick. You let him do it?"

"What could I do?" Ted's despair gave way to a flash of anger. Then he reverted to common sense, with that decent, familiar smile that I liked so much. "I couldn't hold him back, Len. No one could. He said the place was cursed, and now he was going to die. 'Look what it did to Len when he went down there. He went nuts on me! He wanted to stay down there alone.' I tried to reason with him, but he said, 'Ted, you're a man of God. You believe in Him, Lenny and I don't. All I know is that the place has killed me. I'll let you see it one last time, then God Himself can have it!'"

"What did you do?"

Ted's face suddenly dropped. He looked as exhausted as I'd felt after my dream. "I went back down there with him, Len. I had to, there was no choice."

"I guess Alvin was angrier than I'd thought," I said. "And more delusional." He had been angry when I'd asked him to leave me alone in the room, but he seemed to have gotten over his fury by the time Ted and I had met him

"He was crazy, buddy. Burning up with fever. I could see it in his eyes; they were like red-hot coals. So I went with him. I wanted to dissuade him, but this was all his, not mine. I just knew I'd seen Jesus in that room, and I had to go back down there and see the place once more. That woman knew our Lord. I could tell, Len. Maybe she'd bore Him a family, or—"

"She wasn't his lover," I said firmly.

"How do you know?"

I shook my head. I couldn't tell him exactly how I knew; I could hardly believe it myself. "I don't know, but she wasn't."

"But she was close to Him. Close the way I am. Her heart was His, I know it. I went along with Alvin. I tried to offer him anything, but he kept saying the room was cursed and those things in it were cursed. I offered him money and help. I prayed and I bargained with him. I told him I'd get him to the hospital in Istanbul. I'm on good terms with all the big medical people there. I'd fly him back to the States. I'd do anything for him, but it just didn't do any good.

"He had everything down there already—cans of gasoline, solvent, matches, rags! He struck the first match in front of me. I grabbed him; I was ready to kill him. But he had all the strength an angry dying man can grab on to, and he used every bit of it, despite me.

"It was awful! You can't imagine it. The bodies of those people dissolved into this river of horrible dark jelly in front of my eyes, and all I could do was watch. I don't know how I got out alive, but I did. I swear this to you, Len. On my love for you, I swear it!"

He took my right hand, bringing it briefly to his lips, then softly held it. I was touched by him. He looked into my eyes.

"I love you, Len. I didn't come to kill you, but to take you here. Believe me when I say that."

I clutched his hand, barely able to speak. I could still feel the heat coming from the burned site; the wind started to blow ashes on me. I started crying. Suddenly Joshua's violent death, even Benjy's, began to make some barely discernible sense to me, if only to bring Ted to me. "You do love me?"

"Yes, Len. I love you as I've loved my wife and kids—and as I wish to love the whole world. I swear that. And with the help of Jesus Christ, I love you, too."

"Then I believe you."

I sat with him, holding his hand. I put my lips on his soot-stained forehead. "What happened to Alvin?" I whispered.

"Man, he's dead. He went up with them—bang! I saw it just before I managed to hoist myself back up alive. I tell you, the sonovabitch planned it; he was waiting for you to come here before he did it. I guess he flipped out. Funny how people go nuts and don't even know it. This place makes you crazy, Len. We need to leave. Our work's done here, buddy."

Back at the tent, we washed ourselves and changed into some fresh clothes. I still felt in a state of shock, like I had been returned to all the violence I'd experienced before: everything started moving very slowly around me, stalked by that image of the three bodies melting in the room, that trinity of agonized beings touched by something so far outside myself, whose very flesh had become a part of me and who had held my own life and death in their thin hands. Ted only hovered over me like a figure made out of shadows. He smiled at me, as if we shared a secret that would now bond us forever. But I felt as if I could put my fingers straight through him.

It took us two days to get back to Istanbul. We stopped several times and Ted got out of the car and called his wife from pay phones. We spent the night in one of the towns, in a guest house that was not a whore house. This time we slept together but hardly said anything. Ted prayed a lot. I could see his mouth moving.

I asked him what he was praying for.

"Forgiveness. I want to be forgiven for what I've done. And thanksgiving. Just a regular prayer of thanksgiving. I want to thank God that He has allowed me to live through this. And I want to thank Him for you."

"Me?"

"Yep, you brought me to all of this. Years ago I discovered that the idea of prayer was to learn who you really are. It's like therapy you do with yourself. Now, back in that strange room, I finally learned it. I learned that all those years when I was driven close to suicide about sucking dick and sex and getting fucked, that wasn't important. What was important was that I did *not* know myself. I couldn't face my own place with God."

"What's that?" I asked.

"It's the place we're born for, buddy. Nobody can take that away from you, no matter *how* they try. I learned that, down there in that room."

I smiled. I wasn't sure what to say. But I knew I could have told him something very close to that, even without coming to Turkey.

chapter twenty-one

*I*t was evening when we checked back into our old hotel in Istanbul. The desk captain was as cordial as ever. He asked about our trip, and if we wanted to go to another *hamam.*

"I don't think so," Ted said. "I just want to soak in the bath here."

"Very well, Sir. How long will you be staying with us?"

The question hit me, making me realize I had no idea how long I'd be there, or what part of my life would come next. All of my life had been propelled towards the next thing: school, research, my next project, and the one after that. But now?

"We'll leave tomorrow," Ted said, without looking at me.

We took our luggage up on the elevator ourselves. The room we had was on a higher floor than before. The harbor and the rest of Istanbul seemed more distant, a faint glow of lights in a dark veil below our windows.

As soon as we put our suitcases down, Ted started to undress, without looking at me. I felt embarrassed suddenly, like I, an unbelieving Jew, was encroaching on his very Christian need for privacy. I sat quietly on one of the two beds in the room, gazing away from him.

"I'd really like to blow you again," Ted announced, down to his boxer shorts.

I snapped out of the isolated feeling I was in. "Huh?"

He smiled wickedly, melting me. "Wanna shower with me?"

I got up off the bed, took my clothes off, and followed him into the shower. When I got in, he had the water on at a perfect temperature, exactly cool enough. He was covered in soap and very hard.

He lathered me down, starting with my chest and then my crotch, legs, and feet. The shower spray washed the soap off and his tongue followed it in reverse order: my feet, then up to my legs, until he hit my balls. I thought I was going to cream inside, just experience one of those out-of-body orgasms that wash all over you, the way the soap and the shower did.

He was on his knees, the swelling head of my cock at his lips. He was lavishing it with his tongue, but even under the warm shower, I heard a low, soft noise coming out of him, like the flow of a murmur. It had the suggestion of words in it. Maybe he was thinking out loud. Or praying to himself even. The murmuring continued even when he took a little more of me into his mouth and began to suck me. When he took more in, the strange sound stopped. The head of my cock approached the back of his throat, then he lowered himself more, taking me all the way down to the lull of my organ, right there at the testicles.

I felt weightless, the way you do when you're diving into your own relaxation and a man is expertly sucking you. Looking down, I kneaded my fingers through his hair, softly touching him. Then I noticed, on the small of his back, toward the beginning his left buttock, a welt, slightly raised, about three inches in diameter. I reached over, able to touch it.

He took my hand, guiding my fingers away from his back and towards his cock. I played with him, lightly stroking him. His stubby dick was vibrating with heat.

I withdrew from his mouth, pulled him up to me, and we kissed deeply, then got out the shower. I dried him off with a large Turkish towel, and spotted the welt again. He turned back and smiled at me, looking like a hunky satyr, all coppery hairy-limbed, bristling with sexual energy, beautiful.

We got on the bed. Carefully, I touched the welt on his back again and began to stroke it softly. This time he allowed my fingers to remain there. While we both sucked one another, his hand reached over for the back of my lower right calf. He pulled it toward him, caressing the area tenderly, keeping both his hands there as he climaxed in hot big gushes in my mouth. A moment later I repeated the same thing with him, with smaller gushes.

That huge silence after sex grabbed me, making me feel dead and disconnected again. Finally, I asked him, "What *did* you do down there?"

He did not answer me. Instead, he looked directly into my eyes and I found myself wandering into the unexpectedly deep sky-blueness of his. They were so clear, bright, unquestioning. I felt overwhelmed. I closed mine and got closer to him, inhaling the intoxicating sweetness of his clean, hairy skin. I hugged and kissed his firm chest, licking his nipples, his big shoulders, his underarms. He became ticklish, laughed.

My hand grazed the welt at his butt; he jolted up. "Watch it! I scraped myself really bad getting out of there."

"Sorry," I apologized. "Maybe you should have it looked at. You said you knew some doctors at the hospital. We can do it together."

"No." He smiled for a second, guiltily. "That's the least of my problems."

"What's the most?"

He shrugged. "Maybe you guessed it. I'm going to have to leave you soon, Len, and go back to the world I can't leave."

"Why can't you leave it?"

He drew away from me. "Because I need more than you can offer me, buddy. You or anybody else. That's the shitty part. I've fought this and fought it. And each time I try to make any kind of a clean break, I come back."

"To your wife?"

"It's not just June. She's a good Mormon girl, but it's not just her."

That gray, disconnected feeling I'd had, the after-shock from the site and so much else, returned. I got up to look out the window at the night glow of Istanbul. Suddenly, I thought about the handsome young man who'd come in to shampoo my hair and the busy café where Ted and I had stopped for dinner earlier, just outside the city. It was noisy but friendly, filled with all the human colors of Turkey. I got back into bed with Ted. Ted was sitting up, smoking.

"I'll have to give all this up again," he said. "Go back to being the Christian husband in Salt Lake City. It's not so bad, really." He stumped out his cigarette. "Queers always think that being a husband and a Christian is kind of a weight on you, but it's really a weight *off* you. I can be like everybody else, just maybe a little kinkier."

I looked at him. He was very serious. His eyes narrowed.

"I love shopping malls and school sports," he went on. "And those kind of fast food places where you don't have to worry about what you look like, because you know you look the same as everybody else. I can watch my kids, and love them. It feels natural, Len. It's like being inside a popular TV show. Can you understand that? You're not the smart big-deal guest star, just the plain guy next door who's on every week."

"But you're queer."

He shrugged. "Don't bet the world on that, buddy. Tomorrow I've got an early meeting, so I won't wake you up. I'll be back about two, then we can head out back to the airport, if that's all right with you."

"Sure," I answered immediately.

What else was there to say? That I wished I were dead and with Alvin Jurrist in that cursed room? Ted got up and went to the john. I heard him pee, then gargle; the gargling noise reminded me of all the insane questions I'd be asked back in New York. How was I still alive? Why were there so many corpses now attached to me: Josh, Benjy, those people in Queens, even Alvin Jurrist? I was now either a murderer or an accomplice. That poor pregnant woman in the house; that geek Tommy Lee, even Tillman. I'd be hunted forever.

The best thing would be not to go back, but how could I stay alone in Turkey? I'd quickly run out of money and excuses for being there. But more puzzling, how much longer would the substance keep me alive? My growing fatigue and that after-shocked, shadowy feeling, like wading waist-deep further into a mud bog, made me believe not for very long. I had known guys with AIDS who had fought it hard and almost died. Then, after a certain amount of time, they did die. They just gave up. None of them, however, had been as healthy as I was, despite that sucking bog of fatigue into which the substance seemed to be leading me.

I got up once more. There, out the window, was Istanbul again. I opened it slightly, and a fresh breeze scented with the night, carrying distant Turkish music, came in. Suddenly, remembering Akbar and the beautiful young men at the *hamam*, I could actually imagine myself staying there. I felt good. I turned and saw Ted. The reddish hair on his big, sun-dappled chest glowed. He switched off the light, then lit a cigarette with some matches by the table. I watched him blow a continuous chain of perfect gray smoke rings, floating up to me in the deep purple evening. I walked back to the bed and he parted the sheets for me. I got in and fell asleep.

Just like that.

When I woke up the next morning, Ted was gone. I showered, put on some clothes, then sat, thinking for a moment, recalling my feelings from the night before about Istanbul. I was afraid of my limited energies, but quickly made up my mind to call Akbar's phone number. It rang several times, and he answered.

"How are you? I wanted you to call, Len. I'm glad."

I smiled and asked him if he could come over. He told me sure; he'd be there in an hour, towards noon. "Good. Please come. I'll pay for a taxi."

"That's not necessary. I can take a bus. There is one close to me, and it goes right by your hotel. Don't worry. Everything will be fine. Believe me. God takes care of these things, I know."

I hung up feeling really good again. Suddenly, I had a workable plan: I would take care of Akbar, even bring him to New York with me for whatever time I had left. He was sweet, endearing, handsome. The fact that he had been disabled gave him a nobility that so many of the young men I'd met could not match.

Still, how long did I have to live? The next time I died, I was sure I was not going to come back. At least, not as Dr. Leonard Miller.

I decided to write a letter detailing everything that had happened to me: my murder in the lab, my and Josh's abduction, his death and the death of Benjy at the hands of crazed fundamentalist terrorists. That was the only word I could use for them; the same kind of Christian fundamentalists who had smugly tried to blame September 11 on gays and lesbians, had killed me. And all of this happened because I was investigating a human substance that regenerated itself, a substance close to God Itself.

The idea suddenly hit me: I had become a part of that substance. God was the whole form of the universe, from the smallest aspect of it to the largest—and *It* was that consciousness, that will, that holds this amazing thing together. I knew it. I'd experienced *It* myself. But how? How had I, an unbelieving, kinky cocksucker, despised by orthodox Jews, fundamentalist Christians, Moslems, Hindus—all of the cults and sects that have killed for millennia in the names of their own angry, spiteful gods—how had I become a part of this great strange substance?

The question haunted me, and I still had no answer for it. Except that in this vast scheme of things, so much bigger than I was, no matter how strange it seemed for me actually to be a part of this great thing—*It* could accept it.

And would not question it.

When I had finished the letter on hotel stationery, I realized I still didn't know who to send it to. Thumbing through my address book, no one seemed right. There were people I had worked with at the lab, but had never been close to. And a bunch of fleeting casual sexual encounters—

okay, "tricks"—who had comprised a panoply of sex pigs; I'd been one of them. I could admit that without regret, since I had offered my body willingly to those saintly rituals of outsider sex.

Finally I hit on Manny Tuchman. I knew the Pelican's address by heart, and wrote my own address for the return.

Downstairs, a new desk captain brought out a sheet of Turkish stamps; I bought enough to send the letter to America and handed it to him. "It will get there," he said thoughtfully, "in about a week. Turkish mail can be slow. If you'd like, you can send a telegram. There is a telegram office—"

Just at that moment, Akbar arrived. I hugged him and invited him up to my room. The desk captain looked at me disapprovingly, but did not stop us.

We were alone on the elevator and I kissed him and asked him how he was.

"All right. Sometimes things are difficult, sometimes not. I want to leave Turkey, but do not know where to go. Maybe Paris or Germany. There is no work here for me, no matter how much education I have. And Islam does not look favorably on disabled men."

"Why is that?"

"They only say it is God's will."

We got to my room and I unlocked it. I decided that I needed to do one more thing, just in case.

At the desk in the room, I wrote out a short note on a piece of paper, again for Manny, and placed it in an envelope, sealed it, and handed it to Akbar.

"What is this?"

"It's a note, in case anything happens to me." I had written Manny's name and telephone number on the envelope. "You are to contact this man, and tell him what's inside the note. He'll help you."

He put it inside his pants pocket, without opening it.

I got on the bed where Akbar was sitting and held him close to me, kissing him. It was very sweet, the way he kissed me back.

"Would you like to make love with me, Len?"

"Yes, I would."

He took his shirt off and pants, and I helped him with the buckles to his legs. He got into the bed, and pulled a sheet over his lower body, self-consciously. I got up, took off my clothes, and double locked the door in case the maid came by.

chapter twenty-two

I got back to him and lay there for a moment, partially under the sheet, feeling the delight of having him in my arms with so much silence around us, as if time had stopped and I were touching him through glass. Yet I felt every particle of me reaching towards him. Even without legs he was perfect, singular, beautiful. I knew this throughout myself; if only I could say it so that he might know it: that the feelings I had for him had exploded into a desire miles beyond compassion. They had exploded into everything I had sought before in sex, but had not been able to have really.

But now it seemed here; and I was fully myself, but in a place that felt so strange that it made me a stranger. It was not merely that the tide of my desire was reaching towards him, but that this desire was pulling the corpse of my once-dead self along with a whole, freshly new me—really that stranger—towards Akbar.

I kept holding and touching every part of him, lightly kissing him as if he were some mystical presence, here for my pleasure and consolation, and I had become this tongue that could only speak by lavishing him. An erection felt impossible; my groin felt so removed from my cock and also like an immense heavy stone, a foundation, securing me as I lifted him over me and got his cock in my mouth, pulling it down to fill my throat.

I felt, as I had with Benjy, as if the Universe were pouring down through him, attached to this root of his swelling organ, and I became that total, real existence I had pursued throughout my life, but without the connection to it I'd experienced only since awakening in the morgue. He arched his hips, slightly, then pressed them down again, reaching for the back of my head, massaging it as well as my neck and shoulders softly.

Our rhythm slowly continued until with several quick spasms, clenching and unclenching his small, almost adolescent downy butt, he released a first evidence of salty-sweetness, then burst forth, shooting his cum down my throat like light falling through the depths of an ocean.

He withdrew, moaned, settling in close to me, pressing my face to his chest. His heartbeat slowed, and he touched my forehead, cheeks, and mouth with his lips. I held him as what energy I had left pushed off like a swimmer away from my groin and entered my chest.

I felt weightless. Floating. There is an orgasm which I'd been told happens only in the middle of the brain, and I was surely having it. It wasn't that falling through *nothing* feeling that I was accustomed to having after a climax, but this feeling that I was actually rising up.

Through time.

Sounds, images, and scents I hadn't known in thirty-odd years flooded me. Summer. The Jewish working-class beach in New Jersey where my vacationing parents took me when I was eleven and twelve, in the weeks before summer camp. The smell of salt at the beach—very nose clearing!—and the glistening water; the hot sand. Coppertone suntan lotion. Cigarette butts. The warmth on my back, the coolness under my big trunks.

I wore a loose cotton bathing suit that dragged down almost to my knees, with netting inside to support my almost hairless crotch. I was always getting hard in it and would sneak under the boardwalk to feel myself. There, deep in the shadows, I would push my bathing trunks down, and with them somewhere between my knees and ankles, attempt to jerk off.

That wild pleasure, so forbidden. My pale, small, skinny dick, suddenly stiff and exposed. Spit. My little balls contracting tight from the clammy-damp suit, then loosening from the shocking heat that descended in patterns through the thin cracks in the boardwalk, bringing with it vivid crossings of radiance in the dark.

And the beat of portable radios. Dozens of them on the beach, their sounds twisting in and out of earshot. Every girl and her boyfriend had one, families had them, little plastic-cased transistors. There was always a summer beach song and it played over and over again until it stayed in your brainwaves as an echo of the radio waves that kept it moving along the beach. Stevie Wonder songs, the Supremes, "Heat Wave," of course, and my favorite, "Dancing in the Streets." I could hear the distant percussive *wa-wa-wa-wa* of "Dancing in the Streets." Who didn't want to dance in the streets? In my brain of brains I wanted to dance free and naked, but couldn't. But in the shadows under the boardwalk I could reach that wild-boy, Coppertone-scented closeness with the tiny waiting epicenter of

Leonard Miller's young self, that core pulsing with its own white, liquid light. It was there, waiting to touch me.

And I reached it again, floating up. In Turkey. Back to Akbar, who was kissing me tenderly on my face, just brushing my lips with his, when the door unlocked.

"Sorry," Ted announced after walking in. "I should have realized you were busy." He smiled. "The boy from the *hamam*. Uhh, sure. I remember."

I shielded Akbar with my arms. I could feel his embarrassment. He could not run away exactly. But either could I.

"Would you give us a moment?" I asked Ted. "I'll meet you downstairs in the lobby in five minutes."

"No. It's okay, Len. I'll come back upstairs in ten. But I suggest that Akbar be gone by then, because we need to settle things up. Okay?"

"Sure."

He walked out the door, and I helped Akbar on with his legs. He dressed quickly and I did, too. He turned to me, frowning.

"I'm afraid I won't see you again," he said.

"I want to bring you to America, Akbar. But if I can't, everything in the note will tell you what to do. Please do what I ask, and be careful, all right?"

We kissed briefly, then he left. The door shut.

I waited, sitting on the bed.

Those few minutes before Ted's return seemed to stretch on and on, like time was waiting outside now, eavesdropping. I was ready for whatever was going to happen. I just wanted it to be a surprise, like one of those little quirks you go through in the lab, when the experiment gets screwed up and you're ready to pull all your hair out. That's when the real discovery happens, and, out of the blue, this huge wisdom is dropped onto you.

But perhaps the next real discovery would be no discovery. Ted would come back in and, like a good businessman, just tell me how much I owed him. Then we'd go to the airport together and quietly say good-bye.

That would be a surprise—how was I going to say good-bye to Ted?

It would be hard, almost as hard as saying good-bye to myself, which I'd be doing soon. That thought, too, surprised me, like being pulled out of a movie before the show was over. I'd wanted so much to see more, but at the present I had no real time or energy left with which to bargain. I couldn't even concentrate enough to find an answer. All I could do was stare dumbly at the door.

I watched it, until everything disappeared except it. The door started to open very slowly. Ted's face appeared.

Then Mr. Nathan stepped in, wearing a dark, nicely-cut business suit.

chapter twenty-three

*A*t first Ted couldn't look at me, while Nathan stared angrily down at me. Ted began to cough, then managed to say, "I don't have to introduce you two, do I? Henry, uhh, you see, is my boss."

Henry Nathan's sullen face managed to draw itself up into a weak approximation of a smile.

"I thought so," I said. "I knew you were out to murder me, Ted—I did know."

Ted looked at Nathan, then out the window. "I didn't want to murder you, Len, but you had to be stopped. That thing that made you come alive again, we've been"—he coughed nervously into his hand—"we've been following it ever since it arrived at your lab. It comes from God Himself. We couldn't just let you have it, and do anything with it."

Nathan nodded, approvingly. His forced smile became open and genuine.

"You fulfilled your obligation, Ted. My brother. Despite your sins, your problems—what we all know about—you are my brother."

I looked at them. Ted no longer looked out the window. They were standing close together.

I saw a vague resemblance between Nathan's prim face and Ted's more handsome one. "Brother?"

"Henry's my older brother—by four years," Ted said. "Different dads, same mom." He coughed again, clearing his throat, looking smaller, nervous, embarrassed, and sad.

"Henry was legitimate," he explained. "I wasn't. I was the . . . result of a crazy affair. Something she fell into, like one of those things I . . . used to have. So I'm able to understand it. She went off and had me, but after a time she came back. I was two. She had got tired of living the life she'd lived: always running around, the men, the booze. So she came back to God and Dad, and tried to become a good woman. But there were always those moments when she never let me forget what I was."

"Her child?"

He shook his head. "No, buddy. A reminder. Like something you keep in the closet, out of sight. She saw all of her own weaknesses in me. Her drinking, drugs, sex, stuff she couldn't control. Either she punished me, or ignored me. Dad turned his head and became more bitter and religious."

"He loved God, Ted, that's why he loved our mother. Nothing could stop that."

"But you were the only one who treated me like a good person. You always forgave me, Henry."

"Only Jesus forgives," said Nathan. "You didn't need to suffer because of Mom's mistakes. She tried but she never became a good woman, she just got better at hiding. But you picked yourself a good woman! She only knows the good in you. And you've got good kids, too. Neither of them takes after you. All that's good and godly awaits you back in Salt Lake. June only believes the good about you, so she doesn't need to know anything about this. No one does. Dr. Miller here is already dead. He's been buried."

"What about my passport?"

"Stolen, Dr. Miller, simple as that. The guy who stole it was a notorious drug dealer, Ted found this out and had to kill him. The Turkish police will be in this room in less than an hour. We'll show them the stash of heroin you had, but I'll make sure they hand your body over to me. This time, we'll cremate you. Ashes to ashes, dust to dust. But first, we have to do something."

"What?"

He opened Ted's surgical sample kit, removing a scalpel. "You need to remove your pants," he directed.

I looked into Nathan's smiling eyes. "What kind of sick thing are you going to do now?"

The smile dissolved into the same lightning flash of anger I saw him hit Josh with.

"Don't call me sick!"

He raised the scalpel to my throat. Ted rushed towards us.

"It's okay, Len," he said softly. "Henry just wants to look at that tissue, the one that's kept you alive. I know where it is and know what it looks like. Remember? It's like some kind of cyst; we just want to look at it and then—"

"What?"

"Cut it out of you," Nathan said. "While you're still alive."

"You're crazy!" I exploded. "I won't be alive much longer. Why put me through that kind of pain?"

As he'd done in Tonio's car, Nathan extracted a pistol from his jacket holster, pointing it at me. "You think, Dr. Miller, we're just going to wait around patiently for you to drop dead? And how about that tissue, once you do? Will it die with you, or try to bring you back again?"

"It—it remained on me, alive, after I was dead. But I know it's not going to keep me alive much longer. It's through with me. I know it. I'm convinced—so why hurt me?"

"Are you afraid of pain, Dr. Miller?" Nathan asked, smiling triumphantly.

He was right. I was afraid now, filled with the panic I'd felt in my lab. My head began to throb.

"You don't know what pain is, Doctor," Nathan snapped. "The anguish godless people like you put me through. Shooting my wife Gretchen! Blowing up those innocent people in Queens! Now, either you get your pants down now or I'm going to beat you to a bloody pulp—and then I'll get them down myself."

I stood up, unhitching my belt to let my pants drop. "They're down."

"Good." Nathan put the gun away. "That's very smart, Dr. Miller. The more you cooperate, the easier this is going to be. Where is it, Ted?"

Ted's eyes dropped to the floor. He turned from us.

"The lower part of his right calf. On the back, by his sock."

Standing in my underwear, I closed my eyes. Nathan's hands sped over my calf, stopping at the bump that was so distinct from my flesh. Anyone could feel it. I wanted to kick Nathan's face in, but felt immobilized, turned to stone. Was it just fear? Or, maybe, shame, too, that I was still alive? The two of them made me feel dirty, violated, and the cause of way too much harm to others. Benjy and Josh suddenly appeared before me, their faces dissolving as I opened my eyes.

Ted was in front of me, pointing his old nickel-plated pistol at me. "I didn't want to do this, Len," he whispered into my ear.

I could only look at him, as Nathan got up from the floor.

"Put him on the bed," he ordered. "You're going to cut it out of him."

"Wait a darn second, Henry."

"Don't tell me you're chickening out, Ted. Not now."

"Look, I could kill him for you. God forgive me, I didn't want to, but I could. For you. But this butchery, Henry? How can you ask me to do this?"

"It's not butchery, Brother. Even I can see the tissue's already close to separating. It'll be like cutting off a wart. It's a favor to him."

"Then why do it? If you want to kill him, I told you—he's yours. But—"

"I'm not going to let him die once more with this substance on him. Don't you see, Ted, their ways are devious. They undermine the righteous. You know that! They've seduced you over and over again, but every time you've come back to God."

"I came back to you, Hank. That is the truth. I've always come back to you."

"Because deep inside, Ted, you're godly. And our mother was godly, too. She started out as a Jew and she converted. Dad was a converted Jew, too. So you can say I'm all Jew."

"So was Jesus," I said. "Jesus wouldn't want you to do this. He was all about peace, wasn't he?"

"That's what the ungodly preach," Nathan countered. "Jesus was the sword in the hand of His Father. In the Book of Revelations, it is said that He will bring the final fire. What happened on September eleventh in New York was a part of that. It was a wake-up call. But only one. I am here to serve the Lord, I've already told you that's my real profession. Now, Ted, you know what you've got to do."

Ted's eyes looked at me, then returned to the floor again. I couldn't reach him; Nathan had him. What else could I do?

Hurrying into the bathroom, Ted came back with several bath towels. After spreading them out on the bed, he grabbed my shoulders and pushed me face down on to it. My pants were flopped around my ankles, but I still wore my shoes. I offered to take the pants off.

"You're stalling!" Nathan said. "I know how devious you are."

Knotting each of my wrists tightly with some cheap sisal that he took out of his suit pocket, Nathan tied me to the posts at the head of the bed. The ropes burned. I tried to shift up to loosen them, but Nathan jumped on top of me, bearing down on my shoulders with his knees as hard as he could. I stretched my neck up towards him, but all I could see was the rigid underside of his jaw. Then his face, like a wooden puppet's head, tilted down towards me. He no longer seemed angry, just impatient, as if I were using up too much of his time.

Suddenly, I wanted to pray. I can't explain it, but I wanted to grab at anything to feel that I wasn't completely abandoned. I wanted something *real* that I could have on my side. But I had no idea how to do it, or whom to pray to.

With one hand holding my calf, Ted made a quick, deep cut.

"NOOOO!" I screamed.

Nathan grabbed my face, squeezing my mouth shut. Warm blood oozed out all over my leg. Even with his grip on my mouth, I pleaded.

"Can't . . . y' g' me someth' . . . pain?"

Ted jumped up. "I can't do this!" he said, his voice cracking. "Please don't ask me to."

Nathan grabbed the end of a towel, and crammed it into my mouth. "There! That'll keep him from screaming."

"I can't do it," Ted said. "I mean it. If you want me to kill him, I will. But I just can't do something like this."

Nathan got up. Putting his arm on Ted's shoulder, he kept his gun on me.

"We'll pray together," Nathan said softly. "What I want you to do is get back there by his legs. Keep the scalpel in your hand. I'll pray for you, and I want you to pray with me and feel that God's hand is guiding you."

I became really afraid. I couldn't keep the fear away from me for anything now. Truthfully, I didn't know what fear was before, until that moment. My killing in the lab had been so fast it only brought out panic, not fear. Fear was no longer a quick reflex from the anger in Henry Nathan's voice, reminding me of Josh's death or Benjy's. But it emerged nakedly from Nathan's calmness, as he convinced Ted to do this. I could no longer control my nerves or the tremor in my muscles, but I managed, with Nathan off me, to turn my head enough to steal a glance at Ted.

Ted looked distant. A frozen mask of pity stayed on his face, like he was prepared finally to do whatever had to be done next. He licked his lips and coughed briefly.

"Lie all the way down, Len," Ted ordered. "I'll do what I can for you. I'll give you a painkiller. I have some codeine in my sample bag."

He brought a glass of water and a small bottle of pills over to me. After removing the corner of the towel from my mouth, he pushed two of the pills into it with his middle and index finger. Then he brought the glass to my lips, tilted it back, and let me drink.

"Do you feel better now?" Nathan asked his brother.

"I think so," Ted answered.

"We can pray now," Nathan said calmly, after he had waited a minute or so. Then he got back up on the bed, holding me down again with his knees.

"Lord, we want to thank You for Your bounty and for everything You've given us. We want You to know that Your miracles are not wasted on us, and that those who believe in You and Your Son Jesus Christ will have eternal life and—"

The codeine started to have some effect, and Nathan went on so that his voice seemed only calming and distant. I was glad that he was praying—I could use a prayer. I, too, was grateful for the existence that had been given to me, and I was aware that the substance was no longer mine. It had a consciousness of its own, just as it had in the lab that awful night of shattered glass, and *it* knew only too precisely that moment when it would either join or leave me. I knew that, somehow, it—or *It*—was saying good-bye to me in the same way that I was saying good-bye to myself. I hadn't been called out of the movie before it was over: it *was* over. Those small lights at the edge of me were going out once again. This time, though, I was aware that Benjy and Josh were around, waiting.

With the energy I had left, I managed to turn my head and caught a glimpse of Ted, not easy tied-down on my stomach like that. He was standing down on my left side, below me.

He was clenching the steel handle of the scalpel in his hand—light glinted off the blade—and he was crying. I'd never seen anyone cry like that, choking, trying childishly to wipe his nose with the sleeve of the same hand that held the scalpel. As he approached my right lower calf, I could no longer see him, but I could feel his warm tears running down into the cut he had made in the welt. Salt from his tears stung me as Henry Nathan's words droned on, and I could feel Ted's lips kiss the bare skin next to that place he knew he had to cut.

"So, Lord Jesus, we ask for Your aid in bringing Your own substance, that of Your body, back to You, as we, too, are a part of the substance that is God, and we do this in Christ's name, amen."

Ted grabbed my legs and hugged them, sobbing, loudly.

"Ted, you've got to stop this," Nathan ordered. "I've prayed for him. He's not feeling anything, I know it. Now I want you to do this. I want you to be a man and grow up. Will you? Can you be the man you need to be and do this for me, your own brother?"

The room got darker, as if a cloud had passed over any sun left in the sky outside. I was no longer in Istanbul or the beach of my childhood or my apartment in New York. I was back in my laboratory, no longer worried, incredibly happy. All the men I'd known in my life, my lovers, like Josh, boys I'd known, and a mysterious procession of truly magical, sexual tricks; my parents and teachers; some old girlfriends; even a few eccentric old ladies were there in my lab, too. All the little red and blue lights were twinkling over the sinks and counters, glowing like faces.

But the last face I saw was Benjy's. Smiling directly at me, like he had in the van. Those wise green eyes were so happy with me. I wanted to go with him, to take his warm hand, and I turned to them all and asked them, Please, turn off the lab lights and I'll see you—

"I can't do this!" Ted screamed, and shot Nathan dead.

$\mathcal{T}$ed cut the ropes off me, then pulled his brother's body aside, onto the floor. It made a sharp thud, like a car coming to a sudden stop.

"Please don't die," Ted cried. "I need for you to live, Len. I need that more than I need to live myself. The truth is, I don't want to live anymore." He paused. "I—I'm going to leave June."

The room was getting much darker; a storm was moving in. I could feel it. It would sweep away Istanbul, the whole world. I heard noises outside. The long, plaintive amplified calls of the muezzins from the minarets; the distant sounds and horns from the docks. Ted was next to me, holding my hand, kissing my face.

"Will you take the substance," I whispered to him, "and bring it back to my lab, please? And I want you to take care of Akbar. Would you do that, too?"

I could feel his breath on me.

"I can't. My life's over. Henry's won. I can't be godly, be a part of a normal life. It's a lie. It's over. I can't go on putting my wife and kids, even myself, through this anymore. I learned this, because of you."

I nodded weakly. He was being truthful, finally. How could he go back to that falsehood now?

"There's something I want you to do for me. Please, Len."

I had no idea what he was talking about, until he placed his pistol in my hand and arranged my index finger on the trigger. He crouched in front of me, so that his head was right in front of the barrel.

"Just pull it. Please, buddy. You've got to do this for me. I want it so much. It's the only way I'm going to get out of this."

I heard him, and I felt so bad for Ted. But I no longer had the strength in me to do it; I was glad.

Josh and Benjy and my parents and all of those men and the other people were waiting. They were no longer interested in Ted Richards, but they would graciously see me over that little bump where everyone gets afraid. Maybe Da Vinci and Einstein were waiting, too, on the other side, welcoming me. Along with that *thing* that I knew was God, that was approaching me. I stepped into it, into the vast, vast Substance.

I could do nothing. My cold fingers felt his hand press them together, squeezing the trigger. The room filled with a flash of light, and in it I saw Josh's haloed body jolt and Benjy, roped, hanging there. The flash ended; they were grateful. So was I. All my little working soldiers had left me. Then this warmth came like a blanket, like all the black clouds at once.

Then it stopped.

I'm so glad to be back in the lab again, where I recognize my own place and I'm happy. I feel as if I'd never left it. There's so much to tell you, but how can I bridge the gap between my last awakening and the present? The truth is, I want to tell you everything—and hold back nothing. But will you be able to understand it, and, even more important, use this understanding and make it your own knowledge? Knowledge, please see, comes from the body as well as the mind. I wonder if you can see that. Still, I am at peace now, and that risky, brief experiment that began after my meeting here with yet another death is over.

I'm back where I belong, but I'm no longer a part of what I was. No more work-until-you-break-down-and-have-to-be-put-together-by-experiences-with-strangers! No more crafty, kinky, "creative" sex. You think you might miss all of that, but you don't. The leather parties, the bondage, the chummy get-togethers for dream-eros activities and various chemical ecstasies are over.

So long, buddies.

If you've never been a scientist and known the thrill of instruments and long, working experiments, then you have no idea of the beauty of the mental castles science constructs—or the brain-busting hard work it requires to built them. You don't know what it's like to work endlessly and forget about time. Time is a spiral that collapses on itself, disappearing: I understand. Yes, I do. I know all about an experiment that goes on and on, re-inventing itself, creating novel variations within the multi-channeled discipline of a vast scheme.

I was back in the lab, where I belonged. And it was going beautifully—elegant as light—with others there, too: Josh Moreland, and Benjy Rosenbaum. I have them deep inside me, too. So their auras, their presence, is with me all the time.

And so is Lenny Miller. He's with me, too.

I loved him; but he's dead. His time in that experiment ran out. Mr. Henry Nathan killed him, one way or another. Dr. Leonard Miller is dead; that's all.

But Ted Richards is alive.

He's as alive as I was that evening when *I* woke up in the Bellevue morgue. Ted was being truthful when he said he could no longer put his wife and kids through what he'd put them through, or put himself through that, as well. He had come to that great curved wall in his own road, the one that appears as endless darkness, unless you know which tight passage to walk through.

Ted knew his passage; he'd even made preparations for it. They had started his first moments in that underground room, with the three cousins who had known Christ. Ted had passed out after Eli, one of the two men, had touched him, transmitting to Ted that his future lay with them, that this *was* the place God had made for him. In that secret room, Ted had seen Jesus, and the Resurrection, inside his very self. He'd been born for this difficult place; and it was in their miraculous flesh, through them, that he would achieve it.

In the middle of the night, lying next to Lenny, Ted had got up and after placing his pistol in the waist band of his gym shorts, put a T-shirt on over it, and then snuck out. He woke up Alvin Jurrist, who was already half out of his mind, and persuaded Jurrist to take cans of kerosene, solvent, rags, and matches down to the room with him.

"The place *is* deadly," he told Jurrist. "Len's been hiding from you all the time that those people carried plague. That's what you've got! It drove Len crazy being down there, but he had to see it by himself before it's destroyed. Do you want this to be your legacy to the world, man? Len's already seen it. Wasn't that what you wanted him to do?"

Jurrist was terrified to return to the room, but Ted bullied him into doing it, using a combination of persuasion and brute force. Once down there, Ted hurried over to the three bodies and immediately, with Alvin barely believing his eyes, grabbed Eli by his right inner thigh. This was the very place, next to a man's testicles, upon which in biblical times men swore sacred oaths. Eli's inert body began to squirm under Ted's grasp, but Ted locked him down with both hands and using one of his surgical knives quickly cut off a small section of Eli's groin.

After Alvin saw Ted do this, he panicked and tried to escape. But Ted shot him, then he placed the section of Eli's flesh just below the small of his back, securing it with some surgical tape he'd brought for that purpose. The grafting of Eli's flesh to Ted's body started immediately, prompted by that intense bond which, earlier, had drawn Eli's hand to Ted's head. But Ted, despite his impulsiveness, feared these three beings who'd escaped the boundaries of death. What revenge would they seek on him for forcefully taking their knowledge: a knowledge held within the eternal body itself, and the spirit attached to it?

He set fire to the room and the three ancient bodies, then hoisted his way back up, setting fires throughout the site. He waited outside the smoldering ruins, knowing that Len would find him. When that happened, he covered up his crime with all the lies that he could tell.

On the way back in Istanbul, Ted was preoccupied with what would take place and how to hide it from Lenny, even though he felt so close to him. Ted Richards knew he was ready to die. And he was ready to kill Len Miller, too—but, still, how would he deal with his cunning, ardently Christian half-brother? The same half-brother who since childhood had kindly made a place for Ted, and yet taken it away at the same time. Ted prayed for guidance as he had never prayed before. But an even deeper change, beyond any of Ted's prayers, had secretly taken place in him.

He realized, even before he raised the scalpel to Lenny's graft, that he was now closer to the substance that Leonard Miller had become, than he was to the old Ted Richards. No longer could he honor Henry Nathan's wishes—or do his commands—despite the past that had held them together. Before, he'd been prepared to die, but not to kill his half-brother. He had only wanted to make sure that he and Len Miller would be freed from Nathan's insidious power, one way or another.

But, in those final moments of Leonard Miller's life, there was no way out. Ted's real feelings for Len would not allow him to harm him; and in the end, murdering Henry Nathan would be Eli's revenge.

As Nathan had predicted, the Turkish cops stormed into the hotel room. They found the three bodies and took them to the morgue. An investigation was started, and they waited for the bodies to be claimed. The next day, Sulieman, Ted's masseur friend from the *hamam*, by an agreement transacted earlier on the trip back to Istanbul by phone—and, then, whose myriad details were finalized that morning, before Ted's last meeting with

Nathan—walked into the police station and told them that he had spoken to Ted's wife in Utah and had come to claim his friend's body.

Sulieman also told them that Dr. Leonard Miller was Ted's brother, and he would take possession of his remains as well. In addition, he informed them that Mr. Nathan was a notorious heroin dealer from New York, whose cover was that of a "Christian business man." Since Nathan had a small bag of heroin on him, that he had intended to plant on Len's body, that was all the police needed to hear, and after Nathan's corpse remained unclaimed for several days, they threw him into a pauper's grave.

That evening, Ted "awoke" in Sulieman's small apartment, exactly as Leonard Miller had done in New York. Sulieman took him back to the *hamam*, where he had stored Miller's body in one of the private rooms. There Ted cut the substance from Miller's lower right calf, and put it into a sterile, saline solution.

Ted stayed in Istanbul another day. He spoke by phone to the very disorganized Istanbul police—who would believe almost anything—saying that he was another brother in Utah and that he was glad Sulieman had arranged for Ted's body to be shipped back to the States. Then, with Sulieman's help, Ted got in touch with Akbar and told him that Miller's dying wish was that Ted should take care of him. Ted felt driven to do this. It was the least the could do for the friend who had allowed him to escape his own life. At first Akbar did not believe him, but Ted, persuasive and seductive as ever, with Sulieman nodding seriously at his side, convinced him of his good intentions.

Akbar, Sulieman, and Ted then buried Leonard Miller's body in Istanbul. It lies in an old Jewish cemetery, with other wanderers whose time had ended there, like himself.

Akbar and Ted are now residing in New York, where Ted has taken on another name and identity. Sometimes Akbar calls Ted's wife in Salt Lake City to find out how the kids are, and arranges to send her money, left from the estate of Dr. Leonard Miller, which is now overseen by Manny Tuchman. Akbar has told June that both Ted and Henry Nathan, as well as a scientist friend named Leonard Miller, were killed by bandits at a recently uncovered archeological site near Assos. Their bodies, burned at the site, were never recovered; and Gretchen, Nathan's fierce fundamentalist wife, has remained wisely, stonily silent to any further questions. Since the

Nathans had no children, she also contributes to June's support.

As for the man who once was Ted Richards, he doesn't know how long he has to live—weeks, months, decades perhaps—but now he has acquired the strength inside not to betray himself.

He can accept the place God has made for him, no matter how it is defined, just as he can accept his own destiny within the substance of God. This was revealed to him by Eli, the beautiful man whose hand reached out to him across the ages, and who transmitted to Ted an experience so vast that it left him unconscious.

As for me, I once belonged to a woman named Miriam. She and her two cousins, Eli and John-Luke, were in fact distantly related to Jesus, but in the great design we are *all* related. What I am goes back so far that my origin is indistinguishable from the first moment of Knowing, and I can transmit messages to the elements that comprise me, without the human limitations of words.

I was there when the vast form of God began itself, at that first division in time and matter that became the Universe.

So *I*, within that substance of God which once filled a young woman, now relate this story to you. But exactly what is this substance that so many people have fought over, and what is the God that made it?

God, you must know, is that which *is*, and knows *Itself* forever.

And this substance *is* what *It* is.

And that is all.

The end.

Perry Brass

Originally from Savannah, Georgia, Perry Brass grew up, in the fifties and sixties, in equal parts Southern, Jewish, economically impoverished, and very much *gay*. To escape the South's violent homophobia, he hitchhiked at seventeen from Savannah to San Francisco—an adventure, he recalls, that was "like Mark Twain with drag queens." He has published thirteen books and been a finalist five times in three categories (poetry; gay science fiction and fantasy; spirituality and religion) for Lambda Literary Awards. His novel *Warlock* received a 2002 "Ippy" Award from Independent Press Magazine as Best Gay and Lesbian Book.

He has been involved in the gay movement since 1969, when he co-edited *Come Out!*, the world's first gay liberation newspaper. Later, in 1972, with two friends he started the Gay Men's Health Project Clinic, the first clinic for gay men on the East Coast, still surviving as New York's Callen-Lorde Community Health Center. In 1984, his play *Night Chills*, one of the first plays to deal with the AIDS crisis, won a Jane Chambers International Gay Playwriting Award. Brass's collaborations with composers include the words for the much-performed "All the Way Through Evening," a five-song cycle set by the late Chris DeBlasio; "The Angel Voices of Men" set by Ricky Ian Gordon, commissioned by the Dick Cable Musical Trust for the New York City Gay Men's Chorus, which featured it on its *Gay Century Songbook* CD; "Three Brass Songs" set by Fred Hersch; and "Waltzes for Men," also commissioned by the DCMT for the NYC Gay Men's Chorus and set by Craig Carnahan. His musical collaboration, "The Human City," with Houston Opera composer Mary Carol Warwick, has been performed frequently internationally.

Perry Brass is an accomplished reader and recognized voice on gender subjects, gay relationships, and the history and literature of the movement towards GLBT equality. He has taught workshops in writing and publishing fiction. He lives in the Riverdale section of "da Bronx" with his partner of twenty three years, but can cross bridges to other parts of America without a passport.

Other Books by Perry Brass

SEX-CHARGE

" ... poetry at it's highest voltage ..." Marv. Shaw in **Bay Area Reporter.**

Sex-charge. 76 pages. $6.95. With male photos by Joe Ziolkowski. ISBN 0-9627123-0-2

MIRAGE
ELECTRIFYING SCIENCE FICTION

A gay science fiction classic! An original "coming out" and coming-of-age saga, set in a distant place where gay sexuality and romance is a norm, but with a life-or-death price on it. On the tribal planet *Ki*, two men have been promised to each other for a lifetime. But a savage attack and a blood-chilling murder break this promise and force them to seek another world, where imbalance and lies form Reality. This is the planet known as Earth, a world they will use and escape. Finalist, 1991 Lambda Literary Award for Best Gay Men's Science Fiction/Fantasy. This classic work of gay science fiction fantasy is now available in its new Tenth Anniversary Edition.

"Intelligent and intriguing." Bob Satuloff in **The New York Native.**

Mirage, Tenth Anniversary Edition 230 pages. $12.95 ISBN 1-892149-02-8

CIRCLES
THE AMAZING SEQUEL TO *MIRAGE*

"The world Brass has created with *Mirage* and its sequel rivals, in complexity and wonder, such greats as C.S. Lewis and Ursula LeGuin." **Mandate Magazine**, New York.

Circles. 224 pages. $11.95 ISBN 0-9627123-3-7

OUT THERE

STORIES OF PRIVATE DESIRES. HORROR. AND THE AFTERLIFE.

"… we have come to associate [horror] with slick and trashy chiller-thrillers. Perry Brass is neither. He writes very well in an elegant and easy prose that carries the reader forward pleasurably. I found this selection to be excellent." **The Gay Review**, Canada.

Out There. 196 pages. $10.95
ISBN 0-9627123-4-5

ALBERT

or THE BOOK OF MAN

Third in the *Mirage* trilogy. In 2025, the White Christian Party has taken over America. Albert, son of Enkidu and Greeland, must find the male Earth mate who will claim his heart and allow him to return to leadership on Ki. "Brass gives us a book where lesser writers would have only a premise." **Men's Style,** New York

"If you take away the plot, it has political underpinnings that are chillingly true. Brass has a genius for the future." **Science Fiction Galaxies**, Columbus, OH. "Erotic suspense and action…a pleasurable read." **Screaming Hyena Review**, Melbourne, Australia.

Albert. 210 pages. $11.95
ISBN 0-9627123-5-3

Works

AND OTHER 'SMOKY GEORGE' STORIES
EXPANDED EDITION

"Classic Brass," these stories—many of them set in the long-gone seventies, when, as the author says, "Gay men cruised more and net-worked less"—have recharged gay erotica. This Expanded Edition contains a selection of Brass's steamy poems, as well as his essay, "Maybe We Should Keep the 'Porn' in Pornography."

Works. 184 pages. $9.95
ISBN 0-9627123-6-1

THE **HARVEST**
A "SCIENCE/POLITICO" NOVEL

From today's headlines predicting human cloning comes the emergence of "vaccos"—living "corporate cadavers"—raised to be sources of human organ and tissue transplants. One exceptional vacco will escape. His survival will depend upon Chris Turner, a sexual renegade who will love him and kill to keep himalive.

"One of the Ten Best Books of 1997," **Lavender Magazine**, Minneapolis. "In George Nader's *Chrome*, the hero dared to fall in love with a robot. In **The Harvest**—a vastly superior novel, Chris Turner falls in love with a vacco, Hart 256043." Jesse Monteagudo, **The Weekly News**, Miami, Florida. Finalist, 1997 Lambda Literary Award, Gay and Lesbian Science Fiction.

The Harvest. 216 pages. $11.95
ISBN 0-9627123-7-X

THE LOVER OF MY SOUL
A SEARCH FOR ECSTASY AND WISDOM

Brass's first book of poetry since *Sex-charge* is worth the wait. Flagrantly erotic and just plain flagrant—with poems like "I Shoot the Sonovabitch Who Fires Me," "Sucking Dick Instead of Kissing," and the notorious "MTV Ab(*solutely*) Vac(*uous*) Awards." **The Lover of My Soul** again proves Brass's feeling that poetry must tell, astonish, and delight.

"An amazingly powerful book of poetry and prose," **The Loving Brotherhood**, Plainfield, NJ.

The Lover of My Soul. 100 pages. $8.95
ISBN 0-9627123-8-8

How to survive your own gay life
AN ADULT GUIDE TO LOVE, SEX AND RELATIONSHIPS

The book for <u>adult</u> gay men. About sex and love, and coming out of repression; about surviving homophobic violence; about your place in a community, a relationship, and a culture. About the important psychic "gay work" and the gay tribe. About dealing with conflicts and crises, personal, professional, and financial. And, finally, about being more alive, happier, and stronger.

"This book packs a wallop of wisdom!" **Morris Knight**, founder, **Los Angeles Gay & Lesbian Services Center**. Finalist, 1999 Lambda Literary Award in Gay and Lesbian Religion and Spirituality.

How to Survive Your Own Gay Life. 224 pages. $11.95
ISBN 0-9627123-9-6

ANGEL LUST
AN EROTIC NOVEL OF TIME TRAVEL

Tommy Angelo and Bert Knight are in a long-term relationship. Very long—close to a millennium. Tommy and Bert are angels, but very different. No wings; sexually free. Tommy was once Thomas Jebson, a teen serf in the violent England of William the Conqueror. One evening, he met a handsome knight who promised to love him, for all time. Their story introduces us to gay forest men, robber barons, castles, and deep woodlands. Also, to a modern sexual underground where "gay" and "straight" mean little. To Brooklyn factory men. Street machos. New York real estate sharks. And to the kind of lush erotic encounters for which Perry Brass is famous. Finalist, 2000 Lambda Literary Award, Gay and Lesbian Science Fiction.

"Brass's ability to go from seedy gay bars in New York to 11th century castles is a testament to his skill as a writer." **Gay & Lesbian Review**.

Angel Lust. 224 pages. $12.95
ISBN 1-892149-00-1

Warlock

A NOVEL OF POSSESSION

Allen Barrow, a shy bank clerk, dresses out of discount stores and has a small penis that embarrasses him. One night at a bathhouse he meets Destry Powars—commanding, vulgar, seductive, successful—who pulls Allen into his orbit and won't let go. Destry lives in a closed, moneyed world that Allen can only glimpse through the pages of tabloids. From generations of drifters, Powars has been chosen to learn a secret language based on force, deception, and nerve. But *who* chose him—and what does he really want from Allen? What *are* Mr. Powars's dark powers? These are the mysteries that Allen will uncover in *Warlock*, a novel that is as paralyzing in its suspense as it is voluptuously erotic.

Warlock. 226 pages. $12.95
ISBN 1-892149-03-6

At your bookstore, or from:

Belhue Press
2501 Palisade Avenue, Suite A1
Bronx, NY 10463
E-mail: belhuepress@earthlink.net

Please add $2.50 shipping for the first book and $1.00 for each book thereafter. New York State residents please add 8.25% sales tax. Foreign orders in U.S. currency only.

You can now order Perry Brass's exciting books online at www.perrybrass.com. Please visit this website for more details, regular updates, and news of future events and books.